What Sammy Knew

ALSO BY DAVID LASKIN

The Children's Blizzard

The Long Way Home

The Family

What Sammy Knew

David Laskin

PENGUIN
BOOKS

PENGUIN BOOKS
An imprint of Penguin Random House LLC
penguinrandomhouse.com

LIBRARY OF CONGRESS CATALOGING-IN-PUBLICATION DATA

Names: Laskin, David, 1953– author.
Title: What Sammy knew : a novel / David Laskin.
Description: New York : Penguin Books, [2020]
Identifiers: LCCN 2020004185 (print) | LCCN 2020004186 (ebook) |
ISBN 9780143135500 (hardcover) | ISBN 9780525507178 (ebook)
Subjects: LCSH: New York (State)—History—20th century—Fiction.
Classification: LCC PS3612.A8536 W53 2020 (print) |
LCC PS3612.A8536 (ebook) | DDC 813/.6—dc23
LC record available at https://lccn.loc.gov/2020004185
LC ebook record available at https://lccn.loc.gov/2020004186

Printed in the United States of America
1 3 5 7 9 10 8 6 4 2

Designed by Alexis Farabaugh

TO THE MEMORY OF

Ethel Beane Foreman

and

Ivan Doig

Author's Note

Ethel Beane Foreman and Ivan Doig, to whose memory this novel is dedicated, could not have been more different from me—or from each other—in background, temperament, upbringing or outlook. Ethel, the granddaughter of tidewater Virginia slaves, spent her life cleaning the homes and raising the children of privileged white families, including, in the last decade of her life and the first of mine, my own. Ivan, the descendent of hardscrabble Scots, grew up herding sheep and cutting hay in the uplands of central Montana before going off to university and becoming a writer. Ivan was a friend and mentor. Ethel was our domestic worker. And yet together, in their very different ways, they gave me the strength and love and inspiration to write this book.

Ethel, on whom my fictional character Tutu is based, never had much in the way of worldly goods, but she did have a powerful voice and she knew how to use it. I grew up to the sound of that voice, hectoring, commanding, protecting, instructing. I will never forget the sound of that voice crying out when the news came over her radio that four little girls had been blown up in a church basement in Birmingham. I was nine at the time, old enough to understand that those girls were killed because they were black. It never occurred to me that the Birmingham church bombing had anything to do with the racial dynamics being enacted under our own roof. Ethel told me little about her past—I never asked—but late in life, fifty years after she was gone, I set out to learn everything I could. What I discovered—the places she lived and worked, the churches where she worshipped and sang, the death of her only child, her descent from the slaves of our Founding Fathers and from the Founders themselves—I've given to Tutu. Tutu is imagined—but the stories, both the ones Ethel told me and the ones I managed to uncover, are real, and I've tried to recount them in the voice I knew and loved. Remembering and telling these stories is my way of honoring Ethel's memory, keeping her alive in our world, and, I hope, bringing our world closer to justice. Her life matters.

Ivan's stories of growing up poor and motherless in Montana—shared in the course of many a long dinner—were as strange to me as anything Ethel revealed about her own past, and yet these have touched me as well. Ivan took me under his wing, believed in me, supported me in every way a seasoned writer can support a rookie. Ivan himself jumped the fence from nonfiction to fiction in mid-career, and he (gently) nudged me to consider doing the same.

Ethel and Ivan both had my back in the ways that matter most. Without the two of them, I would not be the writer I am, perhaps I would not be a writer at all, and I would certainly never have been the writer of this novel. That is why I have dedicated the book to their memory. But I'd also like to add here my gratitude for their many gifts, often given unknowingly but always unconditionally.

Save me, O God; for the waters are
come in unto my soul.

PSALM 69

What Sammy Knew

Chapter One

This is how Sam Stein remembered drowning.

He was three years old, maybe four. The afternoon was stifling. Cicadas revved in the tops of the backyard trees like rusty chain saws. Or maybe they were chain saws? The air reeked of grass and gas. "Quit whining," Tutu commanded in that voice like a slap—but he couldn't. He wanted his mother! He was so sticky that his shirt was glued to his back and his undies wedged in his crack like a damp rope. "Kiddy pool!" his big brother Tom screamed and then the even bigger brother Ron screamed it too. "Kiddy pool." But why, Sam wondered, would a kitty need a pool? They didn't even have a cat. Tutu peeled his clothes off and told him to step into his trunks. She kept him steady with one hand on his back—her touch soft from the pearly lotion she was forever wringing into her palms. The pool was a circle of blue. A Wiffle ball, a plastic bat, and a couple of rubber duckies circled one another on the shining blue surface. Sam jumped through the confetti of light that shook down from the trees. His two brothers were already kicking up stars and Sam joined in, hammering his legs through the cool slosh, stomping, marching, spinning, squealing. All three of them were as slick as eels from the baby oil Tutu slathered over their pale knobby backs and shoulders. "Wanna duck, Sammy?" his oldest brother shouted in his face. "C'mere, Sammy. Get the ducky." But whenever Sam reached for the prize, Ron whisked it off, hid it behind his back, threw it up, and swiped it back inches away from Sam's greasy little fist. On the last throw, he lunged and fell flat on his face in the tepid bug-flecked blue. He cried into the water and inhaled and choked. His throat screwed shut like a faucet. Still on his stomach with his mouth and nose submerged, he began to thrash and squirm. And then he quit and lay still.

Sam Stein at seventeen could not possibly remember any of this—but he did. He remembered it like it was yesterday. While stars winked on in the blackness behind his eyes, a shrieking whoop—*"MY BABY!"*—pierced his brain and Tutu—tall, brown, bowlegged Tutu, who hated to be hurried—came charging across the lawn, elbowed aside the paralyzed brothers, scooped Sam out of the pool, and pressed him gasping and then screaming to the gray cotton cloth of the maid's uniform she wore.

Sam remembered drowning—almost drowning—but the rest of them—his mother and brothers—only remembered *"MY BABY!"* From that day on, whenever Sam griped about a bully or a skinned knee or a vile teacher or a devious friend, one of them—usually Ron or Tom but sometimes his mother—wailed, *"MY BABY!"* and laughed in his face.

But not Tutu. Tutu was strict and scary. She rarely smiled and never kissed. She punished Sam relentlessly and cruelly—not with her fists but with her scorn—but she never laughed at him, even when he deserved it. Tutu was the live-in maid—*"I'm not your damn maid,"* she snapped whenever she heard one of them use that word—but Sam knew, had known from the day they brought him home hollering for all his newborn lungs were worth, that he was her boy. Born on her birthday, delivered into her arms by his desperate mother, Sam belonged to Tutu. He and his skinny white ass wouldn't even be here if it weren't for her. It didn't matter what he said or did, how he treated her, or whether he loved her back. He was hers. She was his. For good.

Chapter Two

Should he shave? Sam, locked in the bathroom he shared with his brothers, ran two fingers along his jawline and over his upper lip, but instead of sandpaper it felt more like blades of newly sprouted grass. "I celebrate myself and sing myself—and what I assume you shall assume . . ." No, that was *leaves*, not *blades*, of grass and to judge by his photo Walt Whitman had never shaved in his life. What did it matter? Supposedly, girls loved poetry, and Sam, halfway through his senior year of high school, was finally tall enough to stand next to one and recite Whitman or whatever to her face instead of into her boobs. For the first time in his life, Sam was starting to get some second female looks, as in "Is that really Sam? Scrawny little Sammy Stein?" Scrawny no more, Sam had shot up half a foot since the start of the school year, rocketing in three months from puny to lean to—dare one say—lanky?

"Yes, one would definitely dare," Sam told his reflection.

But he still hadn't kissed a girl. At seventeen!

Well, it was a new year—new decade—or almost. Seven hours to go and 1969 would morph into 1970, senior spring would officially begin, and Samuel Orin Stein would be free to do whatever the hell he liked with whoever the hell he wanted to do it. His college applications were in, his second round with the SATs was coming up in six weeks, AP English and history were ticking along nicely. As long as he didn't flunk anything or get arrested, he was golden.

All he needed was a girlfriend.

Sam turned on the water, washed his face, brushed his teeth, combed his wavy chin-length reddish brown hair, scanned the dense drifts of nose and forehead freckles for the telltale bomb crater of a zit. He got so close to the mirror that their noses almost touched. *Cute as you turned out? Girls will eat you alive.* Tutu told him that just last week—and when it came to appearances, Tutu never lied. What would a girl see? Sly hazel eyes flecked with gold and green. Mouth too big for the concave cheeks. Pale, barely visible eyebrows. Tufts of orange fuzz. And freckles—millions of amber dots that swirled and merged and overlapped in coded patterns.

I love freckles, she—whoever she was—would say.

"Would you like to try one?" he asked the mirror coyly.

Sam braced for the reprimand. Tutu was always on his case for talking to himself in the bathroom, though he never understood how she could pick up his solo mumbling clear across the house. But when he shut off the faucet what he heard was not her raucous imperative but a high thin whine like a dentist's drill. Crying? He opened the bathroom door, flipped on the overhead light in the hall—he'd been in there communing with his cuteness so long that night had fallen—and followed the keening to the kitchen.

"Tutu?"

The room blazed with light. Tonight was his parents' big New Year's Eve dinner party and every surface was mounded with food, bowls, boxes, bottles, jars, utensils. A cast-iron skillet of Crisco sputtered on the stove, but instead of frying, Tutu was collapsed on the patched vinyl bench with the apron pressed to her face. Her knobby shoulders shuddered as she rocked back and forth.

Crying—*her*? Sam had only seen tears in Tutu's eyes three times in his life: the Sunday in September 1963 when four little black girls got blown up in a church bombing in Birmingham, Alabama. The day JFK was assassinated. And when the news came over her radio that Dr. King had been shot. Otherwise she was as impervious as a cop.

"What happened? Are you hurt? Did someone die?"

"Oh, Sammy." She rocked and howled and the words strangled in her throat. "They've gone and fired me, Sammy."

"Who did?"

The wailing screeched to a stop like a needle skidding across a record. "Who do you *think*—Mickey Mouse?" Tutu hated a dumb question. "Your parents, that's who. They told me I'm too old and sick to work anymore. One month and I'm out."

Sam slumped down on the bench across from her and listened with head bowed while she gasped out the story. The week before Christmas, Tutu had nearly passed out after climbing the steep flight of stairs to her attic room. Sam's mother, Penny, a radiologist at the local hospital, insisted she be checked out by a heart specialist. Tutu backed out of the first three appointments, but when she finally submitted, the exam revealed that the valves of her heart were seriously damaged, probably from a childhood bout of rheumatic fever. Climbing steps, hauling laundry, dragging around the vacuum—really anything that elevated the pulse could kill her. The cardiologist had advised Penny to let Tutu go—for her own good—and the Steins chose New Year's Eve to break the news. "Out to pasture, Sammy." The tears were running down her face again. "Don't they see I got bills to pay—money I owe—people who depend on me? How am I supposed to get another job? Who'd hire me at my age? Next thing I'll be pushing up the daisies in potter's field."

"Wait a minute! They can't just get rid of you like that. You're part of the family!"

They locked eyes, Tutu's brown pools rimmed in red and Sam's hazel cat's eyes snapping with outrage. "Family, huh?" She took a pinch of bare ginger-colored skin from under the white cuff of her uniform and twisted it at him. "Does it look like we're related?" She heaved herself to her feet. "Now get out my kitchen, boy." That's what she always called it—*my kitchen*—though not one thing in that linoleum, chrome, Formica, plastic, and knotty pine room belonged to her. "I got work to do."

"But—"

"No buts. I'm not your auntie. I'm nothing but the maid. *Ex*-maid soon enough."

"WHAT DO YOU MEAN *her own good*? That's so"—Sam mentally riffled through his newly acquired SAT words—"paternalistic. Don't you think Tutu can take care of herself? Make her own decisions?"

Sam had been tracking his mother through the house ever since she got back from her final round of party errands, and now the two of them faced off in the dank cinder-block basement outside the liquor closet. The naked 45-watt bulb trapped them in a cone of dirty light. Penny Stein, her back to the locked plywood door, had the key to the kingdom of booze hidden in her fist. "So what's your solution, Sam?" Thanks to the recent growth spurt, he was now tall enough to look down on the straight sharp part in the black helmet of his mother's hair. "*You* wanna do the housework she can't handle anymore? Or watch her keel over of a heart attack while she's schlepping your dirty undies?"

"How about letting *her* decide? Give her the autonomy." Those SAT words were great in arguments.

"How about you mind your own business."

"How is this not my business? Tutu practically raised me."

"Oh for god's sake."

"And if she's so sick, how come she's working on New Year's Eve? Fried chicken and corn bread! What's your theme this year—down on the plantation?" His mother bristled. "Don't you think it's just a *tad* hypocritical having *the black maid* serve soul food to your rich white friends? I mean, this is 1969. Have you ever heard of Black Power?"

"Tutu doesn't need Black Power," Penny shot back. "She's got us. She's one of the family."

"Right. That's why you're firing her. I'll keep that in mind when you get old and—"

"We're not firing—she's retiring!" Sam could tell he'd pushed her to the edge. "She's sixty-six years old. She's got her own place in Harlem. Her brother and sister are there. She'll be grateful."

"She sure didn't seem grateful when I found her crying her eyes out in the kitchen."

"You're going to college next fall, remember, Sammy? You're *raised.*"

"That's a cop-out and you know it." He willed himself not to mist up. "Go ahead—open it." He flicked his eyes toward the liquor closet lock. "I'm outta here anyway, so your liquid treasures are safe."

And with that, Sam clattered up the basement steps, grabbed his coat from the hall closet, and stormed out into the night—the last night of 1969.

Then he stormed back in just long enough to pop his head into the kitchen to say goodbye to Tutu. He stopped dead at the threshold. It was like he'd been electrocuted. Time ceased as Sam got sucked into one of those vortices where the ocean sizzles in your ears and your head floats free and you're convinced you've lived this moment before. He stared, glassy-eyed, and instead of his flinty old housekeeper, there was this strange rangy lady with a gash in her heart and a hole in her pocket standing at the stove singing a song he had never heard but knew anyway—*the darkness deepens, Lord, with me abide.* Sam blinked and the vision cleared. "Happy new year, Tutu! Peace!" he shouted over the hiss of fat and gospel and he was gone again.

Chapter Three

He stumbled down the driveway without plan or destination. He'd probably just end up at Dirty Face's—Dirty Face being his best friend. The guy had a real name—Arnold—but Tutu started calling him Dirty Face because he used to drool when he was little, streaking his chin with dark shiny blotches, and the name stuck. Sam was always welcome, no need to call—the walk was five minutes—but at the foot of the driveway he turned the other way. The wind had teeth and the sky glowed smoky red the way it did before rain—or snow. Damn, he should have remembered hat and gloves. Too late now. If he hung around any longer he'd run into his father, who was bringing back a load of folding chairs in the family station wagon—and no doubt stoking a slow burn over the idiocy of parties. How many New Year's bashes had his father killed with his sneering sobriety?

Sam stalked off, scuffing his shoes against the curb. How could they just axe her like that? He might have worn down his mother, played on her liberal guilt—but his father was a lost cause. Adam Stein's iron will—and tinder temper—made him invincible. "Who the hell are *you* to change the world?" Adam terminated every argument. "Case closed"—as if he was a trial lawyer and not a partner in some stupid toy company. Plastic Crap Unlimited. "Screw him," Sam muttered under his breath. "Screw them both."

The weeping willow across the street—a curtain of pliable sticks that the neighborhood kids used as home base in their marathon hide-and-seek games—was flailing crazily in the wind. God, how Tutu hated that tree. Every time it blew, she prayed under her breath the willow would fall. Why? A grand old tree swaying at the edge of some rich white folks' lawn: what did it matter to her? Just one of her strange notions. Like stepping over sidewalk cracks. Like rolling Sam's thumb in salt when he used to suck it. Like fretting over being buried in an unmarked grave. She'd brought it up again that afternoon. *Pushing up the daisies in potter's field.* Tutu always went on about potter's field when she felt mean and low—it was years before Sam understood that she was talking about a pauper's grave. He remembered her bringing it up the day her friend from Baltimore came by the house. Sam couldn't have been more than ten. While his parents were at work, those women sat in the kitchen all afternoon picking at a plate of fiery crab—*Don't touch, Sammy, you won't like it!*—and talking about down home. He'd hung around eavesdropping, but he didn't understand half of it.

"When the boat stove in, everything went to hell in a handbasket."

"I heard he drank all his money and wound up in potter's field."

"Nobody's putting me in any pauper's grave."

"Aw honey, Leon won't let that happen."

"Who's Leon?" Sam piped up—but Tutu just shooed him away. As he fled sulking down the hall, he heard the two of them cackle and snort and slap the table. "I thought I would die!" That's what Tutu always said when something really cracked her up.

And now she would die. According to his mother, it could happen any moment. Her bad heart would give out and she'd keel over—gone, just like that, and he'd never see her again. Tutu had been with Sam's family his entire life—before his life—but truthfully, he didn't know the first thing about her. She was an old black lady who lived in their attic and devoted herself—crankily—to making their lives comfortable. It shocked him when she talked about needing to find another job. In his mind, Tutu wasn't an employee, she was the boss. She was the one who gave the orders, laid down the law, enforced the rules. She was tough. Nobody crossed her, certainly not Sam. He couldn't even imagine his life without her. But what about *her* life? Sam, racking his brain, recalled her saying that her grandparents had been enslaved. And maybe there was something about a child that died—a son?—but if she told him what happened, he either wasn't paying attention or forgot. Where was she from? What deep current of history or circumstance had unmoored this granddaughter of the enslaved from her home place and floated her north to a family of second-generation Russian Jews? Sam had no idea. And once she was gone—dead or fired, it made no difference—he'd never find out. Tutu. His Tutu. MY BABY!

He walked on at random, shoulders hunched, hands balled in his pockets. What if he did a story about it for the high school newspaper? He was editor, after all—okay, *co*-editor with Dirty Face. Who said they had to fill every issue with football, candy stripers, and teacher of the week? "Local maid fired for bad heart."

Or how about a whole series on maids? Did those women earn minimum wage? What about job security? Pensions? Every maid he'd ever seen was black—what about *their* civil rights? Sam's brain started to hum. He'd make Tutu's plight the spearhead of a movement: Maids' Rights! He'd travel down to Mississippi or Georgia or wherever she was from. Meet her family, find out what happened to the son, dig up pictures of her enslaved grandparents. His AP English class was reading James Agee's *Let Us Now Praise Famous Men*. Sam loved what Agee had done for poor white sharecroppers. Loved the prose, even though he couldn't finish it. Loved the Walker Evans photos. Loved Agee most of all. The tousled hair. The tortured grimace. The cigarette wedged in a corner of his mouth. The tragic death at forty-five. Heart attack, right? Sam would do the same thing for Tutu and her people. "Seventeen-year-old writer strikes gold in tragic story of mistreated maid." That would show them.

Sam was on the second paragraph of his rave *New York Times* review—"in prose as symphonic as Agee's yet as punchy as Hemingway's, young Samuel Stein illuminates the oppressed lives . . ."—when he looked up and realized he had circled the block and was standing in front of Dirty Face's house. The cold had numbed his fingers and toes. His stomach was growling. It was New Year's Eve of his senior year of high school and Sam was damned if he was going to spend it trapped in the kitchen with Tutu while his parents yakked it up with their friends in the dining room. Hadn't Dirty Face said something about a party? Sam strode up the driveway, climbed the steps to the kitchen door, and rang the bell. Two seconds later, Dirty Face was ushering him inside. Their maid, Crystal, evidently, had New Year's off.

Chapter Four

Dirty Face was cooler than Sam, or so he insisted. He had the cool hair—straight and shiny and long enough to flip from his eyes with a toss of his head—and the cool attitude (never show your feelings and sneer at everyone who did) and he hung out with the bottom-rung cool kids (except when they decided he was beneath them and then he hung out with Sam). But coolwise, Dirty Face had one fatal flaw: he was short and as chubby as a toddler. Dirty Face would never be lanky. His butt would never ride high and tight like a basketball player's. His cheekbones would never cast shadows on sunken cheeks. The waistband of his jeans would never gap around flat, rippling abs. And, in the world according to Dirty Face, this and this alone was the reason why his adoration of Tanya Tomsky was not requited. Even though Tanya was the same age as Sam and Dirty Face, she acted like she was twenty-five and treated them like they were twelve. Tanya was too cool even to bother with the cool kids in school. She had raven black hair, olive skin, and long elegant arms that she was forever wrapping around her willowy midriff or draping over the shoulders of tall skinny boys. She slouched. She smoked cigarettes. She wrote brutalist short stories about dwarves and Nazis and hookers. One of her stories had gotten a personalized rejection from *The New Yorker*: "commanding . . . Cheeveresque. . . . try us again . . ." Tanya spent every free second hanging out in the City (no need to specify—if you lived in the suburbs of New York there was only one). She claimed she gave blow jobs to older guys she barely knew—guys in their twenties with their own apartments and drug habits in the City—and, feigning shame, confessed every gory gooey detail to Dirty Face, who relayed it all to Sam. Tanya never seemed to notice the agony this wrought—and Dirty Face was too cool to say anything about it except to Sam, who was too nice or maybe just too clueless to call him on this breach of the cool code. "She lets those horny assholes jizz in her face but she treats *me* like a teddy bear!" Sam had heard it all a million times. Dirty Face acknowledged that his case was hopeless, but he couldn't stay away from Tanya or stop talking about her. Sam didn't get it. The whole thing was starting to remind him of the soap operas he and Tutu watched together every afternoon. *The Edge of Night. As the World Turns. General Hospital.* Once, after the day's installment, Sam had idly asked Tutu how you could tell when you were in love. "You'll know, Sammy," she replied, "and then you'll wish you didn't. When it hurts, that's how you know. The more it hurts, the more you love."

Maybe Tutu was right—love was pain.

But being buddies with a monomaniac was also pain. How do you tell your best friend that his Grand Passion is mind-numbingly boring?

Well, it wasn't going to happen on New Year's Eve.

"Anything to eat?" Sam asked without taking off his coat. Dirty Face's parents were out for the evening, but they'd left a stockpile of snacks and keys to their spare car.

"Everything," Dirty Face proclaimed as he threw open the fridge. The boys stood elbow to elbow ransacking the shelves. "Big party over by school," Dirty Face mumbled through a mouthful of clam dip. "Everyone's invited—even you, junior." The pats to the top of Sam's head would have been patronizing if Dirty Face wasn't standing on his tiptoes. "And the car doesn't have to be back till tomorrow morning. So if we end up totally wasted or something—"

"Or something—"

"We can crash there and sleep it off. Maybe this will be the night I get lucky."

They watched TV until 10:00 p.m.—only dorks showed up early for a New Year's bash—and then set out. Dirty Face, at the wheel, swerved through the empty streets, monologuing like a stand-up comic about his broken heart, while Sam stared out the window and emitted the occasional sympathetic "huh." God, how he hated the suburbs—especially *this* suburb, Fat Neck on Lone Guyland, as he and Dirty Face had taken to calling it. So what if F. Scott Fitzgerald had lived here in the 1920s and immortalized the place as West Egg in *The Great Gatsby*? Fitzgerald made West Egg sound glamorous and sexy and vaguely sinister—"one of the strangest communities in North America . . . this unprecedented 'place' that Broadway had begotten upon a Long Island fishing village"—but that was half a century ago, when bootleggers and flappers swung from the trees. Now it was just a bedroom community stuffed with rag-trade impresarios, pill-popping trophy wives, and their brilliant beautiful Ivy-League-or-bust offspring. Oh yes, and the black maids who raised them. The Steins were hardly alone maid-wise. They were not even the worst. In the fancy part of town (Kings Pit, Dirty Face had rechristened it), where Gatsbyesque estates still "glittered along the water," some families had two maids ("girls" they called them, though most were Tutu's age)—a "day worker" and a "live-in." At least both of Sam's parents had jobs, so they had some excuse for farming out the child-rearing. In most of the families with maids, the dad commuted into the City while the mom holed up in bed all day, watching TV, downing martinis, and rasping orders into the caverns of her immaculate split-level. The "girl" did everything—the mother barely knew where the kitchen was. In most of the families without maids, the moms had jobs to make ends meet and the kids pretty much raised themselves. The rest of the families were the maids' families. (Though nobody acknowledged it, Fat Neck was as segregated as Mobile or Biloxi, with the town's few black people consigned to a little ghetto of wood-frame firetraps that no self-respecting white family would touch with a ten-foot pole.) On paper, it sounded awfully tony—the Gold Coast, the Miracle Mile, Kings Pit, Queens Expressway—but it wasn't. The Steins, like most of their neighbors, were outer-borough strivers who had moved out to the Island when "real" money started rolling in after the war. Their privilege was so new and shallow it threatened to come off in the rain like a bad dye job. Sam's parents had staked themselves out in a newly constructed spec ranch house—but the "ranch" was a quarter acre of clay barely thirty miles from the cold-water Lower East Side walk-up where his immigrant grandparents had taken refuge after Ellis Island. The Steins were comfortable but they weren't rich—not City-rich—and everything they had they had earned. “We pulled ourselves up by our bootstraps,” Sam’s father never tired of saying. “What’s a bootstrap?” Sam never quite had the nerve to ask.

“Sam? Sammy boy? Still with me here?”

“Sure, sure. You were just saying how if Tanya doesn’t let you . . .”

Dirty Face pulled both hands off the wheel and implored the windshield. “See what I have to put up with?” Everyone knew what a terrible liar Sam was—everyone except Sam. “Admit it—you haven’t listened to word one.”

“Sorry—just a little distracted tonight, you know?” He considered telling Dirty Face about the Tutu situation but decided not to. It would just trigger a barrage of snark about being tied to her apron strings.

Regaining the wheel just inches before he collided with the curb, Dirty Face screeched left around the high school ball field, hung a right down a short street, and killed the engine. They’d arrived. Sam got out and squinted up and down the unfamiliar block: little wooden boxes set close together, bare saplings swaying in the wind, evergreen shrubs strung with Christmas lights, parked cars lining both curbs. He could hear the stereo bass—it sounded like “Light My Fire”—thumping across the street.

Dirty Face flipped back his bangs and shot Sam what was supposed to be a devilish grin. “Ready to rock ’n’ roll? Next stop—1970!”

Sam was having second thoughts. Technically, he hadn’t even been invited. Technically, he barely knew Janine, the girl who was throwing the party. According to Dirty Face, the whole thing had been masterminded by Tanya when she discovered that Janine’s parents had gone to Florida and left her home alone. Party house on New Year’s Eve sans grown-ups! Tanya called everyone she knew and told them to call everyone *they* knew and apparently they all showed up. A gathering of the cliques to kick off a new decade—the seventies! Only Sam wasn't part of any clique. He didn't have a crowd, gang, or posse. He was only here because Dirty Face had roped him in.

Without knocking, Dirty Face pushed open the door and disappeared into the maelstrom. Sam, two steps behind, considered making a dash for it—no one would miss him, he could walk home, no big deal—when he heard his name sail out over the din. "Little Sammy Stein! No fucking way!" A sweaty hand grabbed him, pulled him inside, and shut the door.

"Richard? Richard Rines?" What was *he* doing here?

"Look at *you*," Richard shouted, squeezing Sam's shoulders with both hands while he gave him the once-over.

No, look at you! Sam hadn't laid eyes on Richard in six years and the metamorphosis was mind-blowing: from Little Rascal to rock star. How did *that* happen? Four years older than Sam, Richard used to be part of the neighborhood pack that hit the street every summer evening for stickball and hide-and-seek. Back then, Richard was a scrappy little punk, black-haired, green-eyed, dirty, ragged, always talking too close and laughing too hard. Richard was fast and fearless but uncoordinated and uncontrollable and that's what Sam liked about him. Tutu always said Richard was a demon, but he was *Sam's* demon—the only older boy who ever gave him the time of day. And Sam worshipped him for it. When the neighborhood kids played chicken—a gladiatorial contest in which two younger boys mounted the shoulders of two older boys and grabbed and punched and yanked at each other until one of them got thrown to the ground and "died"—Richard always chose Sam as his jockey. Sam remembered the sharp bones that jutted out of Richard's shoulders and the smell of dry autumn leaves that rose off his hair. Riding Richard made Sam feel special, noticed, *included* in a way that never happened with his older brothers, Ron and Tom. Ron claimed Richard was a sneaky little thief who boosted stuff from other kids' lockers and smoked cigarettes in the bathroom. Sam didn't care. Tutu told him the cops once showed up at Richard's house after some funny business with two little girls—she'd heard all about it from the Rineses' maid. Sam was convinced Richard was innocent. He didn't even mind when Richard crashed their sled into a tree and nearly gave him a concussion: flying downhill double decker on top of Richard made it all worthwhile. Richard was the outlaw alter ego Sam wanted to be and be noticed by. Demigod and devil rolled into one. And then, at fifteen, he vanished. There were rumors that he had gotten into drugs, that his parents had packed him off to boarding school—or reform school—that he'd totaled the family car, that he'd made some girl pregnant, that he'd run away to join a hippie commune in Vermont. But no sign of Richard himself.

Until tonight.

Sam took in the shoulder-length black hair, the emerald eyes rimmed in black, the broad straight shoulders, and the little scar beside his mouth. Shaving wound? Knife fight? It was as if the last six years squeezed shut like an accordion and he and Richard were back on that sled careening wildly into the abyss.

"Come with me." Richard had Sam by the elbow and was towing him through the bodies gyrating to "Honky Tonk Women" in the living room. "I gotta show you something." Nothing had changed. Richard might look like Jim Morrison's pretty little brother, but he was the same twitchy, scratchy-voiced, in-your-face trickster he'd been at fifteen. "Come on" was all he had to say and

Sam fell into line: sidekick forever. Sam saw heads turn as Richard steered him through the living room—there was Tanya with her lips plastered to the ear of some tall blond guy; there was Dirty Face putting a bullet through his temple with one finger; there was Janine staring bug-eyed at the cyclone shredding her parents' house; there were huddles of kids too cool to acknowledge Sam's existence—but he didn't stop, couldn't stop. It was as if Richard had been waiting for him so the party could really begin.

As they snaked through the kitchen, someone put a paper cup half full of what looked like cough syrup into Sam's hand. "Punch!" Behind the kitchen was a hallway with three closed doors. Like *Let's Make a Deal*, Sam was thinking: choose the right door and you win the all-expenses-paid week in Acapulco, the wrong door and you get the Sunbeam toaster. But Richard didn't pause to ponder: he opened the farthest door without knocking and stuck his head inside. Then he swiveled back to Sam. "Chug it or you can't come in," he said, pointing at the punch, and Sam did as he was told. He gagged but didn't ralph: chalk one up for the side.

Richard prodded Sam inside and shut the door again. A couple of candles quavered in the draft. Sam could just make out the lumps of bodies sprawled on the floor. A match flared and flame glinted off a long glass tube. "Bong," one of the lumps murmured. "Bingo," murmured another. "Bingo bong." "Big bad bingo bong." Then one of them was coughing and the others were laughing and Richard palmed Sam's head and pushed until his knees buckled and he went down. "Someone pack a bowl for young Sammy Stein here," Richard ordered, and then he fitted a mask over Sam's face and handed him the tube. "Gas mask bongerator," he said into Sam's ear. "Just suck, hold, and try not to explode."

What if I fry my brains and fail the SATs? Sam was thinking. *What if the cops come and we all get busted?* But Richard was already kneeling in front of him lighting a match. Sam sucked until the smoke rose to the top of his skull and snuffed out his cerebral cortex. Then he exploded. Richard got the mask off and pounded his back. "No more virgin, right?"

Right, Sam would have said, but his lungs were burning and tears were streaming down his face.

"Good shit, right?"

Was it? Sam had tried weed once before with his brother Ron—but the only thing that happened was that when Ron cranked up Cream's "Sunshine of Your Love" on the living room stereo he could hear the *woo-doo-doo-doo* of the bass and drums in one speaker and the *wah-wah-wahdle-dah-dah* of the guitar in the other. Was this shit better than that shit? Jimi Hendrix's "Purple Haze" wafted in from the living room. Sam shut his eyes, stepped inside the song—*Accuse me why I kiss this guy*—and let go. Purple shag carpeted the floor of his skull and icicles hung dripping from the sockets. Armies of ants were swarming out of the shag, swirling up the glittering spears and tobogganing down like black snowflakes. His mind's eye, hijacking the controls, zoomed in on one kamikaze snowflake—not an ant at all but Rocky, the flying squirrel from the *Rocky and Bullwinkle* show. Rocky's plane was spiraling down in a plume of smoke and the frantic rodent was screaming "Within you without you" through the hole of his face. Sam felt the back of his neck catch fire and his eyes snapped open. The candle flame multiplied and then merged together to a single tongue of light. *The Lord our God; the Lord is One.* Sam rotated his head. From the bookshelf, rows of stuffed animals stared down through malicious glass eyes. The flounces around the bed frame whispered and fluttered. He felt something in the room with him, shivering the air. A burning, evanescing presence. Time's arrow. Love's archer. Time. Love. Time to make room for the next . . .

"Earth to Sam. Come in, Sam. This is ground control. Can you read me, Sam?" Richard's voice. Richard's fingers at the nape of his neck. Richard's crunchy leaf smell mingled with the dank reek of pot. "You need another hit, laddie."

"Laddie?" Sam croaked.

"Lassie?" Richard croaked back. Sam hated him.

The slimy rubber mask was around his head again and Sam was inhaling another column of toxic vapor.

"All better now?"

Sam spewed smoke, his head ricocheting against the side of a mattress. Was something throttling him? No, it was Richard grasping his shoulders and shaking. Then the shaking quit but the hands stayed put and when Sam opened his eyes Richard's face was so close it was like the sun with a corona of candlelight flaring around its perimeter. Or were the rays—radii?—penetrating the circumference? Penetrating, perpetrating, perpetuating, irradiating. Refulgent, redundant, ephemeral, peripheral, penitential. Two minutes ago, Sam knew the difference—now the words fizzed in his brain like static. "You were always such a baby." Richard's voice—mocking him again? Too close. Too smoky. Hands all over the place. "Quit it, Richard"—what Sam used to say when he was ten and Richard jumped him and tickled until he could barely breathe. It worked. Richard let go and slumped down beside him. The two of them sprawled in the dark with their heads lolled back on the pink bedspread. Then "Street Fighting Man" came on full blast and their heads started swinging in sync with the beat, then their shoulders were swaying in tandem and their legs pressed together and they were moving as one as Richard shouted and screamed the lyrics. Richard Rines and Mick Jagger—their satanic majesties—belting it out in perfect unison. Sam, throbbing, wanted to stand up and strut but he didn't dare. *Thank God for the dark*. Then Richard stopped singing and started to laugh—or maybe it was Sam who started laughing and infected Richard—soon they were both laughing their asses off, so much laughter that Sam got dizzy and thought he might puke.

That's when the world cracked open.

"I'm so sorry," a voice pealed into the sudden incandescence—and in the next second the light was doused. Someone had flicked the bedroom overhead on and then off again. But that ephemeral effulgence was enough to scorch the face of an angel onto Sam's retinas. A halo of wine-red curls. Tiny sapphire eyes ablaze with mercy. Skin like dawn-kissed cumulus. And she was gone—fade to black—but then she returned as a silhouette in the candlelight. A moon to Richard's sun. *"Kim!"* Richard shouted. "Why the fuck did you turn on the light? Don't you know light is death?" Sam, pinned paralyzed to his pants, watched the angel descend. "Richard, I can't believe I found you." The hectoring of "Street Fighting Man" segued into the rolling mumble of "Prodigal Son" and the passages to Sam's brain cleared. "My savior," the angel warbled, stretching herself out on the floor on the other side of Richard. The sarcasm was so thick and sweet Sam could practically taste it. A Southern drawl? "Did you hear that someone spiked the punch with acid?" *A-yuh-cid* was how she said it. "If I start tripping I'm going to freak. You know how paranoid I get." In the candlelight her hair was the color of bruised raspberries—amber glass—sun-glazed honey. Her body was so slight she looked like a ripple of satin beside the tidal wave of Richard.

"Kim—Sam. Sam—Kim." Richard, wedged between, crossed his arms over his chest and gestured from one to the other with open palms. "Relax, you guys. I had tons of punch and I'm not tripping." Richard wiggled his cleft chin. "At least I don't *think* I'm tripping."

Sam leaned toward Kim and opened his mouth. He had the sentence perfectly formed in his head. *Don't worry, Kim, I'll save you.* But all that came out was "Ull."

He could have been gone a year—or a minute. There was a pillow under his neck only it was warm. A marble rolled gently back and forth across his forehead but it smelled like flowers. His eyes opened to red tendrils twining above him. No sign of Richard. No music. No bodies on the floor. Sam was lying on Janine's bed with his head in Kim's lap. *Oh god oh god please don't let there be puke.*

"Welcome back. I've been counting your freckles."

Without thinking, out it popped: "Would you like to try one?" There. He'd said it.

He saw her eyes roll but the lips came no closer. "Nice try, Samuel." Samuel? He liked the sound of it coming from her. "I've been wondering. Who ironed your shirt?"

What? Sam glanced down at himself—pale blue beautifully pressed though now a bit rumpled button-down long-sleeve Arrow shirt, passed down from his brother Tom and blessedly unstained by barf, punch, saliva, or bong juice.

"Your mother or your housekeeper?" Kim persisted.

"Housekeeper," Sam finally allowed. "My mother never irons—but Tutu loves it. She irons everything, even my . . ." Undies sounded too babyish. Jockey shorts too studly. BVDs too queer.

But Kim jumped right back in. "Tutu being the housekeeper? The maid."

Sam blinked and removed his head from Kim's lap. This was definitely not the conversational gambit he'd intended. They should be making out by now! But something told him not to try. "Yeah, Tutu being the maid—though whenever I call her that she blows her top and yells, 'I'm not your damn maid!' Tutu's kind of the family boss."

"I bet," said Kim's mouth, mocking—but the eyes danced and her shoulders shook. "*I'm not your damn maid.* I like that. She sounds tough."

"You have no idea."

"Oh, but I do."

And just like that, the awkwardness lifted and the two of them were sitting side by side on Janine's bed and talking about everything and nothing while their shoulders, just grazing, whispered their own conversation. Kim was also a senior, only she went to the other Fat Neck high school, which is why Sam had never seen her before. "Believe me, I would have noticed you," which elicited a blush and an elbow jab to the ribs. "Did your maid teach you to flirt like that?" Kim was a dancer—ballet, modern, Martha Graham—which explained the long waist, perfect posture, and small leotard-toned boobs—but now she was having second thoughts. "With everything that's going on, dancing just seems so bourgeois." Sam mentally flipped through his SAT flash cards: *of or pertaining to the middle class; materialistic.* "I mean, folk dance is one thing—but all that poofy stuff with toe shoes and tutus and pink tights just seems so . . . so . . ."

"Middle crass?"

Laughter leapt from Kim's eyes to her throat. Sam flushed. Was he funny? Funny was good, right? Anything to keep her laughing—Kim's laugh was the most divine thing he'd ever heard—like a fountain of coins falling through a shaft of sun. Maybe he should kiss her right now while her eyes were closed? Too late. The peals subsided and she was off and running again—so much to tell him.

Of course they had to talk about Richard.

Richard, according to Kim, was decidedly not bourgeois. She and Richard had met that fall at a party in the City. Richard had his own place in the East Village, did Sam know that? No, Sam did not. Mutual friends introduced them. Wow, she had friends in the City. All two of Sam's friends lived on his block. "I think Richard's bi," Kim dropped. "You know AC/DC? He's also obsessed with celebrity, oh my god. He claims to know Allen Ginsberg and Andy Warhol. I think they had sex—Richard and Ginsberg—though you never know with Richard. Half the time he's totally lying."

Bi? Sam started to sweat. Richard had gotten so incredibly handsome. Was Sam bi because he'd noticed? And how the hell did Richard meet Allen Ginsberg? Sam flashed on that greasy graying beard tangled in the cleft of Richard's chin. Ugh. If you're going to do it with an old guy, Santa Claus would have been preferable. By the time he refocused, Kim was two paragraphs ahead. Had Sam heard how Richard got kicked out of college for calling a professor a fascist pig? Did he know that Richard's father was a big-time record producer who practically put Motown on the map? Pretty much every big-name black singer belonged to him. Because of Daddy, Richard knew everyone and everyone wanted to know him.

"So is he your boyfriend?" Sam had to ask.

"No—why?—is he yours?" Kim shot back.

"Not likely when I haven't laid eyes on him since I was eleven."

And Sam launched into the story of how Richard used to live around the corner and even though Tutu hated his guts and his brothers said he was nasty, he had always thought Richard was beyond cool and incredibly funny. Funny, yes, Kim agreed, but maybe not as cool as he thinks he is. "Whatever you do, don't trust him." Then they were comparing notes on families—their mothers both worked at the same hospital, Kim's as a social worker, Sam's as a radiologist—and on being raised by the maid. Kim's was named Delores and Kim was her favorite, just like Sam and Tutu. Delores had grown up in Georgia with ten brothers and sisters and she was super-religious—always praying and singing hymns and listening to recordings of Father Divine. She got married when she was fifteen—two years younger than they were!—and by the time she was twenty-one she had four kids of her own. Then her husband died and she had to leave the kids in Georgia with her mother so she could look for work up north. That's how she ended up with Kim's family.

"How did you find all that out?"

"I asked. You might try it with Tutu sometime. It's not like she was born to iron your pretty blue shirts." Ouch. "That's how I got into Black Power. Because of Delores. Last summer we went down to Georgia together to visit her family."

"Your parents let you?"

"They had no choice. You wouldn't believe what I saw. It's like civil rights never happened. When word got out that a white girl was staying with Delores's family, all hell broke loose. Everywhere I went, these white crackers would block my path and shout in my face: 'There goes the N lover'—I can't say that word but you know what it was. 'Go back to Jew York, N lover!' I swear to God I thought they'd shoot me and Delores both."

Sam felt himself shrinking. If he didn't jump in with something fast, he'd be back to four foot nine. "I'm gonna write about it," he blurted.

"You write?"

He basked for a second in the indigo gaze. "Uh-huh. School newspaper." The dazzle dimmed. "But that's just the start. I'm going write about Black Power." Pause, then he took a wild stab. "I hear the Black Panthers are awesome."

"You know about the Panthers?" Sam shrugged. "I hope you're not just bragging, like Richard. He claims they use the same drug dealer—which is bullshit because the Panthers are totally anti-drugs. Not that I would know anything about that—I can't stand drugs."

"Because they make you paranoid."

"And they make you pass out."

Something Sam could not put into words passed between them. A challenge. An admission. A recognition. Both of them were bluffing—a little. Under Kim's war paint, he could see the princess in pink at the barre. The knock-kneed girl trembling on the high dive. She wanted to jump but she didn't have the nerve. Not yet. He didn't have the nerve either. If they just sat there, they'd talk forever and never get any closer. Sam felt everything slipping through his fingers. They'd talk until they ran out of things to say and then they'd separate and rejoin the party. Friends. Just friends.

He was the one who broke the silence. "Kim?"

"Samuel?"

"Might I kiss you?"

She smiled. He felt his freckles ignite. "You might."

And so he did.

Chapter Five

"Did you meet someone?"

It was ten and a half hours into the new decade and Sam had just staggered into the kitchen, head pounding, heart gushing, lips chafed from the longest first kiss in history. He could still taste Kim's perfume on the tip of his tongue. Not just flowers—lilies of the valley, she told him. Kim, short for Kimberly, Goodman. There was her phone number inked on his palm and miraculously intact. He hadn't invented it.

"Smart to get her number. Does this little honey have a name?"

No way was he going to spill the beans to Tutu. Not one word. If she got wind of the fact that Richard was the one who introduced him to Kim, he'd never hear the end of it.

"Well, you better get in there. They're waiting on you."

The New Year's Day brunch was a Stein family tradition. No matter how hungover, every Stein had to show up that morning for scrambled eggs, bacon, and waffles—a rare treat that only

Tutu knew how to coax from the jaws of the rickety sticky waffle iron. The Steins being Jewish didn't do Christmas. The boys were banned from the annual New Year's Eve bash. But the Day After brunch was a command performance.

When Sam took his seat at the table, the parents as usual were talking about their work partners (the managers who wrangled endlessly at his father's toy business and the male radiology team that lorded it over the two female attendings at his mother's hospital). Then his mother changed the subject to "lovely girls," her euphemism for the ugly daughters of friends and distant relatives she was forever trying to palm off on Ron and Tom—Sam too, now that he'd had his growth spurt. He thought about bringing up Tutu's situation, maybe trying to enlist his brothers—but the deep trenches furrowing his father's face decided him against it. *They had no choice*, Kim had said proudly when he marveled that her family let her go down south with Delores. The way to win with parents, according to Kim, was not to confront but to box them into a corner. Divide and conquer. Manipulate. Bore from within. He blinked and there she was behind his eyes. Had she been teasing when she said he was *adorable*? But if she didn't like him just a little, why did she let him kiss her?

"Not hungry?" Tutu asked when she came in to clear the table. "Cat got your tongue?"

Sam just shook his head and carried his plate into the kitchen. In a way, Tutu was his best friend and had always been. She knew his habits and moods and secrets better than his own mother did. She could read his mind. She had his back whatever trouble he made or got into. But after last night, something was different. He couldn't bear the sight of her in a uniform. *I'm not your damn maid* was her joke but it wasn't funny. If Tutu *wasn't* their maid, what was she? "Quit poking your nose where it doesn't belong," she was always warning him. But hadn't Kim poked into her maid's business?

He knew he should wait before calling. Being desperate was the epitome of uncool—but he *was* desperate.

She picked up on the first ring. "I was hoping it was you. How's your mouth? Mine's still completely numb—I can barely eat."

"Sorry . . . I should've . . ."

But Kim burst out laughing—"It was soooooo romantic once I found the ChapStick"—and Sam knew that everything was going to be all right.

They spoke for an hour, until she had to hang up and pee, and then for another hour until she said that her ear was now as sore as her lips. "You're killing me, Samuel Stein." But she agreed they had to see each other again. Soon. As in that afternoon. She lived three miles away and the streets were slushy from the couple of inches of snow that had fallen the night before. Minor obstacle. Sam put on his galoshes and ducked out before Tutu cornered him. His English class was reading *The Sun Also Rises* and as he headed down the driveway, he pretended it was Paris. Kim and Lady Brett fused in his mind. "Hullo, chaps—how about a drink?" The cobblestone streets were etched in black and silver. The women all wore long scarves and crimson lipstick. He and Kim/Brett found a little round marble-top table in the corner of their café and ordered Pernod—whatever that was—and devoured each other with their eyes until they were so famished for love they had to flee down the avenue and race the five flights up to her flat under the eaves, and with the Eiffel Tower winking through the window, they . . .

"Down, boy," Sam said aloud. And then, "Quit talking to yourself, you idiot." But who would hear? The street was deserted, as usual, and so was the next street and the next and the one after that. Nothing but scoops of frosted shrubs; green stubble poking through the snow; black tracks scoring the white streets. What a godawful place they made him live in. What a godawful family. Did they have any *idea* how smug they were? They all cried when Dr. King was shot but did anything change? They didn't even ask Tutu how she felt. "She doesn't want to talk about it," his mother insisted. But did that mean she didn't care? For years now, every time something about civil rights came on the radio, Tutu switched it off. Maybe she didn't want them to see how upset she was. Maybe she listened alone in her attic bedroom, where she could shake her fist in freedom. Maybe it reminded her of how much she hated being a maid. A live-in. Upstairs was her domain. It was all she had—until they kicked her out.

Sam remembered the few times he'd ventured up to the refinished attic room where Tutu slept five nights a week. Even though it was just a staircase away from the rest of the house, the upper floor felt old and worn and mysterious, as if the suffering past were entombed under the eaves. Gaudy floral paper covered the walls; the trim was painted institutional aquamarine; low-wattage bulbs filtered through cloudy glass shades barely lit the corners of the brown linoleum floor. Fifteen steps took him there, but it was like crossing into a foreign country. He was careful to knock and wait for her permission. When he opened the door, Tutu would be sitting there smiling with the Bible resting in her palms. Happy to see him—happier than she ever was downstairs. Sam liked it up there. He liked being a stranger in his own house, a guest. Tutu's guest. A picture of Jesus crowned with thorns hung by the door and the Lord's Prayer in gothic print was tacked over her bed. "One day, I'm going to take you to my church," she told him. "Show you off to my friends." But that day had never come because Sam's mother was too scared to let him to go to Harlem.

And now he'd never get to go.

The bubble burst and Sam realized he was lost. Kim said she lived on Red Oak Lane, just south of the train station—it sounded simple over the phone, but he'd never been to this part of town and everything looked strange in the flat aqueous half-light. He trudged on through the slush, dreaming himself back to their café. *Afterward*. Kim was reaching for his hands across the tabletop. Sam was wedging a knee between her legs. She had the most beautiful neck—reed thin, petal soft, the skin almost translucent.

"You know I have a boyfriend."

Kim dropped this on him last night but Sam had conveniently forgotten until now. Or did she say *had*? He was suddenly miserable. The guy's name was Brad, he remembered that much. "Brad's a total radical—we went to the March on the Pentagon together." *Yeah, and I watched it on TV between Daffy Duck and Porky Pig.* What if Brad the Rad was with her now, wooing Kim back with his Che Guevara scruff and killer sneer? "And who's this little boy? Your latest recruit?" Sam wanted to turn tail and slink back home—but he was freezing so he kept on walking. And there was her house—a bright blue split-level that looked a lot like his. And there was her face in the upstairs window. Beaming at him. Alone. Sam melted and walked up the shoveled path.

MAKING THE SECOND MOVE was even harder than the first. For starters, he was sober. Second, Kim now seemed way too beautiful to be touched by the likes of him. Third, they were alone—her parents were at a party, her older sister was away, Delores had the week off—which should have been conducive but wasn't. They sat on her bed, a platoon of stuffed animals arrayed around them.

Sam looked at the books and papers strewn around the patchwork quilt. *Soul on Ice. Slaughterhouse-Five.* "In Defense of Self Defense" by Huey P. Newton, Black Panthers Minister of Defense. A tabloid newspaper called *The Black Panther* with the headline FREE THE NY 21 AND ALL POLITICAL PRISONERS over a photo of six black men in berets with raised fists.

"My parents think I've gone crazy."

"You're amazing. *This* is amazing."

"And you're . . ." But she finished the sentence with a kiss.

The only other thing Sam said was "Are you sure?"

The only other thing Kim said was "I'm on the pill."

She winced when he slipped a hand under her sweater. "Your hands are like ice." She took his right hand in both of hers and warmed it, moved to the left. Then she freed herself of the sweater and—no bra!—laid both his hands on her boobs. The nipples shrank and hardened in his palms. "There. That's better." There was a moment of trembling paralysis. Kim unbuttoned Sam's shirt. The muscles on his chest were snapping and quivering as if he were being electrocuted—but so gently. A rash of goose bumps spread into his scalp. "You're shivering," Kim whispered and embraced him, flesh to flesh. Her fingers undid his pants and fly. "To treat hypothermia you have to be completely naked." She stripped off jeans and panties and pulled him on top of her. Sam buried his face in the hollow of her neck and inhaled. He brushed her skin with the tip of his lips. Her throat, her jaw, her cheek, her mouth. She spread her legs and he settled between them. "Getting warmer?" Sam groaned. He didn't know the steps, there was no music—but he was dancing. His fingers wrapped the backs of her thighs. She closed her hand around him and slid him into her. "Slowly," she murmured. But Sam couldn't stop.

When it was over, he felt her cheek wet and cold next to his. He thought it was his sweat—right before he came every pore in his body had opened and gushed like a faucet. But it was tears. She was crying.

"Did I? . . . Did you? . . ."

"No, Samuel." And she circled his back with both arms and pulled him so close that he could feel her heart beating inside his chest. The sweat was chilling him. Her warmth was making him hard again. "It just feels like everything's over. Everything that ever happened in this room is ending."

He was back inside. *Twice*? Sam was thinking. *Was that even possible?* Every heartbeat made it bigger. The dance he hadn't known he knew started again. *Ending?* To him, it felt like everything had just begun.

WHAT TO SAY to the girl who has just relieved you of your virginity? *Thanks? Wow? Today I am a man? How was it for you?* (How *was* it for her? he wondered. How could you tell?) Sam was afloat in a tropical sea of relief, an elixir of blissed-out gratitude pumping through his veins—but there was something else gnawing at him he couldn't name or understand. Apprehension? He had an impulse to call someone and share the news—hand out cigars, stand the guys a round of drinks. But who would he call? And what would he say?

"Good thing you're on the pill" was what popped out of his mouth. Romantic, hey? They were in her kitchen polishing off a bakery coffee cake. "Tutu warned me not to get my little missy in trouble the first time at bat."

"That's what she said? *Little missy?*" They both snickered.

"Yeah—and she was staring me straight in the crotch when she said it." Sam grinned. *"I thought I would die!"* he hollered in Tutu's accent.

"She sounds funny—funny ha-ha, not funny peculiar. But Tutu? That can't be her real name?"

"Nah. Her real name's Nettie, but I couldn't say it when I was a baby. So I started calling her Net-tuh and that morphed into Tutu and it stuck. She doesn't mind."

"I bet. You ever ask her?"

Sam shook his head. Somehow, it was a relief to talk about Tutu. Trying to conjure her up for Kim, Sam saw how strange she was—funny ha-ha *and* funny peculiar. Tutu was a sphinx, an oracle, a fount of arcane knowledge and allusions. She told Sam when he was little that if he kept sucking his thumb his teeth would grow up his nose like tusks. Don't eat hot eggs, it will make your breath bad. If a pregnant woman touches a toad, her baby will have warts. When Sam and his brothers got out of hand, rather than spank (strictly forbidden) or fly off the handle, Tutu shook her head and murmured under her breath, "If he's not just like *that certain party* I know." No matter how they begged, she never revealed the identity of this mysterious stranger (it was years before Sam even realized she was talking about a *person* and not some sort of birthday bash with a clown and twisted balloons). "I used to think *that certain party* was some two-bit hoodlum slouched in a dark alley," he told Kim. "You know—with smoke curling up his pencil mustache, a switchblade in his pants pocket, dandruff salting his greasy scalp. Then I saw *To Kill a Mockingbird* and I thought maybe Boo Radley was that certain party."

Kim stared. "It never occurred to you that she made *that certain party* up just to torture you?"

Never, Sam was thinking—but he didn't want to look like the gullible idiot he was, so he kept talking. "She also had a secret hiding place. That had to be real." Whenever he and his brothers fought over a toy, Tutu used to snatch it and stow it away in her *secret hiding place* and there it would stay until they deserved to get it back. No toy ever returned from sequestration. On her days off, Sam and his brothers combed through every inch of the house and basement searching for their vanished Magic 8 Balls and Mr. Potato Heads. They did everything but pry up the floorboards but the secret eluded them. "And now they're firing her," he sighed.

"What?"

"For her own good, they claim—on account of her bad heart."

"And you're *letting* them?" Sam flinched. She made it sound like it was *his* fault. Something snapped—the mood broke. Kim, suddenly all business, was reeling off facts and figures. Did he have any *idea* how little blacks earned compared to whites? After twenty-five years at the same job, a white worker had savings, security, pension. Tutu had none of that, right? Because she was a black woman. Couldn't his parents see how unfair that was? It was different with her maid, Delores—Kim had seen to that. Delores had worked for the Goodman family for years, but she was scared they'd fire her if she made any demands, so Kim stepped up to advocate for her. Delores hated the horrible uniform they made her wear, and Kim badgered her parents to let her wear own clothes to work. When she told Kim she wanted to eat with the rest of family instead of sitting hunched alone in the kitchen, Kim went on a hunger strike until her parents caved. Delores had paid vacations—including Christmas and New Year's. She wasn't docked for the time she took off to deal with family emergencies. Common human decency, but none of it had ever occurred to

Kim's parents. "Civil rights was not enough," she wound up. "It's on us, Sam. We have to *do* something." Her voice stung him. "Blacks were slaves here for two hundred years—twice as long as they've been free." In a flash she was on her feet—"Wait a sec!"—up the stairs and back with her copy of *The Autobiography of Malcolm X.* The book fell open to the marked page. "Listen to this."

> *In one generation, the black slave women in America had been raped by the slavemaster white man until there had begun to emerge a homemade, handmade, brainwashed race that was no longer even of its true color, that no longer even knew its true family names. The slavemaster forced his family name upon this rape-mixed race, which the slavemaster began to call "the Negro."*

Kim closed the book and stared at him. "What's Tutu's last name?"

"Carter."

"Slave name. Same as Curry. Delores Curry. She told me that half the rednecks in her home county are named Curry. Someday I'm gonna help Delores find her real family—her African family. Wouldn't that be amazing?"

That would be amazing, Sam agreed, but already his mind was drifting back to what had just happened in her bed. He would never be a virgin again. *Forever. And ever. Hallelujah! Hallelujah!* The two of them would fix the world together—later.

As Kim flipped through Malcolm X, Sam kept the jubilation to himself. Were they now officially a couple? He decided not to ask or even wonder. Let it be.

Chapter Six

Oh happy day
Oh happy day
When Jesus washed—when Jesus washed
He washed my sins away

Lean, loose-limbed, twenty-one, Leon Carter folded himself at the waist so he could position his face in the frame of the tiny, chipped bathroom mirror. With a toothbrush held like a microphone before his parted lips, he serenaded his reflection.

Oh happy day

The sweet voice swelled and echoed off the tile. The brown Adam's apple bobbed in the polished glass. Leon's neck was so long and the mirror so small that he had to bend his knees if he wanted to see the top of his face and his hair. And he did. Not that he was so vain—"Self-love is as bad as self-hate," Pastor Ball had thundered to the congregation the day before—but he had to see what Shauna would see. Small head, round and shiny as a bowling ball. Tight clipped hair—"Afros are for hippies," his grandmother was always telling him. Wide-set eyes black and white and lit with the love of the Lord.

When Jesus washed—when Jesus washed
He washed my sins away
Oh happy day

Leon Carter began every day with a song of praise. No matter how low he felt, no matter how weary when he rose at 6:00 a.m. ("*You* tired, child?" his granny hollered if he complained. "Wait till you get to my age!"), Leon sang. He sang to the mirror. He sang to the ceiling. He sang in the shower, swinging from "Oh Happy Day" to "I Got a Woman" when he thought the water was loud enough to drown out the lyrics. He sang in the street on the way to the Sugar Hill A&P, where he bagged groceries four mornings a week for $1.75 an hour, which he was happy to get. But most of all, Leon sang in the dim cramped reverberating storefront church on 145th Street that he and his grandmother attended faithfully every Sunday morning. Leon Carter was born to sing—everybody who heard his voice said so, even Granny, who never said anything nice to anybody—and deep in his heart he knew that one of these mornings he was going to rise up, spread his wings, and get a record contract. But in the meantime, Leon belted it out night and day to himself. "You got to *know* someone, honey," Miss Genevieve, who led the church choir, kept telling him. "Get with the Jewish producers—they're the ones with the funds." But Leon lived in Harlem, packed groceries, sang in church. Who would he know?

"Leeee-onnnnn!" Granny's voice rang out through the closed door.

He buttoned a white shirt over the hard scant flesh, patted down his hair, bent over for one last smile in the mirror (Shauna had to love those dimples), and stepped out of the bathroom into the kitchen. He knew better than to keep Granny waiting—especially on Monday morning.

"Morris is coming for me in ten minutes and there's something I got to talk to you about," she started right in. Morris was his grandmother's brother, a cabdriver who lived a few blocks away on St. Nicholas. Most Sundays after church, Granny fixed Morris and his wife, Lorena, a nice dinner—and every Monday morning, Morris drove Granny back to the big fancy house on Long Island where she lived and worked five days a week, sometimes six. "Quit singing and pay attention."

Granny loved giving orders.

Leon sat head down and neck curled over the table like a brown heron and silently spooned Cream of Wheat into his mouth. The kitchen was just about big enough for a table, two chairs, a stove, and Granny. She stood with her back to the square barred window, which at this hour glared black and leaked in currents of cold, and talked while he ate. Leon had long since learned to tune out half of what his grandmother said—she repeated it all five times anyway—but the gist got through. And this time the gist was: the Steins were canning her. One more month and she was out. "Miss Penny says I'm too old and too sick to work anymore."

"Sick?" Leon raised his head and met her eyes.

"My heart's not what it used to be, child. They're saying I can't handle the stairs." Once she lost her job, everything would be on him. If they were going to make it, he'd have to work another shift at the A&P, get a second job, maybe janitor or gypsy cab. She talked on and on about rent, food, doctor's bills, funeral costs, but Leon, sunk inside his thoughts, was barely listening. The cold from the kitchen window went right through his thin cotton clothes. He started to shiver. Leon had been ten years old when his daddy drowned in the Chesapeake. His mother was lost to him—worse than dead. Granny was all the family he had left—and now she was saying she could keel over any minute.

When Jesus washed
When Jesus washed
He washed my sins away

Leon stilled the song in his head, carried his bowl to the sink, and bent over to embrace Tutu. "Don't worry, Granny, we'll make it through. The Lord's watching over."

But he didn't believe it and he could tell she didn't either.

Leon didn't sing in the elevator on the way down to the lobby or on the freezing dark street as he walked to the supermarket. It was the first Monday in January. Holidays over—back to reality. Bums slumped in every other doorway. Dope fiends jostled folks at the intersections. A rusted corrugated steel curtain hung across the front of the Saints Alive Baptist Church, where he'd sung his heart out the day before. On the avenue, cops straddled horses breathing steam like dragons. Girls in plaid miniskirts skipped to school. Brothers with two-foot-wide fros butted their way into the wind. Song was Leon's constant companion—he opened his mouth and the spirit soared through his throat—but after what his grandmother just said . . . *If Granny died* . . . He wouldn't let himself go down that road.

The cold rose up through the soles of his shoes, seized his legs, clamped his muscles. Leon walked as fast as he could but he felt himself freezing and drowning. *You had to know someone.* He sang like an angel—didn't God hear him? Why couldn't he catch a break? A lucky break. No. If you believed, there was no such thing as luck. Luck came to those who earned it. He had to earn it. He had to meet someone lucky and get *them* to share it with him. He needed a demo. He needed ten minutes with a producer. Sing like an angel and the doors of heaven would open wide. But when? And where? And who would pay attention to the likes of him? Leon scanned the faces coming toward him in the pale winter light. Not a single pair of eyes met his.

A block from the A&P, Leon started to hum softly. It was a new song, "Bridge over Troubled Water," just starting to get radio play—but like every song he'd ever heard, it was his forever.

Chapter Seven

Samuel Orin Stein's diary.

Private property!

If you are reading this, stop now, close the cover and put it back in the drawer.

Yes, YOU.

MONDAY, JANUARY 5

After everything that's happened, I can't believe I had to go back to school. Attendance. Pledge of Allegiance. Social studies. Rancid gym locker. Coach Dykstra's pizza face. Newspaper staff meeting. I am not the same person—but no one seems to have noticed, not even Dirty Face. "Kimberly Goodman—she sounds like a Puritan" was all he said when I told him about us. US. "I promise you Kim is no Puritan," I said, to which he replied, "Please, Sammy, spare me the details." Good old Dirty Face. So I'm going to have to celebrate myself and sing myself by myself.

Headline: Sam Stein Falls in Love. Deck: Aftermath of a Drug-Fueled New Year's Eve Party. Lede: Jan. 1, Fat Neck, NY. At 3 p.m. this afternoon, an extraordinary event took place ["transpired" better? occurred, unfolded, came to pass, got imprinted on the sheets?] in an upstairs bedroom at 3 Red Oak Lane. Seventeen-year-old Samuel Orin Stein, a senior at Fat Neck North Senior High School, lost his virginity.

Sammy Boy, you are soooooooooo immature. I mean, why don't you brag about how many times you did it? But oh god oh god oh god I still can't believe this is happening. And with Kim Goodman—the most beautiful girl I've ever seen anywhere.

Kimberly ("my parents named me for a toilet paper company because it didn't sound Jewish") Goodman. Kim. Not Kimmy—*never* Kimmy. Kimberly Beth Goodman.

And to think we've known each other for less than a week.

Why me?

Why *not* me?

But why did she cry? Did I hurt her? She was not a virgin—she made that pretty obvious. I wonder how many others there have been, aside from Brad the Rad? Was I as good as him? At least you forbore to ask her. Never ask. Sammy Stein, it's about time you learned to keep your big mouth shut (and what a cute mouth it is according to Kim—hold on a sec—I gotta go check it out in the mirror and see what she's talking about).

Okay I'm back. Everything looks just as goofy as ever but as long as Kim thinks I'm cute who cares about the stick-out ears and the ridiculous orange peach fuzz?

JANUARY 12, 10 PM

One week later—but what a week!

Where to begin?

If not now, when?

I know I'm lucky—lucky but insane!

I haven't seen Kim in three days and I'm going crazy. I just called but there was no answer. Where *is* she? There's so much I need to tell her.

To start with, all the stuff about my time at Tutu's place.

And all the stuff I want to tell her but *can't* because Tutu would kill me. Where to begin—where to end????

What's truly weird is how Kim and Tutu have gotten so tangled up together. Actually not that weird considering how obsessed Kim is with the souls of black folk. It's like every other word out of her mouth is **black**—**black** power, **black** panther, **black** pride, **black** history. Naturally, it was Kim's idea that I go to Harlem with Tutu.

Yes, I spent the weekend in Harlem and lo! I'm here to tell the tale.

So here's the tale.

When I told Kim about how Tutu has her own apartment for her days off and how she used to ask my mother if she could take me there, she jumped. "You *gotta* do it, Samuel." (She calls me Samuel which no one has done since nursery school—"Wait your turn, Samuel"—but it sounds so sexy and mysterious when she says it.) Her: "Don't ask permission—just tell them you're going." Me: "But I thought we were going to spend the weekend together?" Her: "We'll have a million weekends. This is more important." Me (but silently): "Nothing is more important." But I knew it would make her happy—and I was curious—so I took the plunge. Starship Parenterprise seemed dubious, but I played on their guilt—*"Her time's running out, you said so yourself"*—and finally they said okay.

When I ran the plan by Tutu on Saturday morning, she seemed kind of taken aback at first—"You mean *tonight*?"—but then she got on the phone and I heard her yelling and screaming at whoever was on the other end to get their ass to the grocery store. Roommate? Auntie? After she hung up, my mother took her aside and slipped her some bills for cab fare. By the time Dad drove us to the train station that afternoon, Tutu was totally cool with the whole thing. "We're gonna have us a *fine* old time," she said as soon as we got out of the car. And we did. Man, did we ever.

I have to admit I felt like a jerk riding the train in with my *maid*—but no one gave us a second look and she just read her Bible the whole time. It was freezing outside of Penn Station and there was this wicked wind blowing down Seventh Avenue (I kept looking for the whores in the Simon & Garfunkel song) and we had to wait half an hour for a cab but I didn't mind because we were in the City and I was storing up everything to tell Kim. We got stuck in traffic around Times Square and Tutu kept muttering about all the porno skin flicks and then this wino tried to open the door of the taxi and Tutu hit the lock button just in time but then she rolled down the window to scream at him: "Step off, fool!" I just sat back and let it wash over me.

"We're in Harlem, Sammy," she said once we crossed 110th Street—but to me it didn't look any different than the rest of the city. More black people on the sidewalks. More liquor stores and check-cashing joints and Afro-hair beauty parlors. But from the way my parents talked about it, I was expecting—I don't know—

this war zone with gun-toting gangs and muggers throwing rocks. Actually, it did get a little weird when we hit 145th Street and there were flames shooting out of a trash can on the corner and a bunch of guys standing around drinking out of paper bags and chucking the empties into the flames in a shower of sparks. "Don't pay those bums any mind," Tutu told me. She must have smelled the fear on me—like sweat. Skinny white boy sweat.

Her apartment is on Edgecombe Avenue (never heard of it before) on a block of brownstones mixed with modern buildings—but a lot of the brownstones were just boarded-up shells and the modern buildings were ugly brick apartment houses with bars on the windows and rickety fire escapes sagging from floor to floor. Tutu lives in one of those. It smelled kinda funky in the lobby, like an old pair of sneakers. The elevator was just about big enough for me and Tutu to stand side by side and it took forever to get to the fourth floor. My lucky number! She undid the locks and threw open the front door and pushed me inside ahead of her, then shut the door and relocked it. She must have seen the look in my eyes when she turned on the lights. It was like being in a time machine with the dial turned back a decade. Every single thing in her living room was something that used to be in *our* living room—green couch, brown leather recliner, even lamps and end tables—all of it jammed into a space half the size of my bedroom. "I bet you never wondered where all your old stuff ended up, did you, Sammy?" she said in that mocking way of hers. "Your mama gave me every stick and plate and doodad—whenever she redecorated, I got the castoffs." It was exactly the way our place looked when I was eight—except for the color picture of blond blue-eyed Jesus on the wall. It made me want to curl up on the sofa with my blanket and watch Looney Tunes (she even had our old TV). The only thing I didn't recognize was a mini-sofa facing our big old green one. "That's my new sofa bed," Tutu said proudly. "Where you'll be sleeping." Everything smelled of Lemon Pledge, like she'd spray-painted the whole apartment with it.

My mother had told Tutu not to go to any trouble—"Just give him a couple of slices of pizza, he'll be fine"—but I was glad that she fixed my favorite dinner. London broil, mashed potatoes, onion gravy, and peas. She told me to watch TV while she cooked—just like at home, only there was no door or anything between living room and kitchen (which was about the size of a glorified broom closet), and when we shoehorned ourselves around the table, *she* was the boss. Actually, she looked like a duchess with her back straight against that rickety little chair and a big glossy wig fluffed around her face. I never noticed before that she has freckles too—like tiny brown ink blots spattered on the yellowing parchment of her skin. "Don't you dare touch that food before we pray," she snapped. "You folks may be godless heathens but in *my house* we say grace before we eat." I can't remember the whole thing but it started with "Heavenly Father" and ended with "in Jesus's name amen." She stared me down until I said "amen" too—and then she smiled and picked up her fork.

We didn't say anything for a while—I just sat there and ate and looked around at her stuff (the only picture she had on the wall aside from Jesus was a faded newspaper cutout of Dr. King standing before a huge crowd on the National Mall). I kept thinking about how Kim said, "Get her talking—find out about her family and stuff," so finally I cleared my throat and went, "Um—you know, Tutu, you've been with us all my life but I hardly know anything about you. How come you never talk about yourself?"

"How come you never asked?" was her reply. "I've been working in white folks' homes for going on fifty years now and not once in all that time has anyone asked me that question." She crossed her arms over her chest and looked me in the eye. "I never could figure out if they didn't care—or if they just didn't see me. Like I was part of the furniture I was supposed to dust. *Don't pay the maid any mind—she loves scrubbing our toilets*. After a while I stopped expecting anything else. But I always had a feeling you were different, Sammy. You know why you're my favorite?"

"Because I was born on your birthday."

She shook her head. "It's your soul. God gave you a sweet soul and that's something you can't lose. Sweet and honest as the day is long. You'd've gotten in ten times less trouble if you knew how to lie, but you don't. And that's a good thing—you better believe it."

Her eyes were brimming and suddenly mine were too, which just made her snort. At least she didn't call me a sissy. Then she changed the subject. "You brought along that black notebook of yours?" Does anything escape her? "I see how you scribble in that little book, writing those stories of yours. Well, when you get home, Sammy, get out that notebook and write *this* down. You know how I always say I have two heads? My mama had two heads too and her mama before her. One head for now. One head for *then*. We never had much of anything. But we do have our stories."

• • •

Sam set down his pen, slipped the diary into the bottom desk drawer, and called Kim. After the tenth ring he gave up, stripped down to his undies, and turned off the light. The cold sheets raised a rash of goose bumps on his arms and legs. He lay on his back staring straight up. No chance of sleep the way his mind was churning. There was just enough light coming through the slats of the venetian blinds for him to make out the crack that zigzagged across the bedroom ceiling. His mother once told him that the plaster had split when Tutu fell out of bed—her room was directly over his—and for years he believed it. Naturally.

Sam lay there with his hands crossed behind his head, willing the crack to heal. Tutu always told the truth—he was sure of it—but he was having trouble with some of what she'd told him late that night in her apartment. "The blood of presidents runs in my veins." Her exact words. Sam shook his head against the pillow. Tutu? Kin to George Washington? She said that her people came from the Northern Neck of Virginia, birthplace of three of the first five presidents—Washington, Madison, and Monroe—slaveholders every one. "Course my folks weren't *from* the Northern Neck. You're not *from* someplace that you were brought to as a slave. See this bright skin? That color came to me from a white master. *Slave* master is what I'm talking about." Tutu claimed that her people and George Washington's people were the *same* people, only *her* people were their secret black bastards. "Maybe not old George himself but some kin of his got children on our womenfolk. They should put *that* in your history books, Sammy."

Sam tried to conjure it. George Washington grabbing the washerwoman by the waist, pulling her down, splitting her open, getting up afterward to dust off his wig, averting his eyes when the little ginger-colored slave baby was born. Tutu's great-great-great-whatever. *Holy Jesus.* But why would she say it if it wasn't true? And that other stuff—the terrible evil stuff he couldn't write, wouldn't write, didn't know how to write. After all that happened, how could Tutu stand working for white folks? *White men.* How could she even look at them?

Sam shut his eyes, forcing himself back to that night in her apartment. It was late. The dishes were done and put away. He wanted to watch TV, maybe catch the end of the Knicks game, but Tutu summoned him. "Sit with me, Sammy." She was at her kitchen table. "Something I need to tell you." So he sat down across from her, praying she wasn't going to make him pray again. "Something bad," she started in, and took a deep breath. "Something that happened to me when I was your age." Sam pictured a bony, shy, bow-legged Tutu, squinting a little, as pretty as she was ever going to be. "I needed work, Sammy. I couldn't stand another day in that cabin with my mama and those steaming tubs of clothes. So I took the bus over to the next town. There was an oyster plant there—fish house we called it—where they hired black folks to shuck. I went around to the back door the way I knew I was supposed to. 'You ever shucked before, girl?' the owner asked. Mr. Norton his name was. 'Yes, sir,' I told him, though it was a lie. 'You prepared to live here?' he asked. Beside the fish house, on the other side of a creek, stood a row of shanties, plank and tar-paper shacks rattling in the wind off the bay. Oyster shells heaped everywhere. 'Girls in the three shacks to the left,' Mr. Norton told me. 'Boys on the right. I'll pay you sixty-five cents a gallon. Sundays off. We patrol those shanties every night—my son Mr. Jamie and me. Any trouble and you're out. Got it?'

"But there was trouble, Sammy. How could there not be? The plant foreman, he locked us in at night and made us do our business in a nasty little pot, but the girls in my shanty kept a shim hidden by the door so they could jimmy the lock when they needed to. There was an empty shanty at the end of the row—everyone whispered about it—and one night I crept over there with a shucker named Crusoe Nickens. Tall lanky fellow, as smooth as silk. All the girls set their cap for Crusoe, but I got him. Or he got me. By Christmas I was carrying his baby. Not that I told anyone, not even Crusoe. I just figured that when the time came the good Lord would look out for me. Meanwhile, I pried open oyster shells ten hours a day six days a week till my fingers cracked and bled. Try as I might, I never could wash that fish stink off.

"Whenever the shuckers made a ruckus at night, Mr. Norton came running down the hill with his shotgun, threw open the shanty door, and fired in the air till the noise simmered down. That was a good night. On a bad night, Mr. Norton sent his son Mr. Jamie. Mr. Jamie wasn't past his midthirties, but he already had a gut hanging over his belt. Stank of liquor too half the time, which only made him meaner. The other girls warned me: 'When Mr. Jamie comes, just pretend you're sleeping. Don't look him in the eye. Keep the covers up.'"

Tutu paused and laid a hand over her heart, like she was pledging allegiance. Her brimming eyes were fixed on the table. "One cold night in January, I got to feeling queasy. I knew the other girls would kill me if I upchucked in that stuffy little shack. I was quick and light on my feet. I could move like a cat if I held my breath. Don't you laugh, Sammy. I was young once too. When I couldn't take the cramps anymore, I put on my robe and slipped out before anyone cracked an eyelid. There was a privy behind the shacks and that's where I emptied my stomach. A voice inside my head kept whispering, 'Go back,' but the sky was full of stars and the cold air settled me. There was a rickety little dock beside the fish house that ran out into the cove. I was halfway down, shivering and clutching my robe, when I heard the boards thud behind me. Footsteps—heavy footsteps. I knew without turning: Mr. Jamie walking off his drunk. 'Who's this little yaller gal?' he said all sly and husky when he came close. 'Let's see what you got hiding under that robe.'

"Nobody could tell yet that I was carrying a baby.

"The dock was slick with ice gleaming at the edges like knives. A couple of boats were tied alongside and one had an anchor pulled up next to the engine. Me and Mr. Jamie stood there staring each other down. The cold air turned our breath to smoke. Every puff was like a bomb going off. My mama used to say that if you're carrying a child and you let another man put his seed in you, it will cripple your baby. That's all I could think about when Mr. Jamie set his hands on the robe and started tugging. 'Time was, all you bitches were free for the picking.' His very words. I pushed him off me and ran.

"I heard the footsteps pounding behind. I heard the curse when his shoe slipped on the ice. I heard the crack and the splash of his body. That water was cold but it wasn't deep. I could have pulled him out. I could have run up to the big house and called for help. I could have roused the men shuckers in their shanty. I didn't do any of those things. I didn't think. I didn't pray. And I did not turn around. I ran back to shore, got the shim, and when my hands quit shaking, opened the lock and slipped into my bed. If anybody saw me, they didn't say a word—not then and not the next day either when they fished his body out of the water.

"It was him or me," Tutu whispered. "That's what I thought at the time, Sammy. But now I know better. It was him *and* me."

She reached across the table to grab his hands, still not looking at him. "Don't you *ever* breathe one word of this to anybody." Tears were running down her cheeks. "Ever."

"Why me?" he pleaded. "Why keep this secret all these years and then lay it on me now?"

"Because it eased my heart to say it. And I know I can trust you, Sammy."

SAM ROLLED ONTO HIS SIDE and pulled the covers over his head. His teeth were chattering. What about *his* heart?

If it weren't so cold, he'd have gotten out of bed, pulled the diary out of the drawer, started writing again. The truth this time. The taxi to Harlem, the cramped little elevator, the cast-off furniture, the London broil and peas: he'd filled page after page, but all he'd done was doodle. He hadn't even gotten to the secret grandson who'd gone to church with them on Sunday morning. Long tall Leon. How had Tutu kept that hidden all these years?

It was obvious. They saw what they wanted to see—Sam no different from his parents. He was never going to amount to anything as a writer until he learned to see the truth: to look into people's hearts. Starting with his own. But how?

An hour passed and Sam was still awake and shivering. He thought about creeping up the steps, knocking on Tutu's door, waking her up. But it would probably just give her a heart attack. "Remember, Sammy," she'd said to him that night in her apartment, right before he fell asleep. "No one's ever gonna look out for you but God." It sounded almost like a threat, but then she leaned over and put her lips on his forehead. She never kissed Sam at home.

When Sam finally fell asleep, he had the drowning dream again. The one where he's lying facedown in the pool and his neck is fused and his lungs are bursting and finally he surrenders and inhales and the water gags him like vomit. Only this time it was different. It wasn't the pool—it was Long Island Sound. He and Kim were running down the dock by the boathouse. Kim was in front, he was trying to catch her. Right at the end, she stopped dead and turned on him. As Sam lunged for her embrace, she stepped aside and tripped him. "Richard!" he heard her call. "Richard, wait!" But he was sinking beneath the rancid surface, heart on fire. Sinking. Suffocating. Inhaling. Choking. Drowning. "Richard, wait!" was pounding inside his head when he jolted awake.

Chapter Eight

I left out the best part. I saw Jesus on the ceiling of her church. We were all standing and singing, and the pastor had his hands in the air—and I looked up for a second and there He was. Just a flash of light between the rafters and then poof! He was gone. But it was Him. I saw the light—literally."

"What did He say?" Sparks were shooting from Kim's eyes. *"Sin no more, Samuel Stein, for the fiery pit awaits!"*

"No message—it was more like a bubble bursting. I was probably just hallucinating from exhaustion. After everything she told me that night I barely slept."

"So now you're a Christian?" Kim's laughter cascaded through the train car. "No more sex till you're married—those are the rules."

Sam looked around red-faced to see if anyone was listening. It was an icy clear Friday midday and he and Kim had cut school to go to an anti-draft rally in the city. Kim's idea. Was it obvious what they'd been up to in her bedroom before dashing to the station? The car was mostly empty—a young mother with a frosted perm swatting at her two squirmy kids, a bleached blonde in a red miniskirt and white go-go boots, a scattering of shifty unshaven men glued to their tabloids—and not a single pair of eyes rose to meet his. They might as well be alone. Sam opened his hand between them and Kim slid her fingers into the gaps between his and squeezed: they were a perfect fit. "Au contraire," he said. "Lots of sex. God is love. That's what the preacher said. It doesn't matter if you're black white yellow or brown—as long as you love God, God will love you back."

"Love is all you need." Kim held his gaze. "Love, guns, and comrades. That's what *my* preacher says."

"And who would that be—John Lennon?"

"No, Vladimir. You know—Lenin, Stalin, Marx?"

"So now you're a Communist?"

"Not a Communist, a socialist, Sam I Am." She gave his fingers one last squeeze. "But I have to hear the rest of the story. What happened to Tutu's son—what was his name, Albert? And how did she wind up out on the Guyland with you crazy Steins?"

Sam beamed. At home with his family, he could hardly get a word in—even when his brothers were away, his parents were so wrapped up in their own business that they barely registered his presence. And half the time Tutu refused to listen to his foolishness—*fushness*, she pronounced it. When did anyone ever ask him to finish a story? So he told Kim everything he remembered, flinging Tutu's life in her face like handfuls of dust. She left her son—yes, his name was Albert—with her mother before the boy was even crawling and went to Baltimore to look for a job. Washing clothes, slinging hash, raising white folks' kids, scrubbing toilets, vacuuming office buildings at night—she bounced around Virginia and Maryland doing whatever work she could get. It killed her to leave Albert behind, but what choice did she have? But even though Tutu only got to see her son twice a year, he knew who his mama was. And she knew what made her boy happy. God had given Albert a gift for baseball. By the time he was five, Albert had taught himself to pitch and hit. By twelve, his arm was so strong that even white folks came to watch him throw. Tutu swore that he could have been a professional if he'd been born a few years later, but those were the days before Jackie Robinson and Willie Mays. No coach. No uniform. No money. No opportunity if you were black. So when he turned fifteen Albert stashed his mitt and went to work on the water like his father and grandfather. Crabbing and fishing was his life—the baseball dream was done. He married a maid called Nanny—"domestic worker," she called herself—and they had a son. Tutu was a grandma before she even reached fifty.

Sam stopped. What harm would it be if he spilled a little to Kim? So he took a breath and barreled on.

"This part's really tough. One Christmas Tutu was back home for a visit, staying with Albert and Nanny. There'd always been bad blood between Tutu and her daughter-in-law—and this time, when Tutu saw Nanny whaling on her little grandson just like her mama used to whale on her, she totally lost it. Tutu pulled a knife and threatened to kill Nanny if she struck that child one more time. They were still screaming at each other when Albert got home. Nanny gave her husband an ultimatum: either Tutu left for good or she did. That was the last time Tutu ever laid eyes on her only child. Two months later a call came in the middle of the night that Albert had drowned while tonging for oysters. He'd slipped off the side of his boat, hit his head, and gone under. Dead at twenty-nine. Tutu blamed herself. 'Divine retribution,' she called it."

"Retribution for what?"

Shit. He had boxed himself into a corner. If he told Kim the truth—how Tutu believed God had taken her son because she'd let Mr. Jamie die, a death for a death—he would be breaching her darkest secret. He couldn't betray her. "Long story," he finally said. "Tutu made me promise. . . ." Kim pulled a face. For a second Sam was afraid that she was going to make him choose—her or Tutu—but she let it drop.

"So that's when she came north? After her son died?"

"Right. With Albert gone, there was nothing keeping her down south anymore. The grandson was lost to her. Her sister and brother had both already moved to Harlem. She felt like her life was over. So she took the train up from Baltimore, signed on with an employment agency, and the first job she landed was us. A year after she moved into our attic, I was born on her birthday. A little freckled bundle of joy." Sam dragged the corners of his lips apart in a crazy clown face. "She's been with us ever since."

"And now they're just tossing her out like a broken toaster?"

"Maybe not. My dad's a total hard-ass but I've been working on my mom. Tutu's too proud to beg, but I've been begging for her. I think they might let her stay till I go to college."

"I have to meet her, Sam. She sounds like she's been through so much."

"Just don't . . ."

"Don't what?"

"You know—don't let on that you know about her drowned son and everything. . . ."

"*Oh, Sam.*" Kim rolled her eyes and turned away.

The car filled up at Flushing—old ladies with bulging shopping bags and swollen ankles, skinny skittering dudes with fros, construction workers with hard hats and yellow vests, a couple of long-haired teens who grinned at Sam and Kim like old friends.

"Do you think those two are heading for the same demo?" Sam whispered, but Kim shook her head. "Nah—I bet they're going to Macy's for some fake tie-dye charged to Mommy's credit card." "I bet they got kicked out of school for smoking dope," Sam countered. "When they start college he'll cut his hair and join ROTC and she'll take up tennis." "Or knitting." "She's definitely gonna major in cosmetic arts—Eyeliner 101, Lipstick Studies, Reflections on Rouge." Sam snorted—he loved it when she was snide. "But who am I to talk?" Kim cut the chatter short with sudden bitterness. "Here I am practically through high school and what do I have to show for myself except a stack of report cards?"

They fell silent as the train rocked through the industrial no-man's-land that separated the dinge of Queens from the glitter of Manhattan.

Kim took his hand again, but she was looking out the window. "God, it's ugly," she breathed. "Maybe instead of demonstrating we should be out picking up garbage, painting houses—you know, *doing* something instead of just yelling about it."

Sam followed her gaze out the window to a tableau from hell: half a dozen trash-strewn train tracks were snarled beneath the sooty brick wall of an immense warehouse in which every window was smashed. Past the wall, a pit cratered like the stump of a rotten tooth. And beyond that, on the western horizon, the Manhattan skyline charted its soaring and plunging graph on the cloudless sky. "I always wondered if these were the ash heaps from *The Great Gatsby*," Sam said, trying to break the mood. "You know—that wasteland with the googly eyes of Dr. T. J. Eckleburg looking down from the billboard."

"I hated that book," Kim murmured without taking her eyes from the window. "Everyone was always drunk and those parties were an epic waste and Myrtle got that pathetic little puppy that peed all over the place. Gatsby was a fraud. Tom was obviously a total fascist and Daisy wasn't much better. She and Tom deserved each other. And the anti-Semitism! Jesus, Fitzgerald laid it on thick with Meyer Wolfsheim. Can you think of a single person in that book who stands for anything good?"

Sam kept his mouth shut. *Gatsby* was the first novel he ever loved. He'd highlighted so many passages the pages were practically translucent. Gatsby's yearning became his yearning—to win and lose everything for love. Sam had practically memorized the final page about the transitory enchanted moment when Dutch sailors first beheld the "fresh, green breast of the new world . . . the last and greatest of all human dreams." It hadn't occurred to him until just this transitory enchanted moment how much Kim reminded him of Daisy.

Sam bent his head until his lips were practically brushing Kim's ear. "Do you think anyone else on this train is in love?" What he'd meant to say was "has just made love" but this slipped out instead.

Kim took forever to turn her face from the window. "Anyone *else*?" she finally said. Her eyebrows had disappeared into the curls of her bangs. Sam felt his cheeks flame and he remembered what Tutu had told him that night in her apartment: "Never be the first to say 'I love you.' You can think it all you want but don't say it. Take it from me, you're asking for trouble."

AS SOON AS THEY HEARD the chanting, Kim broke into a sprint, dragging Sam along behind like a distracted puppy. *"One, two, three, four, we don't want your fucking war."* No demonstrators were in sight yet—just their soundtrack crackling over the racket of a thousand engines. Sam had no idea where he was: everything in the city he loved so much looked the same to him—enormous, treeless, dirty, brown. Sun glinted off the upper windows of the skyscrapers but the bottom of the canyon was already in shadow. Pedestrians rushed through the cold oblivious to the siren song of revolution. Kim, dangling Sam from an elbow, bulleted through them, rounded a corner and there it was: a street sealed off with yellow police tape; cops standing shoulder to shoulder in a solid wall, a baton at the ready in every hand; and at the far end of the block, maybe a hundred demonstrators jammed together like grains of sand in the neck of an hourglass. Over the blue shoulders and black helmets Sam could just make out a thin bespectacled guy standing above the crowd with one clenched fist in the air and the other wrapped around a megaphone. *"One, two, three, four, we don't want your fucking war."* The grains of sand took up the cry. Sam did a quick mental calculation: a hundred protesters, three speakers on an impromptu stage (overturned trash cans with a board laid over them), and forty cops. Which meant (thank you, SAT prep) slightly less than two-fifths of a cop for every demonstrator.

"Excuse me. Coming through. Make way." Kim, without breaking stride, skirted the phalanx of New York's finest, ducked under the tape, elbowed through the bodies, and beelined for the choke point at the far end of the street. Sam could now see that there was a second wall of riot police massed at the other end of the block. *We're nothing but sardines in a blue bathtub*, he was thinking. If those two rows of cops closed ranks, there would be no way out. Sam eyed the guns and batons and wished he'd worn a hat—or better yet a helmet.

"What do we want?" the guy with the megaphone was shouting.

"Peace!" they all roared back.

"When do we want it?"

"Now!"

"What do we want?"

"Peace!"

"When do we want it?"

"Now!"

And then in unison: *"Peace now! Peace now! Peace now . . ."*

It sure didn't sound to Sam like the Movement was running out of steam.

But then came the speeches. The protesters stood huddled in the cold while one by one the organizers harangued them with platitudes. Sam had assumed there'd be some kind of conflagration—a bonfire of draft cards!—but Organizer #1 said burning stuff in public was against some city ordinance, so instead a couple of greasy-haired guys flung the shreds of their draft cards into the air like confetti. "No littering!" a cop squawked through *his* megaphone, and that put an end to that. Organizer #2 droned on endlessly about the plight of the innocent, downtrodden Vietnamese people—he had a slight lisp so "innocent" came out "in-ah-thant." Organizer #3 was all about solidarity and collective action and making common cause. Sam silently dubbed them Three Thstooges. If this was the Revolution, he'd rather be in chemistry class. . . .

Then he heard Kim mutter "Jesus Christ" under her breath and the next second she had shoved through the front-line demonstrators, mounted the garbage can podium, grabbed the megaphone from the Third Thstooge, and opened fire. "Brothers and sisters!" Maybe it was the megaphone, but he barely recognized her voice—it sounded so urgent, so momentous. "The war in Vietnam is not just a war against the people of Vietnam—it's a war against the people of the United States of America. Most of all a war against black people. Did you know that more black Americans are fighting in Vietnam than in any other American war? Did you know that more black soldiers have died in Vietnam than in all our other wars put together? When a white kid gets drafted, he rips up his draft card and goes to Canada. When a black kid gets drafted, he ships out and *dies*." The crowd had stopped shuffling. Even the cops seemed to be paying attention. "But most of the black guys in Vietnam were not drafted—they *enlisted*—yes, they signed up willingly, because if you're black, *dying* in Vietnam is preferable to *living* in America. At least you get paid for it." Laughter rippled; raised fists pumped the air; scattered voices shouted, "Right on!" "Tell it!" "Go girl!" The guy next to Sam elbowed his ribs and asked, "Who is that redheaded firebrand?" "Kim Goodman," Sam responded proudly—but instantly regretted it when he saw the guy—man, actually, because on second look he was no draft-age kid but a balding jowly flush-faced adult—pull a notebook from his pocket and scribble something down. "Or maybe it's Bonnie Goodstein—I dunno, we just met," Sam backpedaled lamely—a terrible liar as always. But Kim was full steam ahead. "Now maybe some of you are familiar with our brothers in the Black Panthers." More murmurs; cries of "Free Bobby!"; more scribbles in the notebook. "Well, I'm here to tell you that the Panthers—not the Green Berets—are the *true* freedom fighters of this country. If you want justice. If you want peace. If you want freedom, you better stand up and make your voices heard. Panthers are being gunned down right now in the streets of America while our black brothers die like flies in Vietnam. The only path left to us is revolution—peaceful if we can, but armed if we must." The soprano static of the megaphone reverberated off the skyscrapers and rained down in shards of glass. "Free Bobby! Free Huey! Avenge Fred Hampton! All power to all the people!" Pumping her fist in the air. "The struggle is ours to win!" Pumping harder. "Power to the people—right on!" Pumping and jumping. "Revolution—now. Revolution—now. Revolution—now."

All hundred of them had their fists in the air with her—all but Sam and the man next to him, writing furiously in his notebook. That's when he lost it. Without thinking, without planning, while the demonstrators were shouting and pumping and the air was exploding with their voices and Kim was brandishing the megaphone like a javelin above her head, Sam snatched the notebook out of paunchy man's hands, buried it deep in his coat pocket, and fled.

FORTY-FIVE MINUTES LATER he was on a downtown street corner freezing his ass off and scanning the faces of passersby from underneath the hood of his parka. He still couldn't believe he'd gotten away with it. Or how easy it had been. When the notebook man lunged after him, Sam squeezed beneath the canopy of raised arms and, shouting, "Narc! That guy's a narc!," melted into the crowd. The man screamed, "Stop that kid!" at the top of his lungs—but the other demonstrators took up the "Narc!" cry and closed ranks. Sam heard the man cursing "You goddamn son of a bitch," as he pushed into the lobby of the nearest building. He expected a herd of cops in hot pursuit but there was nothing. Luck was with him—the building straddled an entire block and there was an exit at the other end into the next street. He zipped across the lobby and out the revolving door, and once he was on the street, he nonchalantly joined the stampede to the subway—rush hour. He thought Kim was crazy when she had insisted on fixing a rendezvous spot downtown in case they got separated—*why would they get separated?*—but now he saw the wisdom in her plan. So there he was on the corner of Second Avenue and St. Mark's Place, waiting for Kim to materialize out of the crowd. The notebook was like a lump of coal burning a hole in his parka pocket. Chuck it? Read it? Hide it someplace? Sam was petrified.

What if she'd said Third Avenue?

"What happened? Why did you take off like that?" Sam spun around—and there she was. He fell into her arms and the two of them hugged each other on the sidewalk while the world surged around them.

"Oh my god," he breathed into her curls. "That was *so incredible.* You had them eating out of your hand. How did you know all that stuff about black soldiers in Vietnam?"

Kim broke from his arms and tilted her head back. "The truth?" Her eyes twinkled. "I made most of it up."

Sam dropped his jaw. Kim punched him in the stomach. And then the two of them were flying down the sidewalk, both of them laughing and talking at once. It was like they'd just been sprung from school—or prison—or battle. When Kim finally calmed down enough to take in what Sam was saying about the guy with the notebook and how he'd grabbed it and fled, she stopped and rounded on him. "You realize that guy was an FBI agent, right? Those pigs have totally infiltrated the Movement."

"Let me show it to you," Sam said, reaching for his pocket.

"No *way*—not here." Kim took his hand and started walking again at a normal pace so they wouldn't draw attention to themselves. They were in the heart of the East Village so blending in was easy—everyone on the street was young, long-haired, dressed like a hippie, and either stoned, tripping, crazy, or all three. Kim stopped at the first phone booth they came to. "Richard lives right around here. I'm gonna call and see if he's home. We can stash"—she looked at Sam's parka pocket—"*it* at his place."

Two minutes later they were racing up the dark crumbly stairs of Richard's tenement building near Tompkins Square Park. The door opened at the first knock and Richard, barefoot in torn jeans and a Hells Angels T-shirt, ushered them in. Kim got a hug and a kiss on the side of the mouth. Sam got a squeeze on the shoulder. Richard, lit up at the prospect of mischief, was even more intimidatingly handsome than at the New Year's party. His long dark hair was wet and his cheeks smooth and ruddy as if he'd just stepped out of the shower. A gold stud Sam hadn't noticed before winked on his left ear. Richard looked like a big cat—puma or leopard—that had escaped from the zoo and wound up caged in a slum.

Sam was still taking in the flat—a long narrow coffin of a room with a single barred window at the far end, a couple of ratty mattresses slumped beside a lumpy sofa, and a green plastic table strewn with take-out cartons, hash pipe, beer cans, rolling papers, weed baggie, tweezers, ashtray, socks, and album covers—when the door to the bedroom opened and a swarthy sleepy guy stepped out. "My Israeli cousin, Eli," Richard introduced them. "He's crashing with me for a while. I've got the bed—he's on the floor, in case you're wondering." *Weird to share the bedroom*, Sam was thinking, but then he remembered how Richard once told him that what he hated most was to wake up alone in the dark.

Eli shook hands. Sam shifted his eyes from Richard to Eli, searching in vain for a family resemblance. Everything about Eli was three shades darker—hair, eyes, skin—and where Richard was chiseled Eli bulged. He couldn't have been much older than Richard, but he looked like a man, not a boy—a man who liked to have a good time and didn't take life, or himself, too seriously. "Shalom Kimmy, shalom Shmuel, please to meeting you," Eli said jovially. There was a gap between his two front teeth and a patch of black hair at his throat. "Reekie is my favorite leetle cousin"—Eli's head did not quite make it to Richard's shoulder—"but with the cleaning he's not so good." He tweezed a sock off the table, wrinkled his nose, and dropped it on the floor.

"Eli here just finished his stint in the IDF—you know, the Israeli army," Richard said. "I'm trying to ease him back into civilian life with some good old American R and R." He pulled a chair up to the table and started rolling a joint on a Grateful Dead album cover. "But what brings you two into the big bad city on a *school day*? Do your mommies know you're playing hooky?"

Kim and Sam flopped down side by side on the sofa—a spring corkscrewed into Sam's left buttock—and launched into the story simultaneously, but Richard interrupted. "Let's toke up first. This is way better than the shit at that party."

Kim waved the joint away but Sam took a hit and passed it to Eli, who passed it back to Richard, who winked at Sam. "Hey, Sammy boy, have you ever done a shotgun?" And before Sam could ask what a shotgun was, Richard stuck the lit end of the joint in his own mouth, leaned over to Sam until the unlit end was between his lips, and then blew with all his might. Smoke billowed into the stoned-out cavity that used to be Samuel Orin Stein: SOS. Richard had a hand clamped around the back of Sam's neck like he was going to head-slam him—then he let go and pulled out the joint. "Count to ten, Sammy." But Sam didn't count.

He didn't explode either, though his head was levitating off his neck. What just happened? Where did all the smoke go? And how did Richard do that without burning a hole in his tongue? Richard took another hit, exhaled, stuck out his tongue, and waggled it at Sam. "See Sammy—no burn—magic! Wanna shotgun, Eli?"

"Lo. I mean nein. I mean nyet. I mean no frogging way."

"Whats a matter, Eli, can't you talk and toke at the same time?" Richard stretched out on a mattress with his back to the wall. "Okay, spill it. What are you two so hot and bothered about—aside from each other?"

Sam was about to jump in, but Kim cut him off. "We were demonstrating against the draft. You're draft age, Richard. How come you weren't there?"

"I pulled number 309 in the lottery." Richard took the last hit and flipped the roach into an ashtray. "Lucky me—*you're free to go, young man.*" Kim scowled. "Anyway, somebody's gotta stay home and roll the joints, right? So what happened? Did you guys get teargassed by the pigs?"

Sam and Kim were like a comedy team, jiggling up and down side by side, stepping on each other's lines, clapping a hand on the other's mouth when they got to a good part. "So I was wrapping up my speech—" "She was so cool. It was all about how black guys—" "And there was this commotion at the front of the crowd—" "Some goon with a notebook was writing down everything—" "And the next thing I knew, Sam had vanished—" "Everybody was going crazy yelling and waving their fists and I—" "What the hell was going on. But the organizer guys wanted to talk to me and I couldn't—" "Stuffed the notebook in my pocket—" "And they were like, 'You're such a fantastic speaker, we could use someone—'" "Jumped on the downtown subway—" "And there he was on the corner of St. Mark's—"

"Whoa, whoa, slow down!" Richard held up both his hands until he finally silenced the two of them. "You mean you, little Sammy Stein, boosted an FBI agent's notebook and got away with it?" Sam and Kim nodded in unison. "That is so absolutely totally fuckin' A cool. Well, cough it up, man, we gotta see what's in it."

Sam fished the notebook—a reporter's steno pad—out of his coat pocket and Kim and Richard pushed in on either side of him to have a look (Eli was passed out on a mattress). It was still open to the page on which the agent had been scribbling when Sam grabbed it. "Curly red hair," Sam read aloud, "apparent BPP affiliation—"

"BPP is the Black Panther Party," Kim interjected.

"Possible liaison between BPP and CU SDS."

"Columbia University Students for a Democratic Society—you know, campus radicals."

"Sophisticated command of facts and data—maybe a CPUSA plant . . ."

"Communist Party of the USA—wait, this pig thought the *Commies* sent me?"

Sam flipped to the previous page. "'Freckle-face school kid'—that must be me—'claims her name is—'" He broke off.

"*Wait*—you told him my *name*?"

"Sorry, sorry—I didn't realize—but don't worry—I made up something . . . see?" He pointed to where the agent had written "Kim Goodman??? Bonnie Goodstein???" "Anyway, we've got the notebook."

"But what if he remembers?" Kim grabbed the steno pad from Sam and started flipping through it wildly. "Jesus," she muttered under her breath, "look at all this. . . ." But Sam was barely listening. How could he have been so fucking stupid? When would he ever learn to keep his big mouth shut? Tutu was always warning him. . . . Now, because of him, Kim would be on some FBI watch list. She'd probably never speak to him again. Inside his chest, it felt like a cold fist was tightening around his heart.

While Kim and Richard huddled over the steno pad, Sam got up and walked over to the window. The vertical bars and zigzag slash of the fire escape gridded the world outside: a torn patchwork of yellow and black windows on the tenement across the street, clumps of neon letters flashing meaninglessly on the shop signs, severed heads of pedestrians floating above the fissured sidewalk. It was like watching a movie through a shattered lens. Even four floors up, he could hear shouts and laughter echoing up from the street: the soundtrack of people with lives. Everyone was having such a blast—everyone but him all of a sudden. Sam felt himself split in two—one Sam stood with his forehead against Richard's grimy windowpane, while the other Sam looked up in wonder from the street below. Enchanted and repulsive, the city licked at his ears. Its infinitude crushed him. He wanted to be the hero but he ended up the clown. The traitor. The rat. The plug slipped and he felt himself spiral down the drain.

"This thing is a gold mine," he heard Kim say.

"We could sell it—or trade it for a shitload of drugs." Richard sounded like a kid on a treasure hunt.

"No *way*," said Kim. "This is my foot in the door—a free pass."

"To what?"

"The BPP, you idiot."

"You're gonna use this to infiltrate the Panthers?"

"Not infiltrate—*join*. They don't usually trust whites—but with this!"

"Are you really that into the BPP or are you just trying to get a black boyfriend?"

The two Sams instantly merged back into one quivering whole. He still had his back to Kim and Richard but his ears were cocked to their every breathy syllable. *I already have a boyfriend. Don't be a jerk, Richard. Sam and I are going to fight for justice together.* Kim didn't say any of that—she didn't say anything at all. Sam turned and there she was sitting hunched on the sofa with her head bent over the notebook and her ginger curls bobbing in front of her face. At the back of her neck, the hair was parted around a webbed triangle like the pyramid on the back of a dollar bill. Sam wanted to cover that pyramid with his lips and inhale her lily of the valley perfume—but instead he plunked down silently beside Kim and waited. When she finally looked up, she blinked at him twice as if she'd forgotten who he was. Sam felt the deep creep of paranoia but he shook it off. He had to say something, anything, to break into the magic circle that Kim and Richard had conjured around themselves. "Hey, I almost forgot." He forced himself to smile. "This is *so* cool." Tutu had made him promise—*swear*—not to reveal *to anyone* what he was about to say, but Tutu was orbiting in a different galaxy at the moment. "On Sunday morning, after I spent the night at Tutu's place—"

"What? That witch is still alive?" Richard broke in.

"Yeah, she loves you too, Richard." Sam liked the little edge he'd just honed in his voice. "Anyway, we were walking to church and Tutu was taking me down this old elegant street of brownstones and big trees—Convent Avenue, she said it was called. We turned a corner and this tall skinny kid with a really long neck starts coming toward us—dressed all nice for church in a black suit and tie. Tutu's smiling like her face is going to break open. 'This is my grandson, Leon,' she says. And I'm like, *Grandson, what grandson?* Leon had been living in her Harlem apartment since he was fourteen, but she'd never said a word about it. Not to my parents—not to me—*zippo.* I think there was some trouble back in Virginia—I don't know—she just shook her head when I asked. Anyway, the night I came she made Leon stay with her brother so I could have his bed. But she wanted me to meet him. Show him off—you know, like 'Look what a fine grandson I have.' She made us sit on either side of her in church. 'My boys,' she kept saying."

"Yeah, one of each—chocolate and vanilla," Richard snorted, pinching Sam's cheek. "With pink sprinkles. So what's he look like, this Leon? Is he hot?"

"I don't think he's your type," said Sam.

"Richard doesn't have a type," Kim cut in. "Black, white, guys, girls. He's an equal opportunity slut."

"Not slut, honey—luuuuvaah-boy."

"Anyway, hands off Leon—and don't tell anyone I told you. Tutu would kill me."

"So why'd you say anything?" asked Richard, grinning like a tabby cat. "Death wish?" Sam groped for an answer, but Richard waved him off and started rolling another joint. "Relax, junior, your secret's safe with us."

Chapter Nine

So is she your girlfriend or what?"

Sam and Dirty Face were hanging out in the high school newspaper office, though "office" was a bit of an exaggeration for the basement storage closet that had been equipped with a couple of desks and a battered manual typewriter. The best thing about having an office, Sam discovered, was keeping other people out. The previous editor had stenciled "Staff Only" on the door in red, and Dirty Face, who did the paper's layout and design, had added a raised fist, also in red. Above that, Sam had tacked the Viet Cong flag—a gold star on a red and blue background. Dirty Face christened their closet the People's Republic of Fat Neck High. Mr. Coffin, the paper's faculty advisor, kept warning Sam to remove the flag before the principal saw it and expelled him, and Sam kept ignoring him. When was the last time Mr. Tower had waddled down from his throne room under the bell tower to the grimy bowels of the school basement?

"Girlfriend? Yeah, I guess," Sam said after thinking about it for a while. "I mean, we're together and everything—but we never talk about, you know, our status."

"Girlfriend-ish?" Dirty Face suggested. "Girlfriend-like? Quasi maybe semi sorta until someone cooler comes along type of girlfriend?"

"Something like that."

"What do you see in her, anyway?"

Sam delivered an ocular thunderbolt, which Dirty Face deflected with palms crossed in front of his face. "Innocent question, man."

"For starters, she's beautiful and smart and funny and not afraid to speak her mind—"

"And she puts out." Dirty Face dodged another thunderbolt. "Just sayin', Sam. Kim Goodman's got a reputation, you know?"

"She's not some sleazy hippie chick if that's what you're thinking. You should have heard her speak at the protest. Everyone was blown away. Believe me, Kim is going places."

"With or without you?"

Sam let out a sigh. "That remains to be seen. She's about a hundred times smarter than me—and a thousand times braver."

"Which, let's be honest, isn't saying much."

"Funny, Dirty Face, but let's be honest—not that funny."

"Have your parents met her yet?" Sam shook his head. "Well, why don't you invite her over for dinner sometime? That should clarify things."

"Or end them." Sam could just hear his mother crooning, *Oh, Kimmy, what a lovely girl!*

Behind their closed office door, Sam and Dirty Face had a couple of books open and a half-typed page rolled into the typewriter—but the truth was, they weren't doing squat. Even though it was only the third week of January, senior spring had officially begun and Sam was making the most of it. He'd been waiting all his life for this season. Two and a half months to go until college acceptances (or rejections) arrived. A sorta maybe girlfriend. An office. And more freedom than he knew what to do with. As long as he showed up to class occasionally and didn't fail anything, he was golden. So why wasn't he dancing on the ceiling? It was that *sorta maybe* thing. Night and day, Kim was all he ever thought about—but all Kim ever thought about was that FBI steno pad. They'd left it at Richard's place "for safekeeping" (as if anything was safe in that firetrap), and every time he saw Kim she had a different scheme for what to do with it. "I think you care more about that notebook than you care about me," Sam had told her the other day—but Kim just shrugged. "You think you love me, Sam," she said, "but it's just the sex. Wait till you do it with someone else." *But I don't want to do it with anyone else*, Sam was thinking.

When he and Kim had gotten together on New Year's Day, Sam felt as if he'd vaulted from childhood to adulthood in a single bound. It was like discovering he had wings. He pitied anyone who wasn't *them*. Now, half the time with Kim, he might as well be back in kindergarten. *Just the sex?! JUST?!*

"YOU MUST BE SAMMY'S GIRLFRIEND," Tutu said with a big grin when he and Kim waltzed through the kitchen door that Friday afternoon. Sam felt his face flush.

"And you must be Mrs. Carter," replied Kim, without skipping a beat.

Tutu's smile withered. "You might as well call me Tutu. Everyone else does."

"Sam says you've been with his family forever. You must like it here." Tutu let that pass. Sam had warned Kim not to bring up the job situation—but that didn't mean she wouldn't. A beat of silence dropped and then Kim went on, "It's crazy that they still make you wear a uniform. . . ."

"Keeps my own clothes clean," Tutu said through pursed lips.

"Yeah, but our—" Kim paused, searching for the right word—"*person* said it changed everything when she started coming to work wearing what she wanted."

"And who would that . . . *person* . . . be?"

"Delores Curry."

"Oh, so you're Delores's little girl?" Kim nodded and Tutu rolled her eyes. "I hear your mama's waiting on her now."

"Well, not exactly. But you know there's no law that says you—"

Tutu cut her off fast. "How about you step your sassy pink ass out my kitchen and run along and play with Sammy." She had her fists on her hips and was glaring like the sun on an August day. "I don't need a lecture. My conscience is raised as high as I want it."

"I told you she was scary," Sam said once they'd scooted down the hall and shut the door to his bedroom.

But Kim was effervescing. "No, I love her. She's exactly how you described her." She put her hands on Sam's shoulders and pushed until he fell backward on top of his little boy bed. Then she sat on his stomach and started undoing the buttons of his shirt. "She told us to run along and play, didn't she?" Sam grabbed the hem of her green sweater and lifted. Kim never wore a bra, so the prize was his without the struggle. "So long as you keep them nasty freckly hands off my sassy pink ass!" Kim and her breasts collapsed on

Sam's knobby chest, both of them laughing so hard that the bed squealed.

Sam heard Tutu's transistor radio crackle to life in the kitchen. "She's drowning us out," he said, but Kim wasn't paying attention. She'd kicked off her shoes, wriggled out of her jeans, and now she had Sam pinned to the bed with her knees on his shoulders and her curls cascading down on his face. It was exactly how Richard used to pin him to the ground after they'd rolled down a hill like a pair of logs strapped together. "Say uncle!" Richard would wheedle as a string of spittle dangled from his lips—though somehow Sam always got free just in the nick of time. But now Sam was reveling in being a prisoner. Kim slid herself down his torso, dusting his bare skin with her hair and grazing his mouth with her lips. Two tugs and she had his pants on the floor and his dick in her hand. She wrapped it in her fist like a microphone but instead of singing into it she put it *there*—not inside where he was dying to go but pressed up against the secret little hood she'd taught him about. Before Kim, Sam had barely heard of the clitoris—he thought it sounded like a brand of mouthwash—but now he knew it was the key to the kingdom, the still point of the turning world, the stairway to heaven. "That certain party," Kim had taken to calling it. "Not yet, Samuel. You can't come inside till you pay a visit to *that certain party*." As she reared back, twirling him in slow circles, Sam started to pant. She felt like drenched plush. Her breasts swayed as she rocked her torso over his. His open hands covered them and the nipples wedged between his fingers like cigarette butts. Sam's entire existence—everything he'd ever thought or wanted—was pulsing at the end of his dick. He bucked beneath her, begging. *Now, now, NOW.* At last she slid him down the slippery slope and he was home free.

Down the hall, Tutu was banging pots and pans for all she was worth. As his brain went white then black then burst into rainbow flames, Sam thought he heard *"For the love of God"* float down the hall and curl under the bedroom door like smoke. He didn't care.

"WHAT'S YOUR FIRST CHOICE?" Penny Stein asked Kim as soon as they sat down to dinner. She didn't have to specify. Getting into college was all the parents ever talked to him about. GPA, SAT, AP, safety, stretch, legacy, drag—they had the jargon down pat. Every night they regaled Sam with horror stories of kids who hadn't gotten in anywhere and had to settle for community college—"a fate worse than death," as his mother never failed to point out.

"I'm going to Barnard," Kim replied blithely. "I can't imagine being anywhere but the City."

His parents exchanged a look. Good liberals though they were, Adam and Penny Stein abhorred the student protests that had torn apart Columbia and Barnard, the affiliated women's college, in 1968. The son of one of their friends was in the Columbia chapter of SDS and all he ever talked about was revolution, strikes, riots, sit-ins, teach-ins, demonstrations, rallies, underground newspapers, and making common cause with the oppressed peoples of the world. The friend was practically in tears the last time Penny saw her. "SDS was bad enough, but now campus radicals are threatening to blow up the administration building and god knows what else," Penny reported back in horror. "What are those kids *learning*? That's what I'd like to know."

"Barnard, huh?" Sam's father said, helping himself to more

of Tutu's roast chicken and onion gravy, the Steins' standard Friday-night fare. "It used to be a good school—but these days who the hell knows anymore."

Now Sam and Kim exchanged a look.

"What are you planning on majoring in, Kim?" asked Penny Stein with a forced smile.

"Sex ed," they heard Tutu mutter in the kitchen.

Sam's and Kim's eyes welled as they struggled not to giggle. The parents took no notice.

"Political science," Kim answered when she could trust herself to speak. "My dad's a lawyer—and that's what I'm thinking about too." Sam was relieved that she didn't add "So I can join the Black Panthers' legal defense team," though he knew that was her dream. *We dodged that bullet*, he was thinking. Maybe we can talk about something safe, like basketball or origami or their upcoming ski trip on midwinter break.

"Kim's father's a huge Knicks fan, just like you, Dad." Sam paused to see how that went down. "Looks like they're having a pretty good season."

Everyone seemed happy to talk about the Knicks for a while. Kim made a point of complimenting Tutu's cooking and offered to help clear the table, which elicited a snort of derision. The parents were starting to gripe about their work partners, the cue that Sam was free to leave the table, when Kim butted in to ask Mr. Stein what line of work he was in. She listened politely and even egged him on with a few leading questions as he embarked on a disquisition into the vagaries of the toy business—the price of plastic, the relative profit margins on dolls, games, and novelty items, how discount chain stores were turning the industry on its head. "We've moved almost all our manufacturing overseas in the past few years," Adam Stein said proudly. "Mexico, Malaysia, Singapore—labor is just so much cheaper overseas."

"No unions," Kim put in sweetly.

"Right," Adam agreed heartily.

"No child labor laws or restrictive regulation." She was starting to sound like a prosecutor.

"Humph," he allowed, not sure where Kim was going.

"Some kid gets mangled in a machine, you toss him—or more likely her—and bring in a replacement, right?" Sam tried to signal by wiggling his faint, barely visible eyebrows, but she ignored him. Nothing turned Kim on like political debate.

"Those kids are lucky to have jobs and they know it." Sam could tell his father's fuse was lit. "They *love* us over there. Before we opened our factory in Malaysia, there was nothing. People were starving. Living in the gutter. Eating garbage off the dump."

"What about all the people eating garbage over here because they lost their jobs to cheap overseas labor?" Kim's voice jumped an octave higher. She had Sam's father cornered and she knew it. As long as she didn't start swearing.

"I'm *providing* jobs—not taking them away. Do you know how many people my company employs? Including Sam every summer, and he's happy for the work, aren't you, Sammy?"

Whatever Sam was about to reply, Kim beat him to the punch. "There are people who would *kill* for that job. People with families. They're suffering so Sam can chalk up another feat on his college applications."

"What do you know about it? Have *you* ever gone hungry?" *Here it comes*, thought Sam. He'd heard the tirade so many times he could chant it word for word like a prayer. How Adam Stein's immigrant grandfather had come over from Poland with five dollars in one pocket and an onion in the other and gone to work in a stinking sweatshop on the Lower East Side. How Adam, after growing up in a Bronx housing project, had put himself through college by juggling four different jobs. How he succeeded not because he was *better* or *smarter* but because he *worked harder*. How Sam and his brothers had no idea how lucky they were or how good they had it. And now these spoiled privileged college kids—so-called campus radicals—wanted to rip it apart and give it all away. As if communism was the answer to anything. Look at Poland today! Look at Russia! No, America wasn't perfect. Yes, he believed in civil rights, goddammit. Black people deserved a break so they could pull themselves up by their bootstraps. (In the kitchen, Tutu cascaded cutlery into the sink and turned the tap on full blast.) But that didn't mean blow it up and burn it down. Capitalism coupled to democracy—that was the one winning combination. A rising tide lifts all boats. In the entire history of the world, nothing had ever rivaled the land of the free, home of the brave. If they didn't like it, they could move to Moscow and try starving with Comrade Igor.

"Is that why you're firing Tutu?" Kim broke in. "So she can be free?"

"You need to learn to mind your own business, young lady," Adam barked, looking daggers at Sam.

"Freedom should be fair," Kim soldiered on. "Workers should be partners, not wage slaves. It doesn't have to be about winners and losers. You could turn your business into a collective. Share the profits—spread the wealth. No one gets rich but no one starves."

Adam glared at her. "I notice you don't have any problem enjoying the profits. Or being waited on like a queen. Everyone thinks they can change the world when they're young. Then they go to work and reality bites them in the ass."

"Adam!" Sam's mother, Penny, was flapping her hands above the table as if clearing smoke. "I'm sure Kim is just trying to apply what she's learning in social studies class. All the kids are doing it these days. It's called being relevant."

"Well, she shouldn't talk about things she doesn't understand."

"And *you* do?" Sam was as startled as any of them by the sound of his own voice. He'd never taken on his father in a fight like this. Not once. "Just because you read *The New York Times* and watch Walter Cronkite every night, that makes you an expert on current events? Kim and I have been—"

But he never got to the end of the sentence. The sputtering fuse reached Adam Stein's powder keg and the dining room blew sky-high. Adam was yelling about ungrateful spoiled little brats who didn't know the meaning of an honest day's work and Sam was yelling about how sick he was of being treated like a baby and Penny was yelling about how she could not tolerate such disrespect under her own roof and Kim was trying to get a word in edgewise but no one could hear her over the racket. Suddenly, as if a referee had blown a whistle, Adam quit yelling and turned eerily calm. There was a moment of crystalline silence, then Adam said with a deadly sneer that if they didn't like the system they could get the hell out of his house and try their luck in Hanoi or Havana or wherever the hell. At which point the walls began to spin. Sam was pushing his chair and grabbing Kim by the arm and Penny was telling them to sit down because Tutu hadn't served dessert yet and Tutu came rushing in with a plate of brownies—Sam's favorite!—but Sam and Kim were already down the hall on the way to his bedroom and Sam slammed the door shut while Kim looked at him with burning eyes and without saying a word to each other they grabbed their coats and headed back down the hall and when they reached the kitchen Tutu erupted, "You've got no business doing your mama and daddy like that!" but Sam didn't even stop to say goodbye and the minute they got outside they started running, hand in hand, with their coats open to the cold night air and they didn't stop until they were both doubled over and gasping.

"I hate their guts," Sam croaked when his heart stopped pounding in his ears.

"It doesn't matter," Kim said, squeezing his hand. "*You* won—*we* won."

Sam squeezed back but he couldn't stop trembling.

Chapter Ten

You bitch. You fucking bitch. I know you're lying."

"Herb, please. Keep your voice down, for god's sake."

"You listening up there, Kimberly?" Kim, huddled next to Sam on the floor of her bedroom, clasped her hands over her ears—but the shouting bored into her brain. "Why don't you come down and tell your mother what a fucking lying bitch she is." The voice roared up the stairwell. *"I know you can hear me—you and that little cocksucker you're shacked up with."* Something smashed.

Kim pressed against Sam's bony back and burrowed her face in his neck. "Don't move. Don't breathe," she whispered in his ear. "Make believe we're somewhere else." Another crash and then her mother's piercing scream. *"Don't you dare . . . don't you dare."* Kim and Sam, cocooned in a corner with a horde of stuffed animals, trembled against each other. Her pink and white painted bureau was pushed against the door. The curtains were drawn and the room was dark except for the faint phosphorescent pink of Kim's ballerina snow globe night-light. "Is it me?" Sam asked. "Should I go?"

Kim clung tighter and shook her head into his neck. Sam couldn't know she was crying.

This wasn't supposed to happen—not in front of a stranger.

When Kim and Sam had turned up at her house on Friday night after fleeing the Steins', everything had been cool. She told her parents that Sam was a school friend who'd had "some trouble" at home and would be crashing with them for a couple of days. "Trouble?" Stocky, balding Herb Goodman cocked an eye. "What, they catch you smoking dope?" Sam blushed as only a freckle-face can blush. "Well, we're liberals around here, aren't we, Kimberly? We all want to change the world. You can smoke all the dope you want as long as I don't have to smell it. I think you kids are onto something—it's a bullshit world."

"There's a spare room in the basement," Kim's mother, Bev, chimed in.

"And no hanky-panky or you're out on your ear," Herb growled.

"Thank you, Daddy. Thank you, Mommy. Sam won't be any trouble—he's super-studious."

"Yeah, well, obviously he's no jock." Kim cringed as her father gave Sam's scarecrow frame the once-over. "Don't they feed you at home, kid?"

"Oh, Herb." Bev's auburn curls bobbed around her neck. It killed Kim how much she looked like her mother.

That was Friday night.

Kim and Sam spent most of Saturday hunched at the kitchen table, pretending to study while Sam wrote draft after draft of a letter to his parents and they whispered together about what he should do. Her parents went out to a dinner party that night—Delores had the time off from Friday night until Monday morning—so she and Sam had the run of the house. Sam kept whining about calling home—"My mom and Tutu will be worried sick"—but she talked him out of it. "They threw us out, remember? Let them twist." They scarfed down scorched, gluey frozen chicken potpies in front of the TV, had sex before an audience of scandalized stuffed animals, and showered together afterward. "What—you've never done your pubes?" Kim squeezed out gobs of green shampoo slime and lathered him up, and then of course they had to do it in the shower. She'd barely gotten him back in the basement when her parents stumbled back at midnight.

That was Saturday.

The trouble started at dinner Sunday night. Her father, drinking steadily, kept chipping away at Sam—"Harvard, eh? You think you're some kind of genius? City College was good enough for *me*." And when Sam didn't rise to the bait, Herb turned on his wife. The steak was overdone. The tablecloth had stains. The cheese-stuffed potatoes smelled like shit. "Well, if Kim hadn't guilted you into giving the girl weekends off—" "Delores is not a *girl*!" "Stay out of it, Kimberly. . . ." At which point Herb slid a hand under his plate, flipped it upside down in one smooth movement, and ground the greasy food scraps into the stained tablecloth. "Looks like you got some laundry to do." "You bastard!" Herb Goodman was a short man but his wrath filled the house. Pugnacious at the best of times, he became murderous when anyone challenged him. Especially anyone female. His wife had a scar under her left ear from a broken wineglass he'd thrown at her right after they were married. Kim suffered a concussion at ten after he slammed her head against the bathroom tile. Her older sister, Wendy, broke her arm when he pushed her down the stairs her senior year in high school. "She slipped on the ice," they told everyone—and everyone believed it. Wendy was in college now and rarely came home. Kim had long since learned to barricade herself in her bedroom during her father's eruptions. They never lasted long—and afterward he always begged and Kim always forgave. Actually, she blamed her mother more for putting up with the violence than her father for fomenting it. It was their family secret. No one outside knew or suspected. Until now.

Sam sat at the littered dinner table saucer-eyed and paralyzed. Kim could tell he'd never seen anything like this. Before it got any worse, she grabbed his arm and dragged him up the stairs after her. "Just ignore it," she said through her teeth on the way up. But the racket they made dragging the bureau in front of the bedroom door pushed her father over the edge. The first plate smashed. "I'm calling the police," her mother started screaming. "Why don't you call your boyfriend," her father screamed back. Another volley of crashes. On the floor of her bedroom, backed into a corner, Kim toppled over into fetal position and pressed a pillow over her head. She clamped her jaw to stop her teeth from chattering. Inside her brain a mosquito was wailing, "*Just shut up shut up shut up shut up shut up*." Kim felt Sam wedge himself against her back and his arms wrap around her. She rolled so they were face-to-face. His breath was sweet like he'd been chewing on a stalk of grass. His forehead felt cool and smooth against hers. She moved the pillow so it covered both of their heads. Downstairs, the voices rose and fell like sirens. She sagged into Sam. He was like a pond—so still. He would never turn on her—she felt it the first time he kissed her. He'd never tear her down just to make himself feel bigger. She brushed her lips on his. Poor Sam. He was scared to death. He had no idea.

. . .

THE HOUSE WAS DEAD QUIET when they woke up together in the middle of the night. She could just make out the whites of Sam's eyes in the pink glow of the night-light. They looked at each other for a long silent minute and then, silently, Kim started to undress him. She put her mouth on his and moved down. His chin felt like velour. His neck tasted of salt. Under her lips, his nipples were cold and hard like pebbles. She closed her mouth around the head of his dick and then pulled back so she could watch him writhe and arch and clutch at himself. She took it deeper. She felt the cap throb against the roof of her mouth. "Kim Kim Kim," he whispered, thrashing his head from side to side. He had his palms on her head. His neck was curled back so far she thought it would snap. She lifted her mouth away and looked at his white body glinting in the light. Like a marble statue. Like a flower. Like a wisp of smoke. When she lowered herself on top of him and slid him inside, he gasped like he'd been stabbed. He was hers. He was nothing. A boy in agony. Two thrusts and he melted, dying inside her.

THEY CREPT OUT THE FRONT door together in the freezing hour before sunrise. Kim had crammed a backpack with clothes, books, and her two favorite stuffed animals. The streets were empty. The houses were dark. They marched hand in hand, not daring to speak. Her feet stepped to the revolutionary rallying cry of Jefferson Airplane's "Volunteers." Free. They were free and alone. *Anything can happen now*, she thought. *Anything at all.*

Chapter Eleven

Dear Mom and Dad,

Thanks for the nice childhood. You've been terrific parents until Friday night, when you said some really unforgivable things. You both always taught me how important it is to be welcoming to guests so I was unprepared for your rudeness.

Dad, you recommended that we try our luck in Hanoi or Havana, and I've decided to take the advice. Not literally—but I am moving out and going underground. Don't worry, I'm planning on finishing high school and going to college next fall (assuming I get in). Don't look for me. Don't try to stop me. I don't need your money or your patronizing attitude. I know you think you love me, but I don't see how that's possible, since neither of you really has the slightest idea of who I am or what I believe in.

From now on, all communication between us will go through Tutu. If you fire her, we're done. If you try and track me down, it's over. Here are my conditions: Don't ask around. Don't report me to school. Don't try to bribe or threaten my friends. I have a place to live, I know how to take care of myself, I'm fine. I'll pass messages to Tutu as long as she keeps her job. She doesn't know where I'm living so don't try to coerce her. We'll all be better off this way—and maybe one day you'll see things from my point of view.

Until then, so long and have a nice life.

Your son, Sam

That was the letter Sam carried folded in his back pocket. He'd spent the weekend drafting and redrafting it until Herb Goodman's explosion derailed him. Now that he and Kim were fugitives, there was no time to fix it up, make it bite harder. Still, it was bound to set his parents on their asses. Sam pictured the two of them reading it. *What the hell does he mean "going underground"?*

The sky was just getting gray when they reached the downtown shopping street. Kim stopped at the first pay phone and dialed Brad the Rad's number. He was the only one they knew who had his own car. The plan was for Brad to pick them up in town and drive them to the Steins' place so Sam could get his stuff. They'd figure out the rest after that.

Half an hour later, Brad's beater sputtered to a stop in Sam's driveway. Monday morning. The house was dark except for a yellow blaze in the kitchen window. The door was unlocked as usual.

Sam pushed it open—should he knock?—and there was Tutu, sliding her iron up and down the shiny runway of her ironing board and singing along to her gospel station like nothing had happened. He stopped at the threshold. Was she friend or foe?

"Where have you been? Your folks are half-dead with worry." But Sam shook his head and left the kitchen without saying a word. He set the letter in the middle of the dining room table, where they couldn't miss it, and went back to the bedrooms. "Child? Child?" Tutu shouted down the hall. "You come back in here and explain yourself!" "In the bathroom!" Sam shouted back. But he wasn't. He was in his parents' room pulling twenties from the billfold his father kept stashed in the top dresser drawer. Then he tiptoed to his own room, grabbed his backpack from the closet, and stuffed it to overflowing with whatever he could grab.

"I saved you your job," he announced flatly when he was back in the kitchen.

"You *what*?"

"You'll understand when they get home and read the note. Thanks to me, they can't fire you now. But you gotta promise me you won't say anything."

"I'm not promising shit!" Sam stared—he'd never heard Tutu curse before. "You come creeping in here like a thief in the night and steal all those clothes and books—it's criminal."

"Like the way you stole your little grandson?"

"How dare you!" Tutu reared back and he thought she was going to hit him—first time in his life.

"I thought I could trust you." Sam's voice broke but he couldn't help it. "I thought you were on my side."

"When you start paying my salary, I'll be on your side. Till then, I'm doing what they ask me to do."

"Yeah, well if it wasn't for me, you wouldn't *have* a salary. You'd be out in the cold. You owe me, Tutu!"

"I don't owe you squat, boy. You put those clothes back and get your ass to school where it belongs."

"I'll do whatever the hell I want!" He'd never before raised his voice to her. "I'm not a child anymore, in case you haven't noticed. From now on, I'm not taking orders—not from them or you or anyone."

Tutu sank down onto the patched vinyl bench by the kitchen table. "Listen to you, Sammy. You don't even sound like yourself. That little girl has—"

"Kim's not a little girl—she's a—"

But she brushed him off. "This isn't about her. Girlfriends come and go. But the good Lord only gives you but one mama and one daddy. That's it. You're not getting another pair. You can run and hide—I'm not stopping you. But you pain them that brought you into the world, and that's on you forever."

"*Me* pain *them*? Were you even *here* Friday night? Didn't you *listen* to what he said? *You can get the hell out of my house and move to Cuba*. They're sick of me. They never wanted me in the first place. They'll be better off without me. All of you will."

"You know that's not true. Nobody's sick of you. But you and that gal of yours need to learn some respect. The Bible says—"

"I don't care about the Bible. And neither do they. All they care about is money."

Sam turned his back on her and made for the door but her voice followed him out. "Wherever you go, they're gonna track you down, and when they find you, they're gonna put you in reformatory where you belong. Lockdown, Sammy. That what you want?"

He spun his head around and snapped, "It couldn't be any worse than living here."

And with that, Sam pushed his way outside and kicked the door shut behind him. "Freedom!" he muttered under his breath, but his lower lip was trembling. His parents could rot in hell for all he cared. But he hated himself for the way he had spoken to Tutu. He had half a mind to go back and apologize, but Brad's car was coughing in the driveway and Kim was gesturing frantically from the front seat. So he opened the back door, threw in his pack, and then jammed in beside Kim in the front. "Welcome, comrade," Brad boomed. But Sam ignored him. He had his eyes on the kitchen window, where Tutu stood with tears running down her face.

"I USED TO BE OBSESSED with this place when I was little," Sam told Kim as they sat shivering side by side on a bench. "It was the ducks—after I read *Make Way for Ducklings* I always wanted to come here and look for baby ducks."

"No ducks today," Kim murmured. The sky was milky, the temperature in the midtwenties. The trees were bare. The park was empty. "No maids. No kids. Just us comrades."

"Frozen comrades." They grinned at each other. Despite the cold, they were loving every minute of it—cutting school, running away, hiding out, going underground—alone, together. The park bench faced Long Island Sound—"the most domesticated body of salt water in the Western Hemisphere," in Fitzgerald's famous formulation—and across the slate gray expanse rose the elegant span of the Throgs Neck Bridge. Bridge, salt water, ducklings, deserted park: it all sounded terribly romantic except that the water was so polluted it would blister submerged skin and the bridge with the beautiful name connected the shoddy row houses of Queens with the brutalist housing projects of the Bronx. So much for the fresh green breast of the new world.

Now what? Or, more to the point, where? That was the question Sam and Kim had been batting around all morning. Sam was for taking their chances in Greenwich Village—wandering around Bleecker Street until they found some hippies to crash with—but Kim said the whole flower-power thing was finished—hippies had morphed from love children to drug-crazed cultists who'd sell you into white slavery for a heroin fix. Delores had her own place in the suburb's black neighborhood—but Kim didn't want to risk getting her in trouble. Homeless shelter? Hole up at the Y? Get a job and rent a room in one of those Queens row houses? Hitchhike south? Light out for the territory? Going underground sounded so cool until they actually found themselves scrounging around for their next meal.

Right around the time their fingers and toes started to go numb, Kim had a brainstorm: move in with Richard and Eli. Sam thought it was crazy but she won him over. There were those two mattresses on the living room floor where they could sleep. They'd commute to school on the train, like all the Fat Neck businessmen but in reverse. Brad would pick them up at the train station in the morning, take them to school, and drive them back in the afternoon. When they ran out of money they'd get jobs. Richard would keep their secret—Kim had enough dirt on him to see to that. And anyway, between clubbing and making new "friends," Richard was hardly ever home at night, and Eli was usually too zonked to know or care who was crashing at the place.

There was a pay phone at the entrance to the park and Kim

made the call. Sam could hear Richard's raspy surfer-dude voice through the receiver. "No problemo, kiddo! Your secret's safe with me. Mi casa es su casa." And that was that.

They hitchhiked to the Fat Neck train station, caught the 3:20 local to Penn Station, took the subway downtown, dragged their stuff through the tarnished silver streets of the East Village, skirted Tompkins Square Park, rang Richard's bell, climbed four flights through clouds of cabbage, garlic, and marijuana reek, and went underground.

Chapter Twelve

The first night, Sam slept fitfully. Even after Richard and Eli quit partying, the upstairs neighbors kept rampaging back and forth across the ceiling and bursts of shouting and what sounded like gunshots drifted up from the street and a smeary glow irradiated the curtainless window and ants or roaches or bedbugs or worse swarmed up from the mattress. The alarm went off at six o'clock and he and Kim fell all over each other in the tiny filthy bathroom. It took over an hour to get to the Fat Neck station, and of course Brad the Rad wasn't there so they had to pay for taxis to their high schools, which consumed a serious chunk of Sam's filched cash supply. After two days, he swore he would never ever be a commuter. How could his father have endured the soul-crushing routine all those years?

ON WEDNESDAY AFTERNOON, his mother showed up at school. She didn't come in—anything to avoid a scene in front of strangers—but Sam spotted the family station wagon hulking amid a fleet of rich kids' sports cars in the student parking lot. He thought of ducking back inside, making a run for it out the back door. No. Better not to act like a criminal. So he sauntered up to the passenger door, staring her down all the way, and got in.

"I *told* you—" he started, but she laid a hand on his arm. Were those tears in the corners of her eyes? She looked small inside her puffy red parka. Small and scared. "See?" Sam spread both arms out, shaking off her hand. "Alive and well—and studying! Look at the books!"

"Sam. We . . . I . . . you scared us to death." She looked like she was going to lean over and hug him, but she didn't. "Okay"—she was breathing hard—"you made your point, honey. Now it's time to come home." *No apology? No we-were-so-blind?* "I know your father said some things he shouldn't have. People lose their tempers, you know? But that's no reason to—"

"You really don't get it, do you?" His voice scraped his throat. He wanted her hand back on his arm. He wanted her to cry again. "You can't just crap on people and expect them to fall into line. You—"

"I'm not people—I'm your mother. It's my job to take care of you."

"Yeah, well, I think you need to resign. I'm raised—you said so yourself."

"At least tell me where you're staying. Be reasonable, Sam. *If* we think it's safe—you and Kim could—"

The word "Kim" in her mouth made him burn. "I don't need your permission. I told you already—Tutu's looking out for me. I'm doing everything right—but I'm doing it my own way. Why can't you trust me?"

Because you're such a baby. Because you're such an idiot. Because I'm your mother and I love you.

"I *do* trust you, Sammy. Really. But you hear all these stories—kids getting into drugs. Crazy politics. Blowing stuff up. It's a dangerous world out there. You have no idea."

"Nothing's gonna happen." Her eyes narrowed—she'd never heard him use this tone before. "And if something does, I'll come home. Okay? I promise. But this is something I have to do."

"It's all your father's fault," she said, staring straight ahead with her hands on the wheel. "If only he could control his temper." Then she started the car.

"What? You're driving me to reform school? Prison?"

"No. I'm taking you home." But before she could put the car in gear, Sam was out the door. He didn't slam it. He didn't stride away. Instead, with one hand on the rim of the passenger window, he bent at the waist until his head and shoulders were back inside the pocket of warmth. "Don't make it worse than it is, okay, Mom? You can't control me anymore. You think you can but you're wrong."

Then he withdrew. He didn't turn but he raised a hand over his head and kept walking.

Penny Stein watched her last son stalk away. When he disappeared behind the hedges, she shut off the car, got out, and crossed the parking lot to the high school entrance.

On Thursday afternoon and again on Friday, Sam scanned the lot, but there was no sign of her. Of course. There was only so much time she could take off from work.

Then came the weekend. Sam and Kim pooled their money and splurged on breakfast at a diner on Second Avenue. The best bacon and eggs he'd ever tasted. Endless cups of muddy coffee in chipped white fat-lipped mugs. They found a hardware store and laid in industrial-strength insecticide and cleaning supplies. They scored some secondhand sheets, towels, and blankets at the local Salvation Army. Kim drew up a rotating chore calendar and tacked it to the wall: shopping, cooking, dishwashing, housecleaning. "Like a kibbutz," said Eli. "A collective," said Kim. "Let's call it Casa Riccardo," suggested Richard, who'd been running with some coke-sniffing Italian aristos. "How about Zee Reekie Project?" "Dick's Hole," Sam chimed in and they all howled.

The days were getting longer but it was still freezing on the streets—a cold more pitiless and penetrating than anything Sam had known in the suburbs. There was no place to hide from the wind. Airborne garbage scoured the canyons like flocks of crows. Inside, the radiator hissed morning and night, turning the apartment into a sauna. Sam didn't care. He was enchanted at being free and unsupervised in the City for the first time in his life. The Saturday streets were like a giant polar party. Everyone was wrapped in streamers of riotous wool and alpaca. Eyes peeped from between scarves and hoods, checking him out, challenging him, greeting, inviting, dismissing, lusting, probing. Each block housed a library of stories. On the sidewalk, foreign languages faded in and out like nighttime stations on a car radio. Sam knew it was a tight narrow island but the cityscape felt infinite—brick and stone and glass and asphalt and wrought iron endlessly replicated in every direction, all of it teeming ceaselessly with people and cars. He was intoxicated and flattened. He wanted to rush down every street, sample every cookie in every bakery, eavesdrop on every conversation even he if he had no idea what language they were speaking, stalk random beautiful strangers on their mysterious rounds to clubs and cafés and dark little closet bars and bedrooms humid with flowers and rumpled sheets.

Lovers, haters, vendors, buskers, pushers, preachers, crazies, hippies, saints, models, spies, runaways, bums, junkies, flunkies, wannabes, has-beens, wash-outs, paranoids, poets, rockers, mockers, punks, cons, soldiers, winos, debutantes, and deadbeats—all of them freezing together on the patchwork jingle-jangle sidewalk. Sam felt himself spiraling up to heaven like a helium balloon.

Two Saturday mornings in, Sam and Kim strolled over to the funky radical bookstore on St. Mark's Place. He scanned the poetry shelves in the back for anything by Frank O'Hara or Gary Snyder, while she flitted restlessly from political science to history to comic books. When Sam caught up with her, Kim was standing by a rack of underground newspapers (*Rat, Kudzu, Avatar, The Other, The Organ, Vortex, Zapp, Splat, Bent, Hung, Lilith, Off Our Backs*) chatting up a tall skinny whiskey-colored guy with a red Afro and strawberry freckles. "Sam—Jeff. Jeff—Sam." They shook hands.

"Jeff was telling me about this alternative printing press a couple blocks away," Kim said breathlessly. "It's where *The BP* gets distributed from."

"The what?"

She lowered her voice. "*The Black Panther*—you know, the party's newspaper? Wanna come check it out?"

Sam looked from one to the other. Jeff slouched and winked. Kim was glowing. Sam felt a blade twist in his gut. Had she really fallen for this caramel character in the last two minutes? Should he tag along just to make sure nothing happened? That would be so uncool.

"Nah—I'm gonna get back. Big calculus test on Monday."

"Calcu-*whut*?" Jeff's face split with mirth.

"Yeah, I know." Sam hoped he sounded nonchalant. "But if I fail, I'm toast."

"Okay, see you later then."

"Yeah, man, later."

And out they waltzed.

Shit. Fuck. Piss. Sam was muttering under his breath like a crazy person as he kicked down the sidewalk. How could she just ditch him like that and go off with another guy? He walked blindly, crossing avenues and plunging down random side streets until he found himself in a part of the Village he'd never seen before. Beautiful brick and stone houses lined the blocks. Trees etched black shadows on the sidewalks. The streets had names like English lapdogs—Barrow, Perry, Bedford, Charles, Bethune, Christopher. Sam turned down the last because there were more people on it—all of them young men with tight pants, willowy waists, and leering eyes. Shops hawked leather jockstraps, studded cat o' nine tails, and executioner masks. Shuttered bars sported names like Ramrod, Blue Boy, Hidey Hole, Scrotum, Up Yours. So subtle. "Whatsa matter, sugar?" a teetering linebacker in high heels, purple miniskirt, and yellow wig hooted at him. "Can't find your daddy?" Richard would have had a snappy comeback—but Sam just turned tail and fled. The laughter rang in his ears all the way to Seventh Avenue.

It was dark by the time Kim blew back in. She didn't even take off her coat. Didn't greet Sam. Didn't sit. Didn't seem to realize where she was. She just stood there in the middle of Richard's dumpy living room with her arms wrapped around her tiny torso and her eyes fixed blankly on the window bars. She didn't say a word but Sam could tell she was on fire.

He made believe he was still studying—but in fact he was holding his breath, waiting for her to crack first. Finally, she dropped her dazzling eyes to his face. "Weatherman" was all she said. "I just met the Weatherman."

Sam waited a couple of beats, then a couple more, and when she still didn't say anything else he piped up: "What—is it going to snow?"

Kim burst out laughing, collapsed on the sofa, and started motor-mouthing. "Oh my god, it's happening, Sam. Right here right now—and the Weatherman is making it happen."

He raised his eyebrows and spread both palms out beside his shoulders. Huh?

"Okay, okay, lemme back up. Remember Jeff?" *How could he forget?* "The guy with the red fro? So after the bookstore, Jeff took me to that printing press and sure enough there were bundles of *The Black Panther* stacked all over the place. It's gotta be the coolest underground newspaper ever—like a blueprint for revolution, you know? Anyway, Jeff and I volunteered to help load papers into the back of an old hippie van—and when we got through, the guy nodded us into the back room so we could meet this lady—woman—whatever—this dark-haired hatchet-faced revolutionary earth goddess. Hardly bigger than me—but oh my god she has an aura about her. Lee is what everyone calls her—not her real name—her whatchacallit?"

"Nom de guerre?"

"Right. Nom de guerre. Nom de guerrilla—I'm not kidding, Sam. This is real. There's a war going on out there—multiple wars—all connected. Vietnam, Harlem, Oakland, Indians on the reservations, Palestinians on the West Bank, women everywhere—they're all fighting against the same system. And now is the time for us to rise up and bring it down. I know we're just kids but kids can change the world. I mean, who else if not us?"

"So the hatchet-faced goddess lady—Lee? She's the Weather boss?"

"No—yes—I don't know—I think she's only in charge of one

cell. Anyway, she sizes us up—me and Jeff—and she says, 'Who are you guys?' And I say, 'We're whoever you want us to be.' I guess that was good enough because that's when she keyed us in to what's going down. Okay, listen. The Weatherman is not about rain and snow—it's about revolution. You know Dylan's line about not needing a weatherman? That's where the name comes from. And right now, on starship earth, the wind is blowing to global insurgency—armed uprising—radical action—marching in the streets!" Sam thought she was going to levitate. "You know about SDS?"

"Students for a Democratic Society? The guys behind those sit-ins at Columbia—Harvard—that SDS?"

"Yeah—well, from what I hear *that* SDS is over. Peaceful protest—compromise—playing footsie with the pigs—all that shit is history. The only way to win is to beat the man at his own game." Kim stood, stripped off her coat, dropped it on the floor. "You gotta hear Lee tell it—she knows everything. Everything, Sam! She took me and Jeff to this brown—" She caught herself. "To this pad in the Village which is like Weatherman central command. The Weather Bureau. They've got a plan—oh my god, it's so brilliant. No more demos. No more sit-ins. 'If it's only talk, it's not revolution': Lee's words. It's time to fight—to start blowing stuff up—*their* stuff—you know, banks, courts, draft boards, police stations, military bases. Whatever it takes—as long as it gets on the evening news. That's the key. It's *all* about the media—I totally get that now. The press went crazy last fall when the Weatherman blew up a statue of some fascist old cop in Chicago. No one was hurt but from the television news you'd think it was World War III. The media are our best weapon."

"*Our?* So now you're on board with bombing?"

Kim let that slide. "Nobody's gonna die except ideas and

statues. It's not about killing people—it's about the circus, the coverage. The medium is the message. Attention is everything! The more outrageous we are, the more attention we get. The more attention, the more followers. One well-placed bomb is worth a thousand peaceful protest marches. Can't you see? We light the match—but the media are the gasoline. They're fighting half the battle for us. More than half. Once the news hits, kids are gonna rise up everywhere and join us. High school students like us—we're the vanguard. When it starts it's never gonna stop. This whole fucking thing is gonna blow."

"And the Weatherman is gonna make it blow? You—and this Lee lady—and Jeff—and a buncha other kids playing with matches?"

She shook her head. "No." The flush dimmed. She quit pacing. "Weatherman alone is not enough. But with the BPP—"

"The Panthers."

"With the BPP fighting alongside us, we'd be unbeatable. They already have a national network. They've got a newspaper—chapters in every city—zillions of members. They've got guns and they know how to use them. If only we—*I*—can get the Weatherman and the Panthers to join forces, we could do anything—*everything*!"

"Okay—now I'm lost. What does the BPP have to do with any of this? I thought the Panthers were like *un-gawah—black powah—right on*! But it sounds like the Weatherman is more like—you know—white power? punk power? guerrilla theater with real bombs? Why would they team up?"

Kim took a deep breath. "FBI pigs say the Panthers are violent extremists—but they're not. For them, it's not about violence, it's about *resistance*. Self-defense. They're *saving* lives, not taking them. When some shyster landlord kicks an old lady out of her apartment, the Panthers are the ones who get her back in. When a supermarket charges double in the ghetto, the Panthers show up and set things straight. They're giving free breakfast to hundreds of kids every day. Free doctors and lawyers too—you name it. They don't *talk* about justice—they *enforce* justice. Fight the power by seizing the power. Do you have any idea how many innocent black men, women, and children are gunned down every year by trigger-happy cops? The pigs are waging *war* on black people, no different from Jim Crow, no different from slavery. But the Panthers are fighting back. Arming themselves and using weapons to protect their lives, families, property, and rights. Policing the police. You know what put the BPP on the map? A couple years ago, thirty of them marched into the California State Capitol building carrying rifles and Magnums. Can you picture it? Dudes with fros armed to the teeth and marching in the halls of power. The police couldn't lay a finger on them because the right to bear arms is protected by the Second Amendment, though whoever wrote that one was definitely not thinking about black dudes pointing Magnums at state troopers."

"James Madison," Sam interrupted.

"Huh?"

"James Madison—he was the author of the Bill of Rights." Sam had been boning up for the American history AP test.

"Right. Madison was cool with civil rights, except when it came to his own slaves. Anyway, the Weatherman and the Panthers are the *perfect* combo—the revolutionary dream team—only . . ."

"Only?"

Kim sighed. "I went up there this afternoon." Sam drew a blank. "You know—to the BPP chapter in Harlem."

"You went to Harlem? Alone?"

"No—Jeff went with me."

"So—what—now *he's* your boyfriend?" The second Sam said it he regretted it.

"Jesus, Sam, why do you have to be such an asshole!" Suddenly she was blazing. Sam's heart took off at a gallop. *If she had a gun, she'd shoot.* "I'm talking about *revolution*—changing the fucking world—and all you can think about is having a *girlfriend*? Why'd you leave home, anyway? You haven't gone underground—you're just playing house in a slum. I thought you were different—I really thought I could trust you!" She bolted for the bathroom and slammed the door. "Fuck you, Sam!" He sat there stunned. It was the first time she'd turned on him.

Eli, roused by the racket, stumbled out of the bedroom in his underwear. "What happen? Keemee sounds really peaced up." "Off," muttered Sam. "Off what?" "Pissed *off*, not up." But Eli just shook his head and pulled a beer from the fridge. Richard had still not come back from wherever he'd been the night before. Sam felt like crying—or battering down the bathroom door—or punching Eli in the face. He was on the verge of storming out—revolution my ass! let *her* see how it feels!—but where?

Kim stayed locked in the bathroom so long that Sam was convinced she'd slit her wrists. Finally, he heard the shower splutter on and ten minutes later she emerged wrapped in a towel with her hair streaming down her face. She sat down next to him on the sofa and put her wet head on his shoulder. The smell of shampoo made his legs tremble. Eli, hunched over a magazine, kept darting his eyes over to see if the towel had slipped off Kim's boobs.

"Sorry . . ." she started, but Sam put two fingers to her lips.

"Don't—"

"No, but I want to explain. It's not you. I'm just upset over what went down in Harlem."

With Jeff, Sam was thinking but didn't say.

"When we got to BPP headquarters, two women in black leather jackets and berets came outside to check us out. Women are in charge now, Jeff told me, because all the men are either dead or in jail. The Panther 21 trial has practically wiped out the New York chapter. They let Jeff go inside with them—he's like one-quarter black but it's enough—but I had to wait on the street. People started to heckle—you know, like I was revolutionary Barbie or something. Finally I pounded on the door and someone let me in—Jeff had vanished. The lady goes, 'Whoa, the sistah's still here.' So I say, 'Yeah, the sistah wants to make a deal.' I told her about the steno pad you grabbed off that FBI pig. 'It's yours,' I said, 'on one condition: from now on, Weatherman and BPP band together—common cause!—with me as the liaison.'" Kim shook back her wet curls and hitched up the sagging towel. "But she just looks me up and down and snorts. 'Okay, honey,' she finally says. 'We definitely need to rearm. So you come back with that notebook *and* a crate of Uzis and then we'll talk.'" Kim clamped her chin between thumb and forefinger and squeezed. "Jesus, Sam, what am I gonna do? I don't even know what a freaking Uzi looks like."

At which point Eli dropped the magazine and sprang to his feet. "Uzi? Uzi?" he squawked. "Israeli submachine gun—that Uzi? Who wants Uzi crate? I know where to find."

Chapter Thirteen

Early the next morning, Sam put on his nicest clothes and tiptoed out of the apartment. He'd been feeling guilty about how mean he was to Tutu when he went home to get his stuff, and he decided to make amends by showing up at her church. Besides, he had to hear Leon sing again.

The prospect of navigating Harlem by himself was alarming, but if Kim could do it, he could. So he took the train uptown, endured the side-eye and muttered cracks after all the other white people got off at 96th Street, and exited at 145th Street. "Never *ever* leave the train at that stop," his mother warned him whenever he went to the city alone. *How bad could it be?*

Up on street level, the sun was bright, and the sidewalks were a multicolored parade of ladies in hats and gents in overcoats. A couple of little kids giggled and pointed—"Hey, freckle-face!"—but everyone else was too busy meeting and greeting and hurrying to church to pay him any mind. "Religion is the opiate of the masses," per Karl Marx. But not one of the masses Sam passed on the sidewalk looked drugged. Maybe dope was the real opiate of the masses? On the wall of a boarded-up building on St. Nicholas Avenue, someone had spray-painted "Capitalism Plus Dope Equals Genocide" with a stencil of a black man jabbing a hypodermic needle into his arm. So what did religion plus capitalism equal?

He walked and looked and tried to look like he wasn't looking. On the avenues, stuff for sale was spread across the sidewalk—frayed old magazines, cheap handbags and luggage, gaudy wigs, knock-off watches, tie-dyed dashikis, velvet paintings of African beasts and black superstars. Reflections brimmed and quivered like water in the shop windows. Heads floated by in the buses. Sam swam through it all without stopping.

He was so lost in thought that he nearly walked right by Tutu and Leon waiting for him outside the narrow storefront that was now the Saints Alive Baptist Church. "That's the best you could do?" Tutu said by way of greeting, giving his rumpled khakis and unironed white shirt the once-over. She looked like Queen Elizabeth in her matching blue coat, hat, gloves, and shoes. At least Leon seemed happy to see him. He was taller than Sam remembered and rangier—his perfectly pressed dove-gray pin-striped suit fell short of wrists and ankles, his Adam's apple bobbed restlessly above his shirt collar. When they shook hands, Sam thought he detected a little skyward roll of the dark brown eyes. "Well," sighed Tutu, "maybe Jesus doesn't care how raggedy you look—but I sure do." And with that she swept them inside. There was no bragging about "my boys" this time. No greetings from Miss Lila or Miss Mary Jane or Miss Jolene. Tutu slid into the pew, followed by Leon, followed by Sam. *Church—again! My grandmother must be rolling in her grave.* Someone two rows back sneezed what sounded like "White boy!" Sam felt his face go scarlet. Tutu wouldn't look his way, but Leon leaned over to whisper, "She got up on the wrong side of the bed, is all. Nothing a little praise and worship won't soothe." For which he received a jab in the ribs from his grandmother, and this time Sam definitely saw the eyes roll. Co-conspirator!

An ancient lady in huge fake pearls tottered over to the organ, the white-robed choir rustled to their feet, and the service began. Someone shouted out a hymn title—"Hush"—and the choir laid down the first line and then the rest of the congregation joined in.

Hush.
Hush.
Somebody's calling my name.
Hush.
Hush.
Somebody's calling my name.
Oh my Lord, oh my Lord, what shall I do . . .

Sam stood when everyone else stood and sang when everyone sang and clapped when they clapped. He hummed the words he didn't know. Leon, standing beside him, hit every note in a resonant tenor and when he swayed from side to side, he and Sam brushed shoulders. Sam felt his feet starting to dance. Then the preacher took his place at the pulpit, raised his palms over his head, and made them quake like leaves. "Brothers and sisters in Jesus, welcome to God's house on this refulgent winter morning!" Sam caught Tutu's eye as they all took their seats again and she gave him a little nod. *Praise the Lord!*

Sam raked the stamped-tin ceiling with his eyes, but Jesus refused to show Himself again. Must be on account of all those godless Commies and unrepentant dope fiends he'd been hanging around with. He sized up Leon out of the corner of his eye. Had he ever smoked dope or had sex? Unlikely. Certainly not on Tutu's watch. Leon had a couple of years on Sam—but he still seemed to be on the other side of the great chasm. His cheeks were smooth and shiny, his dense coiled hair about a week out from a crew cut. Sitting there with his hands folded in his lap and his eyes on the preacher, Leon was at home and at peace in God's house.

Sam tuned back into the service when he heard the name Job repeatedly intoned by Pastor Ball. "Can faith in God survive the worst punishment God can inflict? I'm not talking about humbling and chastisement—I'm talking about *devasTAtion*. CaTAstrophe. *Total* loss of EVerything and EVeryone you value. God strips it all away like *that*"—he snapped his fingers—"and you love Him still? Do you? Would you? That's what happened to Job. Job was the perfect man—he had it all—money and children, land and happiness—and God let the Devil take it all away because the Devil bet against him. 'There's nothing perfect about Job except his money,' the Wicked One jeered at God. 'Take his property, kill his family, cast him to the gutter, and I wager that the perfect man will curse thee to thy face.'" The pastor opened his Bible and read: "'And the Lord said unto Satan, Behold, all that he hath is in thy power; only upon himself put not forth thine hand.' Old Satan didn't waste any time. The Devil went and killed Job's servants and burned up his sheep right quick. He sent a great wind from the wilderness to carry off Job's sons. He tore down his house and ripped up his fields. And what did the perfect and upright man do when he had nothing left? Did he curse God to his face? Did he sink into despair? Did he sign his everlasting soul over to the Devil? No. Job tore his clothes, shaved his head, fell on the ground, and prayed. Yes, that's right, brothers and sisters, Job *worshipped* the God who had let Satan lay him low."

"Amen." "Praise the Lord." "Blessed be the name." The souls were kindling.

"Now, didn't the good Lord make a wager on *us*? Weren't *we* like Job when God and Satan rolled the dice? We had land—a whole continent! We had riches and children and contentment—and God let the Devil take it all away and make us slaves. He took our homes and children. He took our freedom. He took our very bodies. Naked—outcast—enslaved! The Devil has had his way with us for all these many years—and the Devil's not done with us yet. Why? Why us? Job asked the very same thing—and listen to what God replied: 'Then the Lord answered Job out of the whirlwind, and said, Who is this that darkeneth counsel by words without knowledge? Gird up now thy loins like a man; for I will demand of thee, and answer thou me. Where was thou when I laid the foundations of the earth? declare if thou hast understanding.' Now I stand before you with the Lord's own challenge: Declare if thou hast understanding. *Declare*! Who among you dare to question God? Did *you* see the foundations of the earth laid down? Did you? Did you?" He pointed his index finger from face to face. "In the darkness of your ignorance and sin, you have the same choice as Job. You can curse God to His face or you can praise Him. You can loot and burn, you can pick up a gun, you can taunt the police and blow up buildings—or you can bless the name of the Lord. The choice is yours, I say. Go with the Devil or go with God. Now, who among you chooses God? Who will dare to bless His precious name? Who will cast out hatred and embrace love?"

"I will." "Yes, Lord." "Take me, Jesus." "Glory."

That is not a fair choice, Sam was thinking. *Why does it have to be one or the other—curse or praise, burn or bless, God or Devil? Life doesn't work that way.* But the joyful noise drowned out his brain.

Tutu had one hand in the air and the other on her Bible. She wasn't looking at Sam or anyone else but Preacher Ball. Her shout swelled the chorus: "I will." They all rose, Sam with them, and the choir broke into song again.

I'm so glad Jesus lifted me.
I'm so glad Jesus lifted me.
Satan had me bound; Jesus lifted me.
Satan had me bound; Jesus lifted me.
Satan had me bound; Jesus lifted me.
Singing glory, hallelujah! Jesus lifted me.

"Now, who among you brothers and sisters in Jesus has heard of potter's field?" the preacher resumed, segueing into his sermon. Sam saw Tutu snap to attention. Potter's field was one of her favorite subjects. Whenever she was feeling sorry for herself, she used to mutter about it under her breath. *They're not going to bury* me *in potter's field. Once they haul you off to potter's field, nobody can find you ever again. Potter's field is nothing but the Devil's ash-pit.* Eventually, he figured out that she was talking about a pauper's grave—but he had no idea until now that potter's field was in the Bible. Pastor Ball laid it out for his rapt congregation: Back in the days when Jesus walked, potter's field was a fallow plot outside the Jerusalem city walls where potters came to dig and cart away the red clay soil. Judas Iscariot bought that clay field with the thirty pieces of silver he got for betraying our Lord. But when Judas went to take possession, his body burst and his guts gushed out on the thick red ground. Divine retribution! From that time forth, potter's field—the Field of Blood, as it was called—became a cemetery for homeless strangers in the Holy Land, a cursed spot where foreigners were tipped without ceremony into unmarked graves. Now Sam understood at last why being buried in potter's field so terrified Tutu. To be buried in potter's field meant you died poor and alone and unmourned, your name and deeds erased as if you had never lived. More than anything in the world, Tutu wanted to be laid to rest in a cemetery plot beneath a headstone set on a green lawn of mown grass. A grave that someone could visit and weep next to and decorate with flowers. And it dawned on Sam what the root of the problem was: money. Pastor Ball declared that if you paid enough into the Saints Alive Everlasting Life Fund, the church would reserve you a burial plot. Double your gift and you'd get a gravestone. From the stricken look on Tutu's face, Sam could tell that she hadn't paid enough. *Once they haul you off to potter's field, nobody can ever find you again.* Sam and Leon exchanged a look, and Leon shook his head just a fraction.

All those years working for his family and she *still* couldn't afford a decent grave?

"We're working on it," Leon told Sam afterward as they walked back to the apartment together. Tutu, lagging behind with Miss Lila, was out of earshot. "Every dollar I bring home from packing groceries, ten cents goes into the Fund. Same with her pay from you all. We're about halfway there."

"How much you need altogether?"

"Five hundred for the grave, another five for the stone."

"So you got enough for the grave already, and now you're working on the stone?"

"We got two hundred thirty between us. Almost halfway to the plot. But now that your parents are"—Leon dropped his eyes—"you know—"

"Not anymore," Sam broke in. "She didn't tell you? They can't fire her—or they lose me for good. I've got them over a barrel."

Leon gave him a look as they walked in step down the avenue. "Let me get this straight. You're—like—*blackmailing* your own folks so Granny can keep her job?"

Sam nodded, beaming. He was expecting gratitude—but Leon kept his head down. "I think she's pissed at you, Sam. No—I *know* she's pissed. You broke the Fifth Commandment—you know, honor your father and mother? She's not gonna be happy till you move back home."

"Well, that's not happening until they apologize."

"She told me you were stubborn. 'You'd never know it to look at him but that boy can fight'—her very words."

"Seriously?" Sam was dying to know what else Tutu said about him—but it would be too uncool to ask.

"Granny cares about you, man. She's always going on about *Sam this* and *Sam that*. It used to make me a little jealous." Leon turned but he didn't break stride. "Until I met you—then I decided you were all right." He shoved Sam with his shoulder. "For a white guy."

Sam grinned but didn't trust himself to say anything.

THEY LAUGHED UNTIL THEY CRIED, all three of them, telling stories over lunch about Tutu's secret hiding place and *that certain party* and how she dug channels in their scalps with her nails when she shampooed them. "She did that to you too?" Leon and Sam asked simultaneously and cracked up all over again.

When the laughter finally died, Tutu heaved a sigh, looking

from boy to boy. "When are you going back, Sammy? They ask me about you every day."

"Tell them I'm fine." His mouth curled in contempt. "I'm keeping up my grades—I even passed the calculus test—that's all they care about anyway."

"Your mama went and called Kim's mama." Sam's eyebrows shot up. "They're thinking about calling the police."

"Let them try and they'll never see me again. You better remind them about the rules."

But Tutu just crossed her arms on her breast and glared. Sam glared back. "You think you got something on me—but you don't." She cut her eyes to Leon for a second. "I didn't *steal* that child, I *saved* him. Isn't that the truth, Leon honey?"

"Aww, Granny, why do we have to talk about all that?"

"Sam knows half the story already—time he heard the rest." With her arms still crossed and her eyes fixed on Sam, Tutu told it. When Leon turned fourteen, she decided to go down to Virginia on a surprise visit. It nearly killed her to see the boy. Leon looked more like ten than fourteen. Nothing but skin and bones, and his eyes kept sliding off to the side like he was scared of something. His mother, Nanny, looked scared, too. Eyes wide and glazed. Mouth twitchy. Tutu thought she must be on dope. Dope or booze or both. Nanny was shacked up with this little slick-haired weasel—skinny but wound tight. He must be the one making Leon and Nanny so jumpy. Tutu hadn't been there five minutes when those two started badgering her for money—to buy more dope, though of course they didn't admit that. "Boy, tell your granny to give us a loan so we can get you a pair of shoes," the weasel kept begging, and every time he opened his mouth, Leon flinched. "I knew right off that something bad was going on. The way he was eyeing my grandbaby—it was just the way that nasty little Richard boy used to look at you, Sammy. Like he was carving you up with his eyes." Now Sam flinched. He didn't want to remember—and when he looked over, he could tell Leon didn't want to remember either. "So I took Leon away and brought him up here. I thought Nanny and that man would come looking—you know, shake me down for drug money—that's all they cared about. But there was nothing. Not a peep out of them."

"Why didn't you say anything?" Sam jumped in. "Leon could have come to live with us. . . ."

"And been the only colored boy in school?" She humphed. "Anyway, your mama and daddy would never have taken in an orphan Negro child. *Don't get involved*: how many times have I heard them say that? They wouldn't even lift a finger when your own uncle got picked up for drunk driving."

Sam knew. "So you just left him here to raise himself?" Leon wouldn't lift his eyes from the floor.

"My brother took him when he could. And after a while he learned to manage by himself, didn't you, Leon?"

"Whatever."

"Don't you sass me, boy."

"Yes, ma'am."

Sam filled his chest with air and let it out.

"Anyway, I don't have to explain myself to you." Tutu's eyes bored holes right through to the back of his skull. "I'm not asking where you're hiding out, you and that curly-head little tramp." Sam reared up but she bulled past him. "And you're not telling anyone anything about Leon. What I did is no concern of yours."

"He's not an orphan," Sam said. He turned, imploring, but Leon wouldn't meet his eyes.

"What?"

"Leon's not an orphan if his mother is still alive."

"He'd be *dead* if I hadn't saved him." She was hollering. "That's the God's honest truth and I don't want to hear another word about it—not from you or anybody else."

LEON AND SAM RODE THE elevator down in silence. Why had he said anything about Leon's mother? He'd been trying to help, but he just ended up making everything worse. As usual.

They hadn't even reached the corner when a little pack of teenage boys closed around them. "Hey, Leon, who's your new friend, Bozo the Clown?" "Hymie the Clown looks more like it." "Welcome to Harlem, Hymie." *"Boo!"* Sam felt the sweat trickle down his pits, but Leon didn't break stride. "Watch your mouths," he spat out in a voice Sam hadn't heard him use before. "Watch your ass," one of the kids shot back—but the pack dispersed at the corner of 145th. The streets were in shadow and the air was chilling. Winter night closing in. Leon, walking fast, had put a couple of feet between himself and Sam. They could have been two strangers on parallel paths. But whenever someone veered too close or stared too hard, Sam saw the muscles in Leon's neck tighten. Out on the street, away from his grandmother, he was a different person. Wired. Wiry. Poke him and he'd pounce.

"Hey, sorry about your—" Sam began as they paused at the top of the subway steps.

"Forget it," Leon cut him off. "One day I'm going back. See if I can help her."

"If there's anything we—I can do . . ."

But Leon shook his head. "You gonna be okay down there?" gesturing at the dark mouth of the subway. "She'd kill me if anything happened to you."

Sam held out his hand and their palms slotted together. "Thanks," he answered, trying to penetrate the mask that had tightened over Leon's face. "I'll be fine."

But he wasn't. At the bottom of the subway steps, a blade flashed out of the shadows and a voice sliced his ear, "Your pockets, muthafucka." In the time it took for the word "mugged" to scroll across Sam's brain, two pairs of hands had completely worked him over. Pockets picked, watch (a bar mitzvah present!) yanked off his wrist, gold chain with the Star of David snapped from his neck. Sam felt nothing, but when his fingers came away from his mouth, there was blood on them. The blade had nicked his lip. *They could have killed me*, Sam thought, but when he tried to turn thought to speech—to scream—his mouth only bubbled as if he were underwater. *Dead in the water.* No, alive on land but broke, with no ID, no subway token, not even a dime to make a phone call. When he finally made his mouth shout, "Stop, thief—those guys mugged me!" no one even turned his way. He thought about finding a cop—but what if they asked his address? What if they insisted on calling his parents?

So Sam stood at the bottom of the subway steps panhandling for change until the man in the token booth chased him off—"You can't do that here, fool!"—and then he slunk deeper into the shadows and tried again. If someone just gave him three dimes, he'd have enough for a token. "Spare change. Please. Spare change. Anyone?" A couple of kids danced around him laughing. "You should be giving *us* change." "Why did you come up here anyway?" "This here is one lost, crazy muthafucka." Most people didn't even look at him. Sam's brain kept grinding out the refrain from "Like a Rolling Stone": *How does it feel? How does it feel? How does it feel?* He was paralyzed. It was pitch-black on the streets now. If he went back up there, he'd be mugged again in a heartbeat—only this time, now that they took from him everything they could steal, they'd probably just kill him.

They?

Finally, an old lady in a shabby brown coat stopped and fumbled in her bag and pulled out a rumpled dollar bill. "God bless you, ma'am," Sam heard himself say.

God?

"You run along home, child."

Home?

How does it feel, how does it feel?
To be without a home
Like a complete unknown, like a rolling stone?

The song looped through his head the whole way back downtown.

Chapter Fourteen

Mirrors lied. Richard had examined himself in enough of them to know their quirks, distortions, and biases. The cracked veiny tarnished glass in his slum of a bathroom was the worst—a fork-tongued skanky little bitch that made every pore look like a crater, every zit like a mountain range, a bloodshot eye like a nuclear blast site. It was noon on Monday—or was it Tuesday?—and Richard was standing naked in the bathroom surveying the casualties from the night before. There were so many hickeys on his neck it looked like he'd been lassoed. The black bristles on his chin were too sparse to raise a respectable beard but too scruffy to be sexy. The whites of his eyes were as muddy as the Mississippi delta. Was that a crow's-foot at the corner of his eye? For Christ sake, he was only twenty-one. "Live fast and die young" Richard's dope dealer was always saying. But what counted in Richard's ledger was not life but looks. Beauty! He pretended he didn't hear the murmurs that rippled in his wake when he waded into the crowd at Max's Kansas City, the downtown hang that was the current epitome of cool. But no one was fooled. Being noticed was practically the *only* thing that mattered to Richard. And to be noticed at Max's you needed two assets: beauty and drugs. To hang with Andy's people you had to have both. Beauty without drugs got you an appraising stare and a bunch of invitations, but unless you coughed up the coke, sooner or later there'd be a collective shrug of bony cold little shoulders. Drugs without beauty got you a slap on the back, a wolfish welcome, a hasty brush-off when the photographers started snapping, and a killer bar tab. But if you had both, you were golden. Andy made sure there was a seat for you in the back room. Keith called you bloke. Lou promised to put you in a song. Patti read her poems to you. Robert asked to photograph you naked. And *everybody* wanted to take you home. Which was fortunate for Richard, since, given where he presently lived, he was not about to take any of *them* home. Still glued to the hideous mirror, Richard slid his eyes down the raw pink skid marks that Cherie—or was it Candy?—had scratched on the marble contours of his chest last night. Stoned out of her fucking mind, but not on weed. Nobody was doing weed in the circle that Richard had fucked his way into. Now it was all about coke, speed, angel dust, amyl nitrate, and heroin. Richard had only been making the scene at Max's for a couple of months—he'd climbed high and fast since reconnecting with Sam at that ridiculous New Year's Eve party—but it was long enough that he was expected to shoulder his share of the high-priced shit. Was it obvious that he was using? He pulled down the lower lids, scanned the stubble around the pouty angel lips, blinked the long tangled lashes. Nothing that a long hot shower and a shot of vodka couldn't flush away. The real pit was not his pores but his pockets. Dough. Cash. Moolah. Dinero. Hamiltons, Grants, and most of all Franklins. If he wanted to keep fucking wannabe stars and sitting at Andy's table and getting his face in *Interview* magazine and maybe, just maybe, publishing his own Polaroids there one day, Richard needed a pot of gold and he needed it fast. All the good things in life would keep on keeping on if he only had a couple of thousand bucks.

The little part-time day job at Daddy's record company was useful for connections, party invitations, and names to drop. But Pops, the big-shot record producer, paid a pittance. Asking for another loan would be humiliating. Embezzling was too complicated. Raiding petty cash not worth the risk. "What are you going to do with yourself?" his father was always asking. "You're not a kid anymore, ya know. When I was your age . . ." *Blah, blah, blah.* "I wanna be famous" would have been the truth—but he knew how lame that sounded. You had to be famous for *something.* Richard was a decent photographer and before he got kicked out of college he'd taken pictures for the student newspaper. He once published a photo essay called "3 A.M." consisting of random shots taken around the city at that exact hour—all-night diners, underground clubs, bums slumped on the subway stairs, Times Square hustlers squinting through their cigarette smoke, drag queens flitting through the alleys, cops prowling the avenues. Gritty, grainy, black-and-white. He wanted to do a series of candid portraits of his new famous friends, but Andy had beaten him to it. Fucking Andy—he'd ruined it for everyone else. Andy could shit in a soup can and they called it art. What was left? What hadn't been done to death already? Politics was a joke as far as Richard was concerned. No way he was going to sign up for the Revolution like Kim. The Revolution was *so* last season. Power to the People with Nixon in the White House? Please. Protest was a waste of time. Hippies were history. Ideals were illusion. War would never end. Nothing was going to change for the better. Why knock yourself out? Live for today, that's what Richard was about. Make it at Max's. And by the time Max's was over he'd probably be dead anyway, so why worry about it?

He turned on the shower and stood there with the water pattering down on his palm, waiting for it to get hot. Sometimes it never did. He was in luck this time—only five minutes of groaning, clanking, and spitting until the spray turned steamy. He stepped in and closed his eyes. The screeching of the pipes raised a welt inside his forehead. Like a soul in torment. No, like a child in torment—a child who would never grow up, never feel safe, never love or be loved. He squeezed his lids tighter. The water was like hot bullets on his scalp. He filled his lungs and emptied his mind. Song titles whirlpooled through the gray matter—"Love Is Strange," "Somebody to Love," "All You Need Is Love," "Where Did Our Love Go." An image of Sam rocking out beside him at that New Year's party floated through the purple haze. Little Sammy Stein. Richard always had a soft spot for that kid. So cute, so smart—and yet so clueless. You could make him believe anything. He even believed in Richard. *Underneath everything, there's not a phony bone in his body,* he'd overheard Sam telling Kim one night. Hah. Not a phony boner in his body, more like. But Sam had discipline—you had to give him that much. Richard could tell that despite everything, he was still keeping up with his homework, high school newspaper, and test prep. Probably end up in the Ivy League. Edit the college newspaper. Score a gig in Hollywood writing screenplays. God, wouldn't *that* be a joke—Sammy Stein hobnobbing with starlets while Richard died broke in the gutter. No way. Sam was too vulnerable to make it big—at heart he was a cream puff, as soft as a snail without its shell. One poke and he'd shrivel. Kim on the other hand was tough as nails. All that Black Panther shit—even if the brothers and sisters blew her off as a spoiled little honky bitch, Kim would land on her feet, find another cause to join—and dominate. Power was Kim's drug of choice. Sam had no idea what he had gotten himself into. They looked good together, Sam and Kim, but what a weird couple. Richard pictured them having sex. Sam on top. Kim on top. Sam's dick in her mouth. Kim's tits in Sam's face—and he was hard in a second. He soaped up and started singing the first song that popped into his head. "*I said, shotgun! Shoot 'em 'fore they run now. Do the jerk, baby, do the dirty now. Hey.*" He aimed it like a pistol—*bam, bam, bam* at the dirty tiles. *Do the jerk, baby.* Kim naked in a black beret, fist in the air, rifle strapped across her boobs, boot heel on Sam's throat. Black Panther my ass.

Whoa. Whoa, whoa, whoa, whoa, whoa. *I said shotgun!* Wasn't Eli always going on about this crate of machine guns that had mysteriously fallen into his lap? Brand-new Uzis smuggled out of Israel by some crazy uncle or cousin or something. Half of what came out of Eli's mouth was bullshit and the rest incomprehensible—but Richard had distinctly heard him say that the "right buyer" would pay a fortune for those guns. What if it *wasn't* bullshit?

Richard shut off the water, shook his head clear, and grabbed a towel. Panthers. Contraband weapons. Radical Kim and gullible Sam. He couldn't see how the pieces fit together—but he'd figure it out. The whole thing reeked of money. Everybody was going to come out a winner—well, maybe not everybody, but certainly Numero Uno. Andy and company would shit a brick.

"Deal making, Dad," Richard told his reflection. "I think I just found my métier."

. . .

"**YOU HONESTLY EXPECT ME** to believe this?" Kim said when Richard and Eli finally finished the story. "I mean, it sounded like total bullshit the first time Eli bragged about the—"

"Not brag—one hundred percent true bullshit," Eli interrupted.

"Whatever." Kim was sitting barefoot on the floor with her hands clasped around her knees. A shaft of afternoon sunlight ricocheted off a window in the tenement opposite and landed on her head, setting her curls ablaze. "So. Let me see if I got this straight. When you were in the Israeli army, you had a buddy who drove an armored truck delivering guns and ammo to outposts on the West Bank."

"Ordnance," Richard put in.

"Delivering *ordnance* to the West Bank—so Israeli soldiers would have weapons to mow down innocent Palestinian women and children—"

"Innocent?" Eli shouted. "Who said *innocent*?"

"Cool it with the politics, you two. You wanna help the Panthers or not, Kim?"

"Yeah," Kim said, "but first I gotta understand what's going down here. Okay—this truck driver buddy is out on a delivery, only when he's done making the rounds he discovers there's one crate of Uzis left over. Someone screwed up and loaded a crate that wasn't on the inventory. . . ."

"Yes."

"So the buddy makes a little detour and off-loads the guns with his uncle—"

"Cousin."

"Cousin. Who happens to be your uncle by marriage?" Eli was

bobbing his head, so Kim kept going. "But then things turn weird. Right after making the drop, your truck driver friend gets killed by a suicide bomber, so now the guns belong to . . ."

"Uncle . . . but *secret*, you know? Only family must to know. Anyone else finding out and"—Eli drew a finger across his throat—"drapes!"

"You mean *curtains*?"

"I said!"

Kim slapped her forehead. "Right. So the guns are hidden in your uncle's garage—but something spooks him—now he wants to get rid of them in a hurry." She had to go through it step by step. "Only you can't exactly toss a crate of Uzis in the trash."

"Like throwing money down the train."

"Jesus, Eli, who taught you English—Jerry Lewis?" Kim rolled her eyes. "Let's just finish this, okay? So when the uncle finds out you're coming to New York, he has this brilliant idea to ship the Uzis to America and make *you* deal with them. He bribes a dockworker to stash the crate in with a shipment of birth control pills bound for *another* uncle in New Jersey who happens to run a drugstore chain. More money changes hands, the guns slip through, and now they're sitting in a warehouse in . . ."

"Neck Tie."

"Teaneck?" Eli nodded. "And you're supposed to sell them?" Nod. "But only to the right buyer?" Nod. "So nobody will be able to trace them back to you or your family?" Nod. "And then you'll go back to Israel with a wad of cash?"

"But first a wad of party with Reekie."

"Okay. Got it." Kim let it all sink in. "So why don't you just sell them to the mob?"

"Because the mob is evil," Richard broke in. "We've got principles, don't we, Eli?"

"Right off!"

"These are A-one top-of-the-line spanking new Israeli Uzis, for god's sake!" Richard sounded like a used car salesman. "We don't want them falling into the wrong hands."

"And you think the Black Panthers are the *right* hands?"

"You made a convert, Kim. The Panthers *need* those guns to protect themselves from the pigs. And I gotta say, Angela Davis is one smokin' hot sistah."

"Why not just donate them? You know, contribution to a good cause?"

"Free?" Eli erupted. "Nothing is free."

"Well, the Panthers are broke—no way they're gonna cough up that kind of money. . . ."

"Oh, but you're wrong, Kim. Dead wrong." Richard's eyes were dancing. "Didn't you hear about the fund-raiser that Leonard Bernstein threw for the Panthers last month?"

"Famous conductor? *West Side Story*? Saturday morning children's concerts? *That* Leonard Bernstein?"

"Everybody at Max's is talking about it. Seems like Lenny and his society wife gave a cocktail party to drum up support for the New York Panthers. I know, crazy, right? All these uptown liberal whities writing fat checks to a bunch of ghetto thugs—"

"Hey, I thought you were a convert?"

"Sorry. *Black revolutionaries*. Anyway, they raised a shitload of cash. The Panthers are flush, baby. I hear they're moving to Park Avenue."

"Very funny, Richard."

"Just think about it for a sec. Everybody wins. The Panthers get their fancy new guns. You get the credit: Kim Goodman, arms broker to the Revolution! Eli gets enough money to party hardy and then fly back to Israel."

"And what do you get?"

Richard split his most irresistible little boy grin between them. "Half?"

Chapter Fifteen

Kim was so cold that her eyes teared and her teeth ached, but she didn't care. She and Sam were alone on the upper deck of the Staten Island Ferry on the crossing back to Manhattan—the only passengers insane enough to venture out into the February blast. But how could they sit out the greatest show on earth? The sun shivered in a sky of pure, dazzling blue. The water, dense and oily, parted like flesh before the blade of the prow. Across the harbor, Liberty saluted their wake. And before them, on the rip-tooth edge of the island, numberless towers fortified the citadel of commerce, their chained glass winking coded messages at the city—the world—the cosmos. One of those banks of windows was her target. The lords of death and wealth still held the keys, but their days were numbered. Their kingdom was tottering. And when it fell, all of this would be hers—theirs—everyone's. The People's Park. Liberation Avenue. The World Peace Center. It wasn't crazy—it was happening. The machinery was in place—or almost. The fuses were wired. The timers ticking. It was a matter of when, not if. It couldn't not work.

Kim felt Sam's frail body trembling beside her. She pressed behind him to break the wind. The only warm thing in the world was the strip of neck between his beanie and collar. She hid her face in the skin and breathed in the sweet boy scent.

Was he one of them?

It was impossible to talk over the wind, so she took Sam's gloved hand and led him back inside the cabin. A cloud of diesel, sweat, perfume, and tobacco enveloped them as soon as they pushed through the swinging door. The windows were fogged but no one was looking outside anyway: napping, riffling newspapers, smoking, muttering, bickering, staring vacantly at the dirty floor, spooning food into babies, the other passengers were utterly oblivious to the miracle of New York Harbor.

"The people," Sam said softly. She raised a quizzical brow. "Everyone on this boat—they're the people, right? Power to *these* people? You seriously think they're gonna rise up and join the Revolution?"

God, he sounded like her father. "I don't know, Sam. I think if they turned on the evening news and saw one of these buildings fall—they'd wake up."

"Yeah, and start screaming about law and order."

"No. If we *acted* instead of just talking about it, we'd get through to them. They're asleep because they think everything's hopeless. But it's not." She lowered her voice. "Before the Panthers, black people were so desperate they were burning down the ghettos. Now the Panthers have given them the power to fight the power and they know it. All it takes is one man—one woman—with a gun to stand up to the pigs."

"They're not pigs, Kim. They're cops. Soldiers. FBI. They've got napalm and nukes, for Christ sake! You really think you're gonna bring it all down with a box of submachine guns and a couple sticks of dynamite?"

"So what's your plan?" She wasn't being sarcastic—she wanted to know. She *had* to know. The day before, at her brownstone, Lee had confronted Kim: *Do you have a boyfriend? Yeah, well, unless he's with us you better ditch him. The stakes are too high now. It's all or nothing—there's no middle ground anymore.*

"I don't have a plan," Sam said, sulking. "I'm a student—not a politician."

"Total cop-out, Sam. If you're not part of the solution . . ."

"Okay. Here's my plan. Make it hot for them—but don't break the law. Gandhi—Dr. King—look how much they accomplished *within* the system. If we just keep marching—"

"That's not a plan—that's the status quo. And what have we accomplished? Nixon's still bombing the shit out of North Vietnam, Cambodia, and who knows where else. FBI pigs are infiltrating every radical organization. The government is trampling on our rights and lying about it. The exact same thing happened in Nazi Germany. We have to do something before it's too late. . . ."

"Yeah, but if we take the law into our own hands, where does it stop?"

"The American Revolution wasn't legal. Those patriots weren't working within the system. Militias, Sam—that's how we kicked out the colonial overlords. The Panthers are a militia too—a self-defense force—only they're black and they have Afros instead of powdered wigs so everybody treats them like a ghetto gang."

"So George Washington was like, 'Up against the wall, you redcoat muthafuckas.'"

When was the last time Sam cracked a joke? Something had died inside him since he'd gotten mugged in Harlem. The voice was deeper—the eyes dimmer. He used to be so funny—so trusting! Now he was wary. He'd bled. He shrank from the darkness but he didn't hide. *Was he one of them?*

"What if you got drafted? Would you serve—or go to jail?"

"Is there a difference? Honestly? I don't know, Kim. Maybe I'd hole up with your friend Lee."

"Go underground—for real?"

"Yeah, but not to make bombs and blow stuff up. What I wanna do is write about it."

"Scribe to the Revolution."

"Sorta . . . kinda . . . yeah. It's the only thing I'm good at."

"So *we're* gonna fight—and *you're* gonna write?" Guilt stabbed her as soon as she saw the hurt in his eyes. It sounded like something her mother would say. She was supposed to prop Sam up, not put him down. Bolster him. Believe in him. And she did. Sam was brilliant! He never had to try, he was so quick, he never forgot anything. Teacher's pet. Teacher's pet with a hard-on. Sam didn't even realize he was sexy, which was the sexiest thing of all. Kim loved how his shoulder blades jutted from his back like wings. She loved the veins that roped down his pelvis and converged at his crotch. She loved how his eyes trailed her across a room—always on her whenever she looked his way. It was so sweet how he never paid attention to what he ate or wore. If it was up to Sam, they'd live on Twinkies, donuts, and ginger ale. But it wasn't up to Sam. That's what was starting to piss her off. At first Kim and the boys had divvied up the chores—like a kibbutz—but after a while it was her giving the orders and them, sullenly, sloppily, doing what she told them. Like a mother. Like a wife. She took care of the food because she couldn't stand the junk they ate—that's what she told herself—but the real reason she shopped and cooked for them was because they *expected* it—all of them. She was the girl and that's what girls did. At least Sam never called her a chick like those assholes in beards and granny glasses. Pussy power! If she was a chick, they were dogs—dumb domesticated animals every last one. Kim had to free herself of that shit—but she knew the boys never would, not even Sam. For all his poetry and romantic soul, he didn't get it. He was as insanely jealous as her father. Sam would die if he found out she'd done it with Jeff—just once, *to get it out of the way*, as they told each other. She hated that she had to hide. She hated that Sam said he loved her. Love! When she knew perfectly well it was just boyish gratitude for sex. He was terrified of being mediocre—they all were—but why did she have to be the one to prove to him he wasn't? Why did he have to own her, control her? Why did she let him? He said he wanted to protect her—all 130 pounds of him. But she didn't want protection—she wanted danger. She wanted to be dangerous. She wanted to stride into Panthers headquarters with that crate of Uzis, pry off the lid, and brandish a gun in the air like a trophy. *Up the Revolution!* Power—not love—was what counted. She would never forgive Sam for seeing her cower and whimper while her father beat the hell out of her mother. No one was going to make her cower and whimper ever again. Not her father. Not Sam. Not Lee. She'd do what she had to, but in the end she, KBG, was going to be bulletproof.

KBG—Kimberly Beth Goodman: her initials but also, as of yesterday, her nom de guerre. And the guerre was here! It was war. How many cells were forming, replicating, dividing, and spreading in the basements and attics of those buildings across the water? Start small. Turn the pigs' weapons against them. One bombing at a time. Issue advance warnings so there would be no innocent victims—they all agreed on that. Blow up a weapons plant in the dead of night. Take out a police station. Torch a draft board. Then do it again in another city. New York. Oakland. Detroit. D.C. Seattle. Seemingly random but coordinated strikes. That's all it would take. Students all over the country would rise up. From colleges to high schools, from ghettos to factory floors—like wildfire. One spark—ten sparks—a thousand sparks, and the whole bullshit system would go up in flames.

Yeah, it was war—but Kim was starting to wonder about the generals. Lee told her if she wanted to be with them she had to give up everything—possessions, family, friends, identity. Fine. No problem. She loved being KBG. She loved Lee. But she wasn't so sure she loved the other comrades. All those goopy self-criticism sessions they insisted on: sitting around for hours in a dark room confessing to their secret bourgeois tendencies, egotism, racism, classism, sexism. Couldn't they see they were just jockeying for power? And all the bullshit secrecy about what was going on in the basement. Kim was in high school—but they were the ones acting like children. Playing with fuses and cotton balls and nails. Nails? Why nails if there weren't supposed to be any victims? No carnage: for Kim, that was nonnegotiable. They were amateurs. They needed the Panthers to show them how to do it. The BPP had it *down*. Self-defense. Grass roots. Community first. Local chapters—national newspaper. Armed foot soldiers. Power to *all* the people. Black and white together: that was the only way they were going to prevail. And KBG was the one who would make it happen.

It all came down to those Uzis. Once she pulled off the delivery, *she'd* be calling the shots. This was their time. Her time.

. . .

KIM WAS SO LOST IN her own thoughts that she didn't even realize the ferry was in the terminal. She hadn't heard a word Sam said in the last five minutes. She was about to apologize but she stopped herself. Apologize for what? Mechanically, silently, they stood and joined the stampede for the exit. The crowd carried them down the ramp and across Battery Park. It wasn't dark yet but lights were coming on in the skyscrapers that ringed the park. From the street, every window looked the same—but behind each square of yellow there was a different person thinking different thoughts and hatching different dreams. The vastness of it was inspiring—soul-crushing—a symphony—a dirge. Kim cast her eyes at Sam. Gaunt. Expressionless. If she told him what she was thinking, he wouldn't know what she was talking about. No one would.

She had the answer to her question: *No, Sam wasn't one of them—but he wasn't the enemy*. He was harmless. And besides, he didn't know anything worth knowing.

A line of cops was fanned out across the entrance to the subway tunnel. Black vests—visored helmets: riot police. Another line blocked off the far side of the park. Was something going down—something she should know about? Before they got too close, Kim grabbed Sam's arm and whispered in his ear, "You go—I have to see someone. I'll meet you back at Richard's in an hour." She let him go and the crowd swallowed her. It would take half an hour to walk to Lee's brownstone—she knew the way. Kim had made up her mind. She was going to tell Lee that she'd gotten rid of the boyfriend. Lie—but where was the harm? Leave Sam out of it. None of his business. None of theirs.

. . .

THAT FRIDAY, WHEN SAM LEFT school, the family car was idling in the student parking lot again—his father this time. *What the hell did* he *want?* Only one way to find out. Sam slid into the passenger seat, just as he had done two weeks before when his mother showed up. His father held out his right hand and left it hanging there until Sam took it. The son tried for the bone-crushing grasp that the father insisted was the way real men shook hands—but Adam Stein's grip was harder.

"Peace?" his father asked, refusing to surrender Sam's palm.

"There was never any war," Sam replied.

"Right. Okay." Adam disengaged and started the car. "So—coming skiing with us?"

It was midwinter break—the week his family always went skiing in Vermont. The five of them when Sam's older brothers were still home; the three of them after Ron and Tom went off to college. "I wasn't planning on it," Sam said.

Adam pulled the car out of the lot. *Political prisoner*, Sam was thinking. They drove without looking at each other. Three silent minutes—then the tirade Sam knew was coming. No—it was the tirade without the tirade voice. His father sounded tired, defeated. Had Sam won? "I've been impressed with you, Sam. I have to say, I didn't think you had it in you. On your own for three whole weeks. Shacked up with a girl and god knows what else. Don't think I missed those twenties you filched"—he turned to wink—"but I didn't think you had *that* in you either." Driving. Running his right hand through his short graying hair. "We got the message, son. Now it's time to come home. A week of skiing—then everything back to normal. We won't even talk about it."

"Do I have a choice?"

Adam thumped both hands on the steering wheel. "You tell me, Sam. I'll pull over right here and let you out. Say the word. You're a grown-up now, right? On your own. Big guy—"

"Dad!"

"Hear me out. You can leave—go back underground, whatever. But there are consequences. Family, Sam. You just get one and it's the only thing that counts. Blood is thicker than water. One day you'll understand that—and I hope when you do, it isn't too late."

"More threats," Sam muttered.

"What?"

"What did you tell me to do when someone threatens me? Cave? Compromise?"

"There are rules, Sam. Expectations. You *owe* it to us. Me and your mother both. Our job is to protect—your job is to respect. You keep your side of the bargain, we'll keep ours."

Sam shut his eyes. He loved those ski trips. No one ever fought. He and his brothers could stay up as late as they wanted. They shredded the mountain all day, no rules, no limits. It was the best thing about his family. It would be so easy. Someone to take care of him again. A week off from all of this . . .

He opened his eyes but wouldn't look at his father. "You don't make the rules. No one does. Everyone makes their own rules. Otherwise, what are we?"

"When I was *your* age, Sam—"

"Please, spare me, Dad—I've heard it all a million times."

Two traffic lights, a left turn, a right at the fork, and they'd be home. Adam drove it in silence and pulled up in front of the garage. They sat there side by side. "Your mother thinks I'm being too harsh," his father said finally. "Maybe she's right." Sam stared straight ahead. "You know." He heard his father breathe. "We'll always be here for you. No matter what."

"That's why you kicked me out?"

"I *yelled*—" He was on the verge of yelling again. "But you kicked yourself out. And now you're back." Sam felt his gut knot up. Nothing had changed. "We're not going to force you. No juvenile court. Your choice, son." His father's palm circled his forearm, squeezing. "We'll hit the road first thing tomorrow morning."

As soon as the kitchen door closed behind Adam Stein, Sam got out of the car, strapped on his backpack, and walked to the train station.

Chapter Sixteen

Leon was buttoning his coat and reaching for the key when he realized he'd forgotten to pray. *Kneel down or it won't count*, Granny's voice rasped at him inside his head—but she'd left the apartment an hour earlier and he was running late already. So he bowed his head in the dark little vestibule, shut his eyes, clasped his hands, and mumbled the first words that came to mind—"Heavenly Father, stand by me . . ."—and then as usual tumbled from speech to song. "In the midst of faults and failures, stand by me. When I do the best I can, and my friends don't understand, Thou who knowest all about me, stand by me." Leon's full-throated tenor echoed off the walls. He opened his eyes, smiling. "I hope you're listening, Lord," he whispered. "Thank you, Lord. Amen." Then he dashed out the door and flew down the stairs. No time to wait for the elevator. It was eight o'clock on a Monday morning. He had four hours to get downtown, find the address on the crumpled little card, meet with Mr. Cohen, and get back uptown to make the afternoon shift at the A&P.

But if God answered his prayer, maybe he wouldn't be bagging groceries anymore. *Thou who knowest all about me, stand by me!*

Leon grabbed a copy of the *Daily News* at the kiosk outside the subway steps. UNDERCOVER COP DROPS BOMB AT PANTHER 21 TRIAL blared the front-page headline. He scanned the box of type beneath the courtroom photo—*self-proclaimed black revolutionaries . . . coordinated bomb attacks on local targets . . . "armed and ready to shoot," according to Police Sergeant Dan Toro*—and turned the paper over to the sports page: KNICKS BLAST BULLETS 115 TO 105. Yes. A month to the play-offs and the Knicks were looking mighty fine. He read until the train came and then stuffed the paper in his coat pocket.

At Columbus Circle, Leon got off the train, fished the business card out of his back pocket, and checked it for the fiftieth time. "Channel Records, 117 West 56th Street. Myron Cohen, vice president and producer. Circle 8-5446." Miss Genevieve, the choir director, had slipped him the card on Sunday after worship. Mr. Cohen was the one who gave Doris Pinkard her big break as a backup—and Doris, who'd sung in the church choir for years, was happy to pass his card along. "Maybe he'll help you too, honey." She beamed. Miss Genevieve loved his granny. Everyone at church did.

Leon surfaced, got his bearings, and started walking. It seemed like a great plan when he woke up that morning—show up at Channel Records, blow Mr. Cohen away with his singing, and leave the rest in God's hands—but now that he was a block away he wasn't so sure. Should he have called for an appointment? What if they laughed in his face? Miss Genevieve told him Mr. Cohen was Jewish—"like all the big producers"—but was that good or bad? "Poor Sammy, born a Jew," Granny was always saying. "If only he'd come to Jesus." But Jesus himself was born a Jew. It didn't make sense. Anyway, Sam had gone to church with them twice now, so maybe he *was* coming to Jesus. Leon shook his head clear as he strode toward Seventh Avenue. Focus. His voice. His song. That's what counted.

The building was old, brick, and dirty with painted-over windows and sagging, rusted fire escapes. *Not much better than Harlem*, Leon was thinking. The elevator at the back of the lobby was a dark shaft screened by a tarnished metal cage. Leon pressed and waited. He heard it and then he saw it: the car hurtled down, slowed, came to rest half a foot below the lobby floor, and then lurched inch by inch up to the level. "Lobby," a deep voice boomed as the cage rattled open. No one got off. Leon, the sole passenger, stepped on. An ancient white-haired black man levered the cage shut without looking at him. "Where to?" "Channel Records, please." The car rose, creaking and swaying up the shaft. They ascended in silence. The cage doors parted on the eighth floor, Leon got out, the bars rattled shut behind him, and he was alone again.

A frosted glass door displayed the name CHANNEL in gilt-edged black letters but there was no buzzer. Should he just walk in? He stood there trying to collect himself. *Heavenly Father . . .* A door slammed down the hall. Heels clicked toward him. He tapped on the glass—no response—and pushed the door open.

The reception area was hot and grubby and so brightly lit it made him squint. In the center of the room stood a big wooden desk with two stumpy couches huddled on one side and an empty aquarium pushed against the opposite wall. Behind the desk were three more doors, all closed. Leon cleared his throat but the receptionist—a white girl in a tight red sweater, brown bouffant hair, and way too much eye makeup—was talking on the phone and wouldn't look at him. He flicked his eyes to the sofas. Should he sit and wait? He flicked to the three closed doors. "Myron Cohen" was painted in black letters on the middle one. That was good. "Hold on a sec," the receptionist said. She hit a button, put the phone down, and reached under the desk. "There should be ten—but you better count," she said, proffering a stack of tan padded envelopes.

"Ten?" Leon stammered.

"You're here for the packages? The messenger boy?" Finally she looked at him. The bundle of envelopes hung in the air for a second and then disappeared back under the desk. "What, then?"

Leon put the card on her desk and turned it so she could read it. "I'm here to see Mr. Cohen. Mr. Myron Cohen?" He cut his eyes to the door and back to hers. "The record producer? Mr. Cohen was a help to Doris Pinkard—from my church?—and I was . . ."

"Mr. Cohen happens to be tied up at the moment," she said, reaching for the phone. "But if you leave your demo tape . . ." She waited, her eyes narrowing inside the rings of black. "No demo?" Leon shook his head. "Well"—one crimson nail nudged Cohen's card back across the desk—"when you make one, mail it. He'll get back—he always does." Then she simultaneously hit the button on the phone and twitched her head toward the entrance. "Sorry—nothing," Leon heard her say into the phone. He felt her eyes on the back of his neck until the door swung shut behind him.

It was all over before it started.

Leon stood in the hall, sweating into the coat he hadn't even unbuttoned. His vision was hazed as if somebody had just punched his head. It wasn't supposed to go this way. Messenger boy! *Nobody owes you anything in this world,* he heard Granny's voice humbling him. *Nobody but yourself.*

Leon started to hum over the anger and he kept humming with his teeth clenched as he rode the elevator back to the lobby. The hymn filled his head but he only allowed one thread of it to escape his sealed lips. *Precious Lord, take my hand, lead me on, let me stand, I'm tired, I'm weak, I'm lone.* He must have been humming louder than he intended because by the time they reached the lobby another voice was humming along softly with him.

"Church-raised—not many like that these days," the operator said as he bounced the cage to a stop. Leon turned to look at the man. Black rheumy eyes—papery brown skin like a supermarket bag—even older than Granny. "Don't tell me," the man went on. "You went up to sing for Mr. Cohen but the girl wouldn't let you in." Leon stared. "You're not the first and you won't be the last. Step back on, son. I know somebody who might help." When they got back to the eighth floor, the man parked the elevator, stepped out in the hall, and beckoned to Leon. "Walk around that corner there till you see 802. Mr. Cohen rents that little closet for his father. Everybody calls him the Rabbi. Tell him Mr. George sent you. First he'll talk your ear off—but then he'll listen. Go on, boy, sing him your song."

There was a number on the door but no sign, no name. Leon stood paralyzed until he heard the muffled voice on the other side: "Come. Open. It's not locked." He obeyed. Mr. George hadn't exaggerated—it was a closet, just large enough for a desk, chair, and a shelf crammed with toppling piles of books, tape cassettes, and records. The man sitting at the desk held a black book open in his knotted hands. Leon knew it was the Bible. "Close," the man said, and Leon shut the door behind him. There was a single window but it faced an air shaft. The sun had never graced this space. There was just enough light from the desk lamp to spark gleams in the old man's eyes—two slits curtained by curling gray brows. "So nu? You want to say or I should guess?" Foreign but familiar—he sounded like half the shopkeepers in Harlem. The man wore a black suit and a white shirt buttoned at the throat with no tie. A white disc like a Frisbee rode the top of his dense springy hair, the same gray as the eyebrows and beard. The eyes were so small, the lids so narrow, the brows so dense, Leon was convinced the man was blind. He opened his mouth to speak but nothing came out. "Okay, I'll guess. Everyone in church thinks you sing like angel. Someone tells you my son will give big break but he wouldn't see you. George in elevator took pity and says you should talk to me. Yes?"

Leon nodded. "More or less."

"Come closer." Leon took two steps forward. He could see the man's eyes now—ignited coals of fire and ash. "Do you believe in God?"

"Yes, sir."

"Call me Rabbi—everyone does, even though I'm no rabbi. No matter—God doesn't care. If you believe, you must pray. Let me hear you pray."

"I pray by singing."

"Me too. So sing."

Leon shut his eyes, slowed his breathing, opened his mouth, and let the spirit move through him, just like in church. "Wade in the water. . . ." He started low. He didn't think. He didn't strain. He let the music out. "Wade in the water. Children, wade in the water." The voice climbed. The air trembled with light. "Wade in the water. God's gonna trouble the water." He opened his eyes and everything went dark again. Neither spoke—but there was no need. A chord—an accord—vibrated and faded between them.

For the love of God. "Mr. Rabbi?" Another beat of silence. "Could you sing what you pray?"

The rabbi put the Bible down gently on the desk. He held his hands before his eyes. His lips trembled and then a single pure note like the upper register of a clarinet, but sweeter and sadder, filled the room. "Shema Yisrael." He took in air and the voice soared. "Adonai Eloheynu." Nasal, almost whining, the note spiraled and spread as smooth as water. Leon, suspended over the precipice, held his breath. "Adonai echad."

As soon as he finished, Leon sang the prayer back to him, blurring the strange words but perfectly hitting the notes, the sobbing cry, the ancient liquid warbling. He stopped and smiled at the old man. "I like that twangy wail. That sounds kinda cool."

"For Jews, our most important prayer," the old man said. "Top of the charts. You heard before?" Leon shook his head. "First time and you pick up—just like that?" Leon nodded. The old man nodded back. "Okay—take chair." There was a gray metal folding chair propped against the bookshelf. "Sit. Listen."

ALL THE WAY BACK UPTOWN, Leon replayed the conversation—monologue really—in his brain. He wished he could have recorded it. The Rabbi said so much—but most of it he could barely understand. *You have a gift*: he remembered that much perfectly. *A gift given by God that would be a sin to waste.* But then it seemed like he tried to talk him out of using it. Why not just sing in church? Sing for your granny. Sing for your girlfriend. No girlfriend? A nice-looking boy like you? Why do you want to get mixed up in the music business anyway? It was filthy. Mean. Nothing but heartbreak. Half the singers are on dope, did you know that? This business is not about talent—it's about money. Connections. Stabbing your way to the top. Or screwing, if you're a girl. Is that the life you want, a nice churchgoing boy like you? No? Then what? Leon laid it out for him: Song was the only thing that made him feel alive. The rest of life was just killing time for money—dirty money and not much of it. Bagging groceries. Driving a cab. Shining shoes. Work all your lifetime and you still don't have a dime. That wasn't God's plan—that was the Man's plan. If God didn't want him to use His gift, He wouldn't have given it. Okay, so let's ask God, the Rabbi said. He'll tell us. They bowed their heads. Leon slid off the folding chair and knelt beside it. *Heavenly Father*, he said. *Baruch Shem*, the Rabbi said. *In thee, Lord, I put my trust*, he sang. *Ya'air Adonai panav*, the Rabbi sang. *The Lord make his face to shine upon you*, he sang. *The Lord bless you and keep you. The Lord lift up the light of his countenance upon you. And give you peace. And give you peace.* By the time they were done, they were harmonizing. Leon didn't even know how he knew the words and music. He rose from his knees and sat again. *You see? You hear?* the Rabbi said. He stretched his hands across the desk and Leon took them—dry small delicate fingers with a fierce grip. *You feel?* Then he let go and rummaged in the desk drawer. A card, another business card skimmed across the wooden surface. *Tell Mo the Rabbi sent you. He'll give you a break—not free but not much. Bring me the tape. If it's good*—it will be good!—*I'll play it for my son.* How much? *A hundred fifty. Two hundred max. God bless you.* And you.

A million songs whirred through his head as the train rocked and shrieked through the tunnel. God would tell him the right one. But where on earth was he going to get two hundred dollars?

Chapter Seventeen

When partying on drugs, timing was everything. If you smoked, snorted, shot, popped, or swallowed too soon, you'd be all fucked up with nowhere to go. If you waited until everyone else was going full blast, you'd never catch up. Too much at once and you'd pass out before the fun started. Too many kinds and you'd barf. The trick was to coordinate liftoff with your entrance, rapture with the music's climax, and the ecstatic second before blackout with orgasm.

Richard's Friday night was off to a promising start. He had smoked a joint with Sam and Eli back in the apartment about an hour before midnight and floated the idea of bringing them along to Max's. Sam begged off because he had to write an English paper ("What, stoned?" "Sure. I get some really high ideas while cool.") and Eli was too engrossed in a *Twilight Zone* rerun ("To make better how I'm spoken English"), so Richard hoofed it over to the club by himself. Fuzzed out and ravenous by the time he arrived, he slipped past the front room's packed booths, dodged into the bathroom to do a quick couple of lines (people were having either sex or heart attacks in the adjoining stalls—impossible to tell which and inadvisable to ask), and bellied up to the bar for a vodka shot or two. The buzz was that David Bowie was going to show up later that night but no one was holding their breath. Richard sucked the last ice cubes, left a twenty on the bar, and sauntered to the back—Andy's domain. He did a quick internal scan before confronting Dorothy, the inner sanctum's crazy dipso lady bouncer. Hands steady, breath sweet, pants tight, dick front and center, coke stash wedged deep in his front pocket, brain. *Brain*? Brain clear spinning warped woofed and welded firmly to his skull. The perfect buzzed state to party with the beautiful people, among whom Richard (quick sideways glance to the mirrored wall) stood out for his pretty-boy cheekbones and quarterback shoulders. Daddy's record label didn't hurt either—but that had only been good for a one-time pass. Richard was on his own now. No problem. He knew the ropes. And he had a little surprise up his sleeve that none of them would be able to resist. Showtime!

Dorothy waved him through, the black door swung open and shut, the front bar roar faded to a distant migrainy hum, and he was in. No Andy tonight. No Lou. No Patti. Maybe they were all at the Chelsea hanging with Bowie? No matter. A black-clad silver-bangled arm rose above the round table, beckoned him over, pulled out a chair. "*Ree*-chard!" Nico kissed his cheeks, Joel pushed a glass in front of him, Jackie winked her (his?) eyes, which looked distinctly rabid in the bloody neon light. Home! It didn't matter that no royalty was in evidence. Even on an off-night, the back room at Max's was better than anyplace else in

New York—in the country—fuck, in the world. What happened at every other club was gossip—here it was *history*. What the women wore became fashion. What the men painted, sang, or wrote determined the avant-garde. What the men and women did together was the real cultural revolution. Fuck Kim and her fucking Black Panthers. Max's was the only radical underground that counted, though the back room *did* eat up whatever Panther crumbs Richard picked up from Kim, Black Power being oh so chic at the moment. And now there was this weapons deal—guaranteed to boost his cool quotient, street cred, and cash stash. Richard Rines—gunrunner to the Revolution, when they'd all written him off as just another pretty face with a hardworking cock.

The regulars were hard at it when Richard joined them—dishing about sex, what else?

"Well, I've been both and had both," Holly drawled, silencing the table. "And I can say that the intensity is a hundred times greater for women. It's like a BB gun compared to a bazooka."

"Bigger bang for the buck?" Larry, a sorta famous AC/DC artist who'd been on the scene before most of them were born, asked.

"Not just bigger, sweetheart. More . . . what am I saying? . . . pervasive? A guy fucks with his dick—a woman fucks with her whole body and soul."

"More orifices, that's for sure."

"So male," Holly sighed. "As if it's all just plumbing. I'm talking about the mind-body continuum."

"So what's better?" Larry was lapping it up. "Up the ass or in the twat?"

"You tell me, darling." That brought down the house—and the next round was on Larry, club rules.

"Anybody know where Andy is tonight?"

"Doing Bowie's makeup, if I had to guess."

"Or just doing Bowie, period."

"As if. Andy never does anyone—he just watches."

"And takes pictures."

"And makes movies—but god, have you ever sat through one?"

"They call it art—but it's more like printing money if you ask me."

"Yeah, well, if it's so easy, why don't you run off a bunch of Franklins so you can quit mooching."

"Mooch? Moi?"

"Oui, cherie, toi."

"The price of fame."

"I hate to break it to you, doll, but the only thing you're famous for is between your legs."

"Did a *single* head turn when you walked past the bar?"

"Of course—I counted six, give or take."

"Well, when it comes to you and heads, it's always more give than take."

Another round of cackles—another round of drinks.

Richard barely touched his glass—he was saving himself for later in the evening. Anyway, it wasn't the same without Andy. It was like they were all playing themselves. Putting on an act. So brittle. So fake. Jackie and Ari, Mick and Bianca, John and Yoko, Andy, Oscar, Liz and Dick were genuinely famous. The rest of them were back-up singers. Rule #1: If you talked about being famous, you weren't. Richard, flatlining, began to wonder why he was here.

"So what have you been doing, Richie?" Candy batted her three-inch eyelashes his way. "Aside from ass and twat." More roaring. "Got a job yet?" Code for drug money.

"As a matter of fact . . ." Every one of them lasered in on his face. This is what Richard loved best. Even if they were mostly just the B-list, he wanted them. Now that he had them, he had to hold them. Spin it out. Make it last. Dangle and dodge. "You know that wad of cash Leonard Bernstein laid on the Panthers?"

"The famous radical chic fund-raiser."

"Throw a bone to the black folks—"

"Before they blow your white ass up!"

"Well," Richard looked around the table conspiratorially, "I've figured out a way to get my hands on it."

"What, you're gonna break into Panthers headquarters and crack the safe?"

"Pull it out from under Bobby Seale's mattress while he's asleep?"

"Turn tricks? Sweetie, that's never gonna work unless you change your sex—"

"And race."

"Hilarious." Richard crossed his forearms on the table and leaned in. He was desperate to do another line of coke but he had to drop his little bomb first. "Have any of you ladies ever heard of an Uzi?"

"You mean like Uzi and Harriet?"

"Scusi?"

"Uzi—who's he?"

"Uzi Americains are so stupeeed."

"I can't eat, I'm feeling kinda Uzi."

"I Uzi love her but it's all over now."

"Yeah, I thought it was pretty funny too." Richard didn't move a muscle; every eye was still on him. "Until a crate of them fell into my lap. Top-of-the-line, brand-new, Israeli automatic weapons." The eyes widened; mental gears spun. "And I know who'll pay top dollar for them. Now, if you'll exc*Uzi* me . . ." He pushed himself off the table and stood.

"Hey, where're you going?—you just got here."

"Business." He winked, making for the door while a surf of voices broke behind him.

He didn't get far. He detoured to the bathroom to snort that line—and when he came out, the mirrored lights of the bar burst in his pupils so he just had to stop for one more drink to bask in the dazzle. His nose was already numb from the coke and after one sip of iced vodka the rest of his head followed suit. Fuckin' A, it felt good to be alive. Richard was admiring himself in the mirror, minding his own business from the top of the world, when a familiar face appeared in the mirror beside his. Nico the Aryan goddess model bombshell actress superstar undisputed A-lister. They winked at each other's reflections. Why wasn't she still in the back with the rest of the crowd?

"Sometimes those people make me want to scream, you know?" The din was so loud she had to put her lips practically inside his ear to make herself heard. Her perfume turned his insides to pudding. "You too?" Richard nodded and Nico's soft smooth lips glided up and down his ear. "And what's all this about Uzis? Are you running guns for the Black Panthers?" It came out Bleck Pentards in her German accent.

Richard kept his eyes on the mirror. The bar was packed shoulder to shoulder. Nico on his left—and on his right a burly guy in a blue pin-striped suit and slicked hair. Not the typical Max's look—more businessman than artiste, in fact.

"I was just bullshitting," Richard shouted. Hyperalert from the coke, he felt the pin-striped shoulder stiffen as their reflected eyes collided in the mirror.

"But I *love* the Pentards," Nico shouted back. Halfway through her sentence some celebrity waltzed in, and everyone quit talking and swiveled to see who it was. The word "Pentards" detonated in the lull. "So sexy."

The pinstripe was definitely eavesdropping. Richard's high began to curdle. "Sexy but dangerous. Honestly, I really don't . . ." He tried to douse his rising panic. What was the problem? No one straight ever came to Max's—the pinstripe was probably just someone's agent.

"You should take pictures of the guns before you deliver—*when* you deliver." Nico, heedless, barreled on full steam. "Andy would publish—your big break, yes?"

The pinstripe's eyes were probing Richard's in the mirror. It was like a pickup—only he had a feeling it would end with him being fucked over instead of fucked. Time to eighty-six this joint.

"Gotta split. See ya round, babe." Richard sprinkled some bills on the bar.

"Hold it, you." The pinstripe swiveled to block him.

"Actually, I'd rather not." Richard had a lot of practice at this. "I already have a boyfriend."

"Yeah? And who's *he* running guns for—the Pink Panther?" This was getting stickier by the second.

"I'd love to stay and chat." Richard leaned in closer. "But you're really not my type." And with that he closed the gap between their faces, planted a kiss full on the guy's mouth, hopped off his stool, and melted into the three-deep bar crowd. He was out the door and back on the street before the pinstripe was done swabbing off the saliva.

. . .

RICHARD CUT THROUGH Union Square Park—catty-corner to the bar—but the junkies were even scarier than being tailed by a gorilla, so he veered back to the avenue, took a left, a right, ducked into an alley, flattened himself in a doorway, checked both directions, and finally started to breathe again. How could he have been such an idiot? Richard assumed that anyone who made it into Max's was some kind of hipster or wannabe—why crash the epicenter of cool if you weren't cool yourself?—but instead, just his luck, he and Nico had plunked down next to the fucking mafia. Who else would wear such revolting cologne? Just the word "Uzi" gave that pin-striped prick a hard-on. By now he probably had Nico tied up in some back room where he and his ginzo goons were torturing her till she squealed. Fuck. Fuck and phooey.

Screw it. He was probably just trippy from all the shit he'd been ingesting. Richard gulped down the cold night air, shook his head clear, and squared his shoulders. *Everything was going to be just fine.* Now that he was sure he wasn't being followed, he took his time getting home. Anyway, there was no place else to go. That was the thing about New York—you plummeted from somebody to nobody just by stepping through a door. Didn't matter who you thought you were—out on the street even Andy was just another muthafucka. Gun muzzle in the small of your back. Hands down your pockets. Hiss in your ear. And you were done—picked clean and kicked to the curb with the rest of the nobodies. *What the fuck?* Richard's new motto. *What the fucking fuck.* Being nobody just meant you could be anybody. Nothing to lose. He could head up to Times Square, hunch under an awning like James Dean, pick up some drunk horny closet-case conventioneer, take him for everything he was worth. He could ride the subway all night with a marble-covered notebook on his lap like a street poet. He could hit the park, cop some horse, bliss out under the trees. How did that Ginsberg poem go again? . . . *angelheaded hipsters burning for the ancient heavenly connection to the starry dynamo in the machinery of night* . . . The machinery of night was humming softly all around him. Wind licked the bones of the deserted streets while high above, in the ceilings of commerce, fluorescent tubes burned like Christmas. A century of soot caked every surface. Old bums serenaded the pavement at the top of their lungs. Night-shift pickpockets sized him up and passed him by. Not a single living organism aside from rats and maggots survived for long out here. If it weren't for his record producer daddy, Richard would be just another maggot, sleeping in a doorway like the rest of the junkies—or even worse, slaving away beneath the eternal flame of industry. According to Kim, those were the only choices capitalism offered—slaver or slave—but Richard wasn't buying it. Politics didn't explain shit. Not anymore. Some new beat was surfacing, vibrating the city, bouncing off the sidewalk, humming in the subway, slamming the bodies on the dance floors. Heavy, monotonous, tranced-out, giddy. *Nothing would change, nothing would last. Pleasure was all that counted. So everybody dance now.* Richard loved it. His beat, his people, his body, his soul. So what if he was born rich? In this new world, no one judged you as long as you could dance. Lucky little ducky Dickie. Handsome, charming, friend of the famous or almost famous.

Friend? Really?

Richard stopped at the rail fence that surrounded the Church of St.-Mark's-in-the-Bowery, a Federal-style dowager dressed in hippie tie-dye. If he had a friend, he could pick up the phone, laugh, cry, crash at his place, meet at a bar, or just stand under the portico of this lost village chapel shooting the breeze till the sun rose.

But, when you came right down to it, was there anyone in this whole humongous heartless city he could count on, except maybe—just maybe—little Sammy Stein?

IT WAS ONE IN THE morning when he stumbled through the apartment door but Sam was still up. "Just finished!" he greeted Richard triumphantly. "How d'ya like this for a title? 'Rich and Famous: F. Scott Fitzgerald and the Cult of Celebrity.' AP English will never be the same."

"You should have asked me for some pointers," Richard said, collapsing on Sam's mattress. "Celebrity is my destiny."

"Wanna hear the first page?"

"Why don't you just start with what you wrote after we did that J."

Sam squeezed out half a smile, stood up from the littered table, and stretched his arms over his head, baring a strip of skinny boy waist where his T-shirt rode up. A little needle of envy pierced Richard. He had four years on Sam. His gut was still flat, his features finely chiseled, his head lustrous with black hair—but for how much longer? In Andy's world, the first little bulge and you were over the hill—unless your pockets were bulging too. He wanted to lean over and twist the little sprigs curling out the top of Sam's tighty whities. The kid was no baby, even if he acted like one half the time.

Sam sat down cross-legged on the mattress next to Richard. Bags pouched his eyes and discs of sweat stained the T-shirt under his pits, but he was stoked with the heat of creation. "I love this book," he murmured, holding the tattered paperback clasped to his heart, "but the more I study it, the more I agree with Kim about the bullshit politics. There's a passage she showed me about black people that I totally missed. Listen to this." He thumbed until he found it:

> *As we crossed Blackwell's Island a limousine passed us, driven by a white chauffeur, in which sat three modish negroes, two bucks and a girl. I laughed aloud as the yolks of their eyeballs rolled toward us in haughty rivalry. "Anything can happen now we've slid over this bridge," I thought; "anything at all. . . ."*

Sam put down the book. "Can you believe he calls black men *bucks*? It'd be like me calling Tutu *girl*. At least Faulkner acknowledges racism—but with Fitzgerald it's unconscious, totally taken for granted."

"You're gonna ace college, man."

"Yeah, if I get in." Sam stood up and started pacing.

"What a crock. Colleges will be *competing* for you. You'll be beating them off with a stick."

"Instead of just beating off, huh?"

"Good one, Sambo."

"Hey muthafucka, you better not let Kim catch you talking that shit."

"You think I'm scared of that little white-ass honky bitch?" Sam cracked his paperback on the crown of Richard's head. Richard grabbed his forearm in both hands and twisted in opposite directions. Sam tore loose, got behind Richard, flung an arm under his chin, and put him in a headlock. Richard reached back with one hand and goosed Sam—whereupon they both toppled over.

Richard was bigger by three inches and twenty pounds and within seconds he had Sam flat on his back with his knees pinning his shoulders. “Say uncle.”

“Fuck you.”

“Say uncle, Sammy!”

“Fuck your uncle.” Sam arched and tumbled Richard off him. They lay panting side by side for a minute.

“So where’s your girlfriend tonight?” Richard asked when he got his breath.

“Who knows.” Sam sighed and rolled over on his side. “She never tells me anything anymore.”

“So you’re just gonna mope around here waiting for her?”

“Unless you’ve got a better plan.”

The second they walked into the bar Sam knew it was a terrible idea. But when had he ever said no to Richard? “My treat—my choice—those are the rules.” So he tagged along, sidekick forever. And now look where he was. What was the name of this joint anyway? Rock Hard? The music was deafening. The sweat and smoke were asphyxiating. The bar was dark as a skull, but every two beats the dueling strobes captured and froze a hundred contorted bodies—all male. He heard them roar and felt them press against him. Warm flesh. Sticky leather. Belt buckles—or boners—jabbing his flanks. A hand locked around his forearm—Richard’s—and dragged him through the press. Shoulders parted. Miraculously, two empty stools appeared at the far end of the bar. Richard grabbed one and shoved the other under Sam. A big bald bartender in red leather and black body hair strobed into view and Richard waved Vs at him with both hands like Tricky Dick. “Two double vodkas!” he shouted over the music.

Richard pounded his but Sam sipped. He wasn’t a drinker. He

didn't want a repeat of New Year's. *You're a reporter*, he told himself. *Just take it all in. It doesn't mean anything. No one knows you're here.* By the third sip he was bobbing his head to the beat. He looked in the mirror behind the bar. Everyone lit in the strobe looked as if he'd been assembled in the same factory. Leather vest. Cropped head. Lean face. Hungry eyes. *How do they tell one another apart?* He dodged the eyes that tried to snag his. Richard was engrossed with the guy on his other side. *Now what am I supposed to do?* By the fifth sip he had to pee. He jabbed Richard with an elbow and screamed, "Bathroom," in his ear. "In the rear," Richard screamed back. The line snaked halfway across the back room. There must have been twenty guys waiting to empty their bladders—or whatever. At least the music was less assaulting. His gaze fell on the head of the guy in front of him—blond hair cut short and a deep furrow where head and neck fused. In gym class, when coach had them line up in squads, Sam always stood behind a kid with that same blond groove at the back of his head. Sean Rourke. *Here? Now?* No way. He turned—and both of them went crimson. "Sam?" "Sean?" Even in the dim light, Sam could see Sean's eyes flicker like slot machine icons—then the tough-guy face cracked open in a grin.

"Don't tell me—you're here undercover—writing about the scene for the school rag. Or . . ." He winked.

Sam opened his mouth but nothing came out. Sean was part of the Irish gang that haunted the park by the Catholic church. His father sold cars at the local Chevy dealership; one of his older brothers had been captain of the football team. He and Sean had never been friends exactly—scrawny boys like Sam gave the Irish gang a wide berth—but the two of them had an understanding. One time in junior high, when their class had its turn in the stinky over-chlorinated pool and Sam dove in and his bathing suit slipped off his nonexistent hips and the other boys pointed and screamed "Stein's a homo!", Sean shut them up. God knows why.

"Listen, Stein." Sean was bouncing from foot to foot. "I know what you're thinking."

"I'm not thinking anything except about my bladder." They were standing next to each other now, shuffling toward the toilet. Sam caught Sean's darting eyes, but he couldn't read the expression. Shame? Merriment? Conspiracy? He'd never noticed how much Sean resembled the photo of Fitzgerald in profile on the back of *The Great Gatsby.*

"Very funny." Sean was shaking his head. "I was about to say, I won't tell on you if you don't tell on me. But you know what? I don't give a rat's ass who you tell. It's senior fucking spring. We're free! At least I am." And with that, Sean clapped an arm around Sam's shoulders and with the other hand chucked him under the chin. "See you around, Sammy." He pushed open the door of the john, turned to fire off one last grin, and disappeared.

RICHARD FOUND HIM SITTING HUDDLED on the curb outside the bar. "I thought maybe you found someone you fancied. Expand your horizons."

"Just came out for a breath of air. It was so stifling in there." *I know what you're thinking.* And he knew what Sean was thinking.

"Totally." Richard sat down next to him. "All those horny hunks in leather pants—I got kinda overheated myself."

Sam bristled. "That's not what I meant."

"Oh c'mon, Sammy. Lighten up. Deep down, everybody's queer."

"Whatever you say, Richard." *Not a word about Sean—never.* "But seriously. You actually like that place? You're handsome—funny—

cool—whatever. No one's gonna say no to Richard Rines. But that bar was the dregs. So—" Sam groped for the word—"ugly."

"Okay. Got it. Next time it'll be the Russian Tea Room." They walked a couple of blocks without speaking. Sam glanced at his friend's perfect profile. Was he offended? Was it *possible* to offend Richard? In the streetlight the jagged scar next to his mouth looked etched in black. A plume of vapor billowed from his pursed lips. "Sam?" Richard broke the silence. "How old were you when my family moved to the neighborhood? Eight? Nine?"

"Something like that."

Richard slowed the pace, heels scraping the sidewalk. "Remember Donna?"

Donna was Richard's younger sister—Sam's age, maybe a year younger. She'd been born with hydrocephalus—water on the brain, they called it, which made Sam think of the specimen bottles of pickled organs he'd once seen at the Smithsonian. The disease swelled her head grotesquely and shriveled her body to a pale limp specter. It killed her when she was nine. Sam's mother made him write a condolence letter to Richard's parents. He hadn't thought about Donna in ages.

"Yeah, I remember," Sam said softly. "You were, what, fourteen when she died?"

"Yeah. God, kids are so fucking mean at that age. *There goes Donna Dumbo. What's inside your head, Donna?* You know why I always liked you, Sammy? Because you were nice to her. Remember the retarded class?" Sam remembered. "Everyone acted like those kids were contagious. But Donna said you used to hang out with them on the playground."

"Because I was such a reject no one else would go near me."

"No, Sam. You were nice. Nicer than me." Richard stopped walking and propped his back against a lamppost. "There were times I wanted her to die. Lots of times. It was so *embarrassing*—the way everyone stared, like the whole family were freaks. When she got hurt she didn't cry—she *moaned*. She didn't even sound like a person. Every year her head got bigger and the rest of her shrank. It was all my parents ever talked about. I prayed that they'd get rid of her. And then it happened. They took her away to the hospital and she never came back. And I thought, *Now no one's gonna call me "freak brother" anymore. No one's gonna point and laugh*. Once Donna was gone, I could be cute. Cute Ricky. It's all I ever wanted. *Look how cute Richard is. What a hottie*. Yeah. You have no idea how good that felt. To be looked at because you're attractive and not some freak? So yeah, Sam, when I walk into a bar and every head turns, yeah." He was breathing hard, staring at the sidewalk. "Freak brother is ancient history. Now it's like *Who's* that? *Look at* him. *Hey, gorgeous*. Okay? You get it now? I wanted her dead, Sam—and then she died. Now I think about her every day—except when I'm too fucked up to think."

Sam was speechless. Richard had always been so wild, so physical. He was constantly in your face—hands all over you, chugging beer, cracking jokes, making trouble. It never occurred to Sam he was carrying all this darkness inside. A surge of heat rose inside him. "You knew you were my hero, right?" Sam waited but there was no answer. Richard pushed off from the lamppost and they started walking again. "When we were kids, I thought you were so—I don't know—crazy. Dangerous. Like nothing mattered. Like you didn't care what anyone thought. Free—you were so free."

"Oh, c'mon, Sam." The grief had evaporated and—boom!—just like that the snarky edge was back. "Why don't you just admit you were in love with me." He threw an arm around Sam's shoulder and squeezed. "Or should we say *are*?"

"Sorry, pal, but you're not my type." Sam let the arm rest heavy on his shoulder.

"Oh, so you have a type?" Sam shrugged off the arm. "Ever done it with a guy?"

"Are you crazy? I was a virgin till Kim and I . . ."

"Ever wanted to?"

Long pause. "I don't know. Maybe. It's weird—but when I got mugged in the subway up in Harlem? I kept thinking about Leon. . . ."

"Who's Leon?"

"You know, Tutu's grandson I told you guys about? It's not like I'm attracted to him or anything. But the whole time I was stranded in the subway, I kept hoping he'd rush down and save me. You know, like a brother."

"Soul brother."

"Whatever."

Half a block of silence. "So, what's going on with you and Kim?" Sam only grunted so Richard pressed on, "It was nonstop boogie nights when you guys first moved in—but now it's like a tomb out there."

"She's starting to scare me." Sam's voice was a thread. "She won't even talk about what she's doing anymore. It's like I'm a spy."

"You know you're never going to hold her." They were striding in step now, both their heads tilted down at the same angle. "She's not the girlfriend type."

Sam felt his mouth start to tremble. "Oh yeah? Well, I think she's someone else's girlfriend now. She barely looks at me."

"You gotta let her go, man. Don't make her hate you."

"I thought she understood everything about me." The words were coming out in gasps. "That first night—when I talked about Tutu and she told me about Delores. It was like whatever I thought, she'd thought before me. We just *got* each other. But now . . ." Sam gulped to get control of his voice.

Silence fell between them again. They were almost back to the apartment. "Okay, Sam, fast-forward five years—no, ten," Richard tossed out. "What do you see yourself doing?"

Grateful for the change of subject, Sam answered without thinking: "Writing."

"Duh." Richard thudded him with a shoulder. "Everyone knows you're gonna be a writer, dude. But about what? And who for?"

"That's the thing," Sam practically wailed. "I wanna be a writer—but honestly—deep down—I'm scared shitless that I don't have anything to write about and never will."

"What about that bar? Gay liberation—the next big thing."

"Ugh."

"What about Kim and the Panthers?"

"She'd kill me—she's already totally paranoid about the FBI."

"What about me?" Sam walked on, shaking his head. "Or Leon? What about Leon?"

"What *about* Leon?"

"You could write his story. 'Leon Washington' . . . "

"Carter."

"'Leon Carter: The Secret Life of the Maid's Son.'"

"Grandson."

"Whatever. Think about it, Sam. Everyone's always going on about power to the people—but who *are* the people? So you do a series of profiles of real people . . . starting with Leon."

"What if he says no?"

"You're never gonna know till you ask him, right? Don't tell me you're chicken."

"Bock bock bah-*gaw*!" Sam cawed at the sky. But honestly, it wasn't such a bad idea.

Chapter Eighteen

Sam stationed himself outside the storefront church that Sunday at the stroke of noon. People passing on the sidewalk gave him either a wide berth or a hard stare but Sam didn't mind. He waited until he saw Tutu and Leon step outside and then planted himself on the sidewalk in front of them.

"Lord have mercy!" Tutu was loud and radiant, as she always was after church. "You look like you grew two inches and lost ten pounds." She dimmed a notch. "You in trouble?"

Sam, beaming, shook his head.

"Well, you better come on home with us. I bet you could use you a home-cooked meal."

Leon took his hand and gave it about a dozen shakes. Sam felt the warmth spread from his fingers to his heart. Their eyes met and held.

The three of them took the long way home. It was a fine day, not yet spring but no longer the dead of winter. Clumps of budded daffodils nodded under the bare trees lining Convent Avenue.

The big blowsy forsythia bush at the corner of the yard in Fat Neck would be in bloom soon—one week of yellow ecstasy before the long drab season of green.

"Your mama's been sick," Tutu told him as they rode the elevator. "Had to miss work and everything—as if you care." She fixed her eyes on his. "Her hair's turning gray too. From fretting over you, Sammy."

"Well, you can tell her I'm fine. See?" He spread his arms out and tried to smile.

"Yeah, all ninety-five pounds of you. One good wind would blow you clear to Jersey." Sam and Leon traded a look.

As soon as she got lunch on the table, Tutu started in talking about her own mother. Did I ever tell you boys about my mama, Miss Hannah? Miss Hannah knew voodoo. Miss Hannah could cure whatever ailed you with roots and potions. She knew how to cast a spell and drop someone in their tracks just like *that*! Once, when I was a little girl, Miss Hannah was walking me to town and a little white boy started chucking stones at us. I pulled back my mouth with my fingers and stuck out my tongue till the boy ran inside crying to his mama. That white lady came storming out like her hair was on fire. "Either you take a switch to that child or I will," she hollered at Miss Hannah. "And I mean *right now*." Miss Hannah broke a branch off their willow tree, peeled down my undies and whipped me good. But after every whack, Miss Hannah turned her head and drilled that white woman with her eyes. I never cried out once. Two days later, the little white boy broke out in pox and almost died. He bore the scars on his face for the rest of his life.

"Miss Hannah's voodoo," Tutu concluded, glaring at Sam. "There's a lesson there, child. When your parents slap you silly, it's for your own good. Blood is thicker than water and don't you let anyone tell you different. You've only got but one mama and daddy. Lose them and you've lost everything."

"That's where you come in, Tutu," Sam shot back. "I haven't lost *anything* as long as you're there as my spy."

"Hostage is more like it," she cut him off. "Did anyone ever think to ask how *I* felt about this little game? Toting messages like some flunky. Going behind their back. It's no different from lying."

"But I did it for your own good." Sam hated the little whine that crimped his voice. "If it wasn't for me—"

"What in God's name do *you* know about my own good?" Tutu's eyes were molten with wrath. Leon, in the middle, tried to signal Sam with his eyebrows: *Back off, man.*

"But I saved you your job!"

Tutu, glowering, rose to her feet. "Did I ask to be saved? Did I?" Sam started to sweat. "You better think about saving your own precious hind quarters before you start in worrying about mine. I'm done spying for you, Sammy. I quit!" She turned her back on him—on both of them—and stormed out of the kitchen.

AN HOUR LATER he was riding shotgun down the West Side Highway in a blue 1963 Chevy Impala with Leon at the wheel. Leon had barely said two words over lunch—but the minute Sam made noises about heading back downtown, he jumped up and offered to drive him. The Impala belonged to Tutu's brother Morris, a cabdriver, but Leon got to borrow it on nights and weekends so he could pick up a little extra cash running old folks around on their errands. Gypsy cab. Sam was happy for the ride. It gave him some time to talk to Leon about the article without Tutu eavesdropping.

Driving in the City terrified Sam—in fact, ever since he flunked his road test, just being in the driver's seat made him antsy—but it seemed to turn Leon loose. One hand on the wheel and the other fiddling with the radio dial, Leon barely even looked at the road and never bothered with his blind spot or rearview mirror. Every time he hit the gas, he cranked up the volume. "When it comes to singing," he shouted to Sam over the music, "a car's even better than the shower." Whatever song came on—"Everyday People," "Sugar, Sugar," "Honky Tonk Women," "Build Me Up Buttercup"—Leon sang along with perfect pitch and perfect recall of every word. Sam grabbed the dial and spun it just to test him. Rosemary Clooney. Frank Sinatra. Sly and the Family Stone. The Supremes. Janis Joplin. The Stones. The Archies. Leon never missed a note, skipped a beat, muffed a word.

"You're incredible," Sam crowed. "You should be on television—like *American Bandstand* or *Ed Sullivan* or something."

"What's incredible? Another Negro with rhythm?"

Sam didn't know whether it was cool to laugh. "No one in my family can even carry a tune—except Tutu."

Leon let that slide.

"It's all about church," Leon said, weaving through the traffic. "When I opened my mouth to praise the Lord, I just hit the notes without trying. It was like I was born to sing."

"That's how I felt when I learned to ski," Sam jumped in. "I was up on this frozen mountaintop and it was like an icicle speared the center of my brain. Don't ask me why—I just knew I could do it."

"Seriously?" Sam nodded. Leon went on, "I thought skiing was something rich white folks did to scare themselves."

"Well, there's that, I guess." Sam spun the dial to the classical station and a Mozart aria fluttered around them. "But for me, it's almost—you know—holy. The only time I really believe in God is when I'm flying down a mountain."

"That's just not *right.*" Leon batted Sam's hand away and twisted until he landed on Wilson Pickett belting out "In the Midnight Hour." "Cold is evil. Cold is death. Cold is the opposite of holy. You oughta come to church more often, man. Empty your mind, open your mouth, and feel the spirit working through you. Plus, it's a lot warmer than skiing."

Sam grabbed the dial. Now Mahalia Jackson was wailing "In the Upper Room." It was like stereo—Mahalia in one ear, Leon in the other. He didn't even strain for the high notes.

"You have any white friends, Leon?" Sam asked when the song was over.

"Nah."

"Why not?"

"You have any black friends?" Pause. "And don't say Tutu cause she's not your friend *or* your family."

"I don't get it," Sam barreled on. "I mean, everybody talks about civil rights, equality, freedom, integration, blah, blah. But there's not a single black kid in my school."

"And there wasn't a single white kid in mine."

Long pause. "Someday We'll Be Together" started playing but Leon let it spin without singing along.

"You probably think I'm just some stuck-up white kid who's hanging out with you because I've got a thing about your grandma."

"No. I think you're hanging out with me because I'm driving your white ass home." They laughed.

"But seriously . . ." Sam took a deep breath and told him about the article. “I’m thinking I’d write it in interview format. Or all in your own words. Like, the story of Leon Carter, as told to Sam Stein. It’d be for the school paper—but that’s just the start. Maybe *Ramparts* would pick it up—you know, the underground rag? Or *The Village Voice*. Or even the *Times* magazine—gotta shoot high, right? First thing, I’d have to interview you—get all the facts straight.” Leon drove on in silence, exiting the highway and nosing the Chevy into the maze of Lower Manhattan. At a traffic light, he turned so he could study Sam’s expression. When the light turned green, he turned away, still without speaking.

“What street did you say you lived on?” he said finally.

“Just drop me off here,” Sam told him as St.-Mark’s-in-the-Bowery came into view.

Leon pulled over but Sam didn’t get out. The radio was still blaring—“Chain of Fools”—and they let Aretha get to the end of the song. Then Leon switched it off. “That article idea? I think it’d be cool,” he said quietly. “Granny says you’re always scribbling away on something. Let’s see what you can do with me.”

“COOL!” WAS STILL RATTLING around his brain when he threw open the apartment door. “Fab news! Leon’s like totally cool with the article.” That’s what he would have said if Kim had been there—or Richard—or even Eli. But the place was deserted. Just a note on the kitchen table in Kim’s plump round little-girl handwriting: “Back soon. ♥K.”

Sam took a breath. Shook the bees out of his head. Grabbed his notebook and a pen. Pulled a chair up to the kitchen table. Sat down. And started writing.

Leon Carter sings like an angel and drives like the Devil's on his tail. And maybe he is. Because Leon Carter is young, black, and male in America—and if ever there was a combination to make the Devil give chase, that would be it.

Now what?

He sat with his pen poised over the page, but no other words came. He read over the three lines, flung the pen across the room, and let his face fall into his palms. *Now what?* Snappy little lede he had there—but aside from driving and singing, Sam didn't know the first thing about Leon Carter. Well, not quite accurate. He knew Leon was lean and handsome. He knew that his father was dead; his mother was messed up on drugs—or something—back in Virginia. He bagged groceries at a Harlem supermarket and drove a gypsy cab and gave his grandmother whatever he could spare so she could buy herself a grave. He went to church on Sunday. What else? Did Leon remember anything about his daddy? Did he have a girlfriend? What were his dreams? His fears? Secrets? Where did he see himself in ten years?

Sam didn't have a clue.

That's why you need to interview him, asshole.

Right. Always a good idea to get the story before you try to tell the story. Ask leading questions. Don't assume you know the answers. Open your ears and your heart but remain impartial. Record, don't interpret. Observe, don't judge. Once you find the story, let it tell you how to tell it.

Isn't that what Mr. Coffin always told the high school newspaper staff?

Sam picked the pen up off the floor and started pacing. He tried to empty his mind—then tried to fill it with facts. He tried to put himself in Leon's shoes, in his skin. Leon was black. His hair was springy. He had a voice so beautiful it made you tremble to hear him sing. He'd been poor all his life. He wanted money! He wanted to count for something, to be somebody who had nothing to do with bagging groceries. He wanted his big break—who didn't? But who was going to give Leon Carter a break?

Sam sat down at the table again and started doodling under the single flimsy paragraph he'd penned in a lather. Smiley faces. High-heeled shoes. His signature ten different ways. What if Leon were writing a story about him? What would he need to know to get it right? That Sam dreamed of being a famous writer? That try as he might, he really couldn't understand Kim's obsession with the Black Panthers? That he was secretly convinced he was a total fraud? That despite everything he still looked up to Richard? But why would he need Leon to tell his story anyway? He could tell it better himself. Couldn't everyone?

Come to think of it, why did Leon need Sam to tell *his* story? It was a kind of theft, wasn't it, telling someone else's story for them? A double theft when it came to black folks. White people had taken everything from black people except their souls and their stories—and now Sam was going to take Leon's story too? The one worldly thing Leon had left—scooped up and cranked out for some high school newspaper? And he was planning on making a *career* of this?

But Leon said he was cool with it. So did that make it right? Who was Sam fooling?

If he had any pot, he would have rolled a joint and smoked it—but Richard was the keeper of the drugs and the last thing Sam wanted was to be caught rummaging through Richard's shit like some pathetic junkie.

He poured himself a glass of water, gulped it down, poured

another. Then he slammed the notebook shut and started pacing again. His father once told him you could extract a core from an ancient tree and map the forest's weather for centuries—wet years and dry years, plagues of insects, fire, flood. Sam didn't care about trees—he cared about people. What if you could take a core of someone's brain? Like Leon. Like Richard. Or even Kim. Who was she really? What did she want? What set her pulse racing when she woke up in the middle of the night? He and Kim lived together, slept together, breathed the same air, but did he really have any idea what went on inside her?

The simple truth was that he didn't know shit about shit. It didn't help that he and Kim hadn't said more than two words to each other in days. The silence was killing him.

Richard was right—he had to let her go or she'd hate him. But would that be any worse than hating himself?

LEON CROSSED THE HALLWAY IN two strides and leaned his long torso into the kitchen, bracing his forearms on the door frame. "Guess what?" His grandmother didn't even look up from her Bible. "Sammy says he wants to write about me."

"Is that a fact?" Tutu guided a string between the two faces of the book, closed it, and folded her hands over the cover.

Leon saw that she was still brooding over what Sam said about saving her job, but it was too late to backpedal now. "Smart as he is, he's bound to write something good. You told me yourself—"

But Tutu raised her palms in the air to stop him. "What I *told* you . . ." lowering her hands to the book again, "is that he's not half as smart as he *thinks* he is. If you had the opportunities that boy has—"

"Aw, Granny."

"If you'd finished school like I told you to." *Here it comes*. "If you quit singing for a second and started listening. If you'd been born rich and white, instead of poor and—"

"You always told me that didn't matter. Who the Lord favors . . ."

"You think that child's your friend?" She wouldn't let him finish a single sentence. "You think he's going to make you into somebody just by *writing* about you?" She was shouting. "I'll tell you what's going to be. He's going to write something that makes *himself* look good. Look good—feel good—just like his parents did with me. 'Good old Tutu—been around forever—part of the family.' They think they believe that. But it's a lie—just like Sammy's lying to you, Leon. I gave twenty years of my life to that family—never sick a day. I took *pride*—you better believe I did. And look at the thanks I get. 'Don't mind her—she's just the maid.' Just the maid! And those civil rights people are no different. Folks who never did an honest day's work in their life telling *me* I need to find some self-respect. *Uncle Tom—Aunt Jemima*." She spat out the hated names.

Now Leon had his palms up. "Not me, Granny. I never said that. I know how hard you work . . ."

"Sammy Stein doesn't even respect himself—so how do you think he's going to respect *you*? I was a fool to believe those people were any different. Don't you be a fool, Leon. Stay away from that boy. Tell your own damn story—or better yet, keep it hid so no one can take it from you. You open your soul to Sammy, and nothing good will ever come of it. Trust me." She pushed herself to her feet. "Now I'm going to lie down. I'm tired to death." She squeezed past him, stomped across the apartment, and shut herself in the bedroom. Case closed.

Chapter Nineteen

All that week Sam spent every free moment in the school library. Leon was coming over for the interview on Friday night, and Sam wanted to be prepared. If he was going to tell this story right, he had to put it in perspective, establish the wider context, dig beneath the surface to the truth that was rooted in history. He needed to go back to the beginning—to slavery and emancipation. Who were Leon's people? How, when, and why did they get from Africa to Virginia to New York? He knew what people would be thinking: Leon—Tutu—they were nobodies. A grocery bagger and a maid. Who cared about their life stories? Who cared about anyone's story? That was Sam's job: to make people care. A century after the Civil War, was there a place for a young black man in America aside from prison or the army? If Leon had a future, the only way to grasp it was to look at his past—his *whole* past. Take nothing for granted. Examine every source. Don't be blinded by the glint of illusion. Isn't that what his

AP history teacher, Miss Koestler, kept drumming into their skulls? Facts are fluid—you're never going to nail them down—so don't try. Gather as many sources as you can and squeeze them until something emerges. Start at the beginning—which in Leon's case meant enslaved forebears on the Northern Neck of Virginia, where (as Tutu had told him and the history books confirmed) three of the first five presidents had been born on plantations worked by her and Leon's enslaved ancestors. If he found out how those plantation presidents treated their slaves and what happened to them and their offspring after emancipation, he'd have the start of Leon's American story.

That was the first problem: there was nothing. Sam scoured the school library for books about the founders' slaves—and came up empty. In the half dozen biographies of the first president, the only mention of slaves was the provision in Washington's will freeing them. One biography devoted a paragraph to Washington's trusty valet Billy Lee, the only slave named outright in the president's will. That was it. Sam tried to summon Tutu's quadruple great-grandmother from the grainy photos of Mount Vernon—but he gave up. To judge by the histories and biographies, the slaves of the founders were an invisible army who did all the work without being seen, heard, recorded, or remembered. It was like black people had never really existed in America until they were emancipated. Lots of stuff in the library about the Emancipation Proclamation and the Thirteenth Amendment—"Neither slavery nor involuntary servitude shall exist within the United States"—but between the Civil War and the civil rights movement, there was a total void in black history except for a single biography of George Washington Carver. Books about the civil rights movement were segregated in their own little nook. They even had *The*

Autobiography of Malcolm X—Kim's favorite book. So Sam grabbed it off the shelf and settled in to read the story of how a two-bit Harlem dope pusher transformed himself into the father of Black Power. He read Martin Luther King Jr.'s "Letter from Birmingham Jail" and the "I Have a Dream" speech that he vaguely remembered watching on television when he was eleven (his parents had asked Tutu to come watch with them but she wouldn't). He asked the librarian to help him dig up newspaper articles about the church bombing in Birmingham, Alabama, that same year—1963. It all came back to him as he ran his eyes down the blurry columns of microfilm from *The New York Times*: Tutu had been preparing their dinner that September Sunday when the news crackled onto her transistor radio that four little black girls had been killed after a bomb blew up their church that morning. Sam rushed into the kitchen when he heard the cry—and there stood Tutu, frozen between the sink and the stove with both hands over her mouth and tears streaming down her face. She shook her head—once—when he asked her what was wrong. The radio played on and on, repeating the story a hundred times. Tutu listened in silence to every word, and Sam listened beside her, trying to take it in. When she served the five of them their dinner, she turned up the volume so they could all hear it perfectly from behind the swinging kitchen door. And no one said a word. They just ate the food Tutu put on their plates and listened to the news reports out of Birmingham until even Sam had memorized those four girls' names: Addie Mae Collins, Cynthia Wesley, Carole Robertson, Denise McNair.

This was history. He and Tutu had lived through it together, each sealed in a separate bubble. Never once had they talked about it—any of it—not then, not after.

Sam read and took notes until the librarian shut off the lights and threw him out—then he trudged the mile to the station and caught the train back to the city. In the suffocating car, mostly empty at this hour, he made a running list headed "Questions for Leon." He decided he'd start with a point where their lives intersected: He'd recount everything he remembered about the Sunday of the Birmingham church bombing and then he'd ask Leon where he was that day, how and when he heard the news, how he reacted, how the people around him took it. Personal, political, particular. Better than just launching in with "So, man, tell me about yourself. Start from the beginning and go up to the present. Be specific. Start." Right? Question #2: Who do you like better, the Mets or the Yankees? #3: Who inspires you more—Dr. King or Malcolm X? #4: Do you have a girlfriend? #5: Any advice for what to do when your girlfriend quits talking to you? #6: Do you know anything about your enslaved ancestors?

Sam erased, crossed out, rewrote, reshuffled the questions so many times that by the end he couldn't read a single word.

LEON SHOWED UP ON FRIDAY evening at six thirty—half an hour late. "No subway service below Fourteenth Street," he apologized at the door. "Some kind of mess-up in the Village." Dressed in a white starched shirt, blue tie, shiny gray suit, he looked like a traveling Bible salesman. As soon as he cast an eye around Richard's tenement living room—which Sam had stayed up half the night before to clean—he slipped off the jacket and folded it neatly on the back of a chair. *What had he been expecting—the penthouse suite?*

When they got through the awkward shuffle by the door, Sam

pulled out a chair for Leon at the decontaminated plastic table, sat down opposite, and cleared his throat. "So." He flipped open a steno pad. "Right." Clicked open his ballpoint pen. "Should we get started?"

Leon nodded, breathing shallowly through his nose. *Did the place really smell that bad?*

Sam unfolded the illegible list of questions and, glancing briefly at the erasure blots and arrows, launched into his memories of the Birmingham church bombing. Leon, silent and motionless, heard him out to the end. "So my first question is—what do you remember about that day? How old were you? Where were you when the news came on?"

Leon stared at Sam for the count of two then dropped his eyes. "You're saying this happened in sixty-three? I was thirteen, maybe fourteen. Can't say I remember much about that time. It was right before I came north with Granny."

"You never listened to the news? Civil rights—Dr. King—all of that?"

Leon shook his head.

"Where were you—on Mars?"

A crease dented Leon's smooth brow. "Nah, I was still in Virginia."

"With your . . ." He was about to say "mother" but he wasn't going to make that mistake twice. "Folks," he finished lamely.

"Look, man. I didn't come here to talk about that." Sam could tell from the strangled voice that he'd pissed Leon off. "That's not part of the story, okay?"

That's totally the story! Sam wanted to yell. But he just mumbled, "Okay," and flipped through his notes. "So you lived in Virginia till you were fourteen? Northern Neck, right?" Leon nodded.

Sam forged ahead, "You study much local history before you left? You know, George Washington, Mary Ball? Tutu told me her grandparents were slaves, which means your great-great-grandparents were slaves. Ever hear anything about whose slaves they were?"

"Nobody talks about that stuff." The crease in Leon's brow deepened. "What's the point?"

"The point?" Sam was incredulous. "It's our history—that's the point. If no one talks about it—"

"*Our* history?" Leon's mouth twisted. "I don't know squat about *your* history—but it's not the same as mine. You don't want to hear my story—all you care about is what's already in your head." His eyes went hard. "The noble Negro standing up to injustice. That's not me. I'm not my *race,* Sam—I'm a *person.*" Sam shrank before the anger. "A person you can't see and never will. The truth? To you, I'm nothing unless you can put on a label on it. Grandson of slaves. Victim of racism. What do you know about it? You're just using me to make yourself feel better. Just like Granny told me. You say you wanna write my story—but it's just gonna end up being about you."

Sam flushed. This was going seriously off the rails. "Whoa—sorry—I didn't mean—"

But before he could finish the sentence, the door opened and Richard came strolling in. He wasn't supposed to be here yet. He'd promised to make himself scarce until eight thirty so Sam could interview Leon in peace—but when was the last time Richard kept his side of a bargain? He looked like he'd just been to a beauty salon—clean shaven, clear-eyed, hair combed, smelling of aftershave. After shaking hands with Leon, Richard plunked himself in a chair next to Sam, tilted it back with his hands behind his head, and amped up the killer grin. "Sam here tells me you're a pretty cool dude." *He had?* "So what's the coolest thing you've ever done?" *Why hadn't he thought of that?*

"Um." Pause. "Well. This is kind of embarrassing." A little smile was twitching at the corners of Leon's mouth. "But a couple years ago—on a dare—I auditioned for *Hair*—you know, the musical?"

"No *way*." Richard started humming the chorus to "Aquarius." "You like that kind of music?"

"No way!" Leon was grinning now. "It was a dare, right? I had no idea you had to take off your clothes and stuff. Granny would have killed me if I got the part."

"Which you didn't?"

"Correct. But they really liked the way I sang. *You could totally do backup for the Four Tops.* Those were the exact words of the . . . whatchacallit?"

"Casting director."

"Right."

Sam sat there chewing the cap of his pen, while Richard and Leon started riffing back and forth about music. Every group or singer that Leon mentioned—from Mahalia Jackson to the Jackson 5—Richard had either met, hung out with, or knew every song they ever recorded. *Helps to have a record producer for a father.* They took turns pinpointing the album on which soul stars like Ray Charles, Aretha, Stevie Wonder, and Etta James pivoted from gospel to R&B. Then they started swapping favorites—"I Was Made to Love Her," "I Heard It through the Grapevine," "Hallelujah I Love Her So"—and soon they were singing bits, alternating lead and backup. Sam, now furiously taking notes, didn't know whether to be grateful or incensed at how Richard was hijacking the interview.

As if on cue, the two of them quit singing at the exact same moment and burst out laughing. "Wow." Leon's eyes were shining. "You sure know a lot about our music considering that you're—"

"A white boy," Richard finished for him. "Yeah, well, my father's Irv Rines, the record producer. Heard of him?"

"Irv Rines is your *father*? I'd give *anything* to meet that man. My number one dream . . ." And he was off and running about how he was born to be a back-up singer because he could hit every note of every song—"It's true," Sam interjected, "I heard him"—harmonize in any genre, memorize a song the first time he heard it. He told them about meeting the Rabbi and how he was going to make a demo tape as soon as he scraped together the money.

"This is incredible," Richard practically crooned. "How come you didn't say anything about this, Sam I Am? I work part-time in my dad's studio," Richard barreled on. *Yeah, like two hours a week.* "I'm sure I could arrange for you to come down and meet Dad. Gosh, once you have your demo, who knows . . . ?"

"I can't believe this," Leon murmured, his eyes liquid. Then he pulled up short. "Your daddy—he's Jewish, right? Miss G at the church said to get with the Jewish producers."

Richard shot him a quizzical look. "One hundred percent certified Semite. If you ask nicely, he'll sing you 'Hava Nagila.'" Richard started singing in Hebrew and clapping along—Sam was cringing—and by the second verse Leon joined in on harmony. "Jesus, Leon," Richard beamed, "you could front for a bar mitzvah band."

"Let's get back to the story," Sam interrupted, racking his brain for what to say next. Two pairs of eyes were trained on his face: okay, Mr. Cub Reporter. "Everybody's got a story, right?" Blank stares. "Boy meets girl—boys loses girl. Boy works hard, studies law, goes to Washington and becomes president—"

"Or crook," Richard put in.

"Or both," Sam added. "Or: boy grows up poor and lonely, moves to the city, gets a job. . . ."

"Meets a famous record producer and becomes a star," Richard finished Sam's sentence, winking at Leon.

"Now *that's* a story I like. But that's not my story." Leon fell quiet for a moment. "Not yet, anyway. I guess I grew up poor—but I never thought of it that way. When Daddy was alive there was always plenty to eat—fish and crabs off his boat—tomatoes and beans in the summer. You white folks are always wanting to pity us—unless you're hating on us—but one's as bad as the other. We look after our own, know what I mean?" Sam nodded, at a loss for what to say. Leon continued, "My story has a hero but it's not me—it's Granny. No offense, Sam, but my granny busts her butt at your house six days a week to give me what I have. Without her—and our church—I'd be nothing. Worse than nothing."

"Yeah, but without our messed-up system you wouldn't need Tutu—or church," Sam said. "You'd be out on your own—"

"But that's where you're wrong," Leon cut him off. "Even if I was rich as Solomon, I'd still go to church with Granny every Sunday. If you can't get with the Lord, you can't get anywhere."

Sam chewed the cap of his Bic pen. "Okay—lemme ask you something else." He tried to ignore Leon's sigh. "Right now your dream is to be a singer. But what about before you left Virginia? Back when you were fourteen, what did you wanna be when you grew up?"

"I know what I wanted to be," Richard butted in. "A fireman! Sliding down those poles. Driving a big shiny red engine."

"Leon?"

Another sigh. "Fourteen? Truthfully, I didn't want be anything.

I wanted to *be* nothing. I just wanted not to be me." Two silent beats. "What about you, Sam?"

He breathed out hard. "I wanted to be Richard." Which got him a little "awww" and a punch on the shoulder.

"And now?"

"Hey, who's interviewing who?"

"And now?"

Another silence. "Kinda like you at fourteen."

"What? With a friend like him?" He nodded to Richard, which got Leon a shoulder punch.

Leon put his jacket back on, shook hands, and headed for the door. "Got a driving job later on," he explained. "Friend of Granny's coming up from Baltimore on the bus. I'm supposed to pick her up at Port Authority."

"You're a cabdriver?" Richard asked.

"Gypsy cab, I guess you call it." Leon's eyes came to rest on Sam. "If any of you ever need a ride anyplace . . ." He fished a couple of cards from his pocket. "Morris Carter. Taxi Driver. 24-hour cab service" was embossed in big black letters; but Leon had penned a line through "Morris" and written his own name in, along with Tutu's phone number. Sam slipped the card into the back pocket of his jeans; Richard laid his on the plastic table.

Sam followed Leon out the door onto the landing. "Is Tutu still mad at me?"

Leon shook his head. "Seems like Granny's mad at everyone these days." His mouth twitched for a second. "Do me a favor, would you? If you talk to her, don't mention the article. Better yet, don't even tell her you saw me."

Sam raised his right hand. "Scout's honor." Luckily, Leon had no idea how bad he was at lying.

Chapter Twenty

Kim stood at the bottom of the stairwell of Richard's tenement building and stared up at the five flights of steps. She couldn't remember the last time she'd eaten—but the smell of piss and beer in the lobby made whatever was in her gut heave. She was trembling all over but she wasn't going to let herself break down. Like her mother. Mother? She couldn't even conjure her face. Having a mother felt like another lifetime. Another girl's life.

Kim sank down on the bottom step, crossed her arms over her knees, and let her head drop—but the second she closed her eyes she saw it. She couldn't blot it out. She couldn't stop replaying it. Where Lee's brownstone stood there was a smoking pile of twisted beams and rubble cordoned off by police tape and fire engines. Flames shot up through the smoke and sputtered in the blasts of the fire hoses. A crowd was pressed up against the tape four deep, but she shoved her way through. She had to be sure. She checked the street sign on the corner—Eleventh Street—no mistake. This was Lee's street—Lee's brownstone—but there was no brownstone. Just the gap in the building façades like an extracted tooth. A voice behind her: "Smell that? Burning flesh." Another: "Like a fucking war zone." Another: "Cops say it could be a gas main—but these days who the hell knows." *Gas main—or pig attack*, Kim was thinking. Or maybe the bomb went off by accident? The last time Kim had seen Lee—around eleven that morning—she was in the sub-basement tinkering with a blasting cap. Was Lee's charred body underneath that rubble? A pair of black cars pulled up. The guys who slammed the doors weren't wearing uniforms, but they got waved through by the men in blue. FBI. That's when Kim split.

This was supposed to be the day—the night—when it all went down. Operation Off, Lee called it. No more firebombs. No more Molotov cocktails. These were the real thing: dynamite pipe bombs designed to decimate, not maim. They were going to be detonated at an army officers' dance in Jersey—"bring the war home." That was Lee's show. Kim was assigned the sideshow—a single bomb tagged for the draft induction center on Whitehall Street in Lower Manhattan. All the bombs were timed to explode simultaneously at midnight. March 6, 1970: the start of the Second American Revolution. That was the plan. Lee had laid it out for her that morning at the brownstone. They had a plant inside the induction center—the pigs were not the only ones who had infiltrated the enemy—and Lee ordered Kim to hand off the bomb to him with instructions on where to place it and how to set the timer. After that, she had to stay off the street for a while to make sure she wasn't being followed; then return to the brownstone to help them load the van for the Jersey attack. Lee had told her to bring back some cotton balls—the watches they were using as timers ticked too loudly and they needed the cotton to muffle the sound. Kim still had the bag stuffed in her coat pocket. Jesus.

It was around five in the afternoon when she walked away from the smoldering remains of the brownstone—now it was nine at night—but Kim could barely account for the time between. She sat on the tenement step trying to reassemble it in her mind. Get a grip. At first she'd been so stunned she didn't know where she was going. She stumbled down Fifth Avenue, and there was Dustin Hoffman striding at her, toward the bomb site. Weird. "Hey, Mr. Hoffman!" she heard a voice shouting. "Do you know who lived in this building?" She didn't wait around to hear the answer. She didn't stop or turn until she got to the subway entrance at Astor Place. There was a safe house in Chinatown where they had all agreed to meet up in case something went wrong. That's where she decided to go—it was all she could think of. But was there anybody left? When she got to the address of the safe house, she stood outside leaning on the buzzer and praying under her breath—*Please, please, please* . . . But the pad was empty—at least no one answered—and her last hope flickered out. Kim didn't have a key—she hadn't been with them long enough. She found a phone booth and called everyone she could think of. Finally, Jeff picked up. They met at a hole-in-the-wall lo mein joint on Canal Street.

"You know about the brownstone, right?" she whispered to him. "Any word from Lee?"

Jeff shook his head.

Kim looked away, biting her lip. "Now it's all on the Panthers," she said grimly. "We need to do the drop. Immediately. Tomorrow."

"We're ready," said Jeff. "Panthers got the bread—you deliver the goods—and we're cool."

"Right."

"But it's gotta be a brother that does the hand-off. No brother, no deal. You know how they are."

She knew. "There'll be a brother," she promised him.

They agreed to talk the next morning to finalize the details; then they separated. Jeff said he was going up to Harlem to lay the deal out for the BPP command. Kim sleepwalked through the slummy downtown blocks to Richard's place. And here she was, squatting at the bottom of the stairs, clutching her knees with her arms and shaking uncontrollably. Her guru was under a pile of rubble—where else could she be?—her cell was obliterated; her own bomb was set to go off at midnight—but what if it misfired like the ones that took out the brownstone? Kim ground her fists into her eyes. Fucking Eli's crate of Uzis. It was all she had left. It was everything. She forced herself to get up and start climbing the stairs. *It's gotta be a brother* rang in her ears as she dragged herself up the steps. Funny. For all her madness about black power, the only black people Kim knew were her maid Delores and Jeff, and he was so light he could pass if it wasn't for the fro. That was going to change once the Panthers had those guns.

She opened the apartment door to find Richard sprawled on the couch with a joint between his fingers, listening to Jefferson Airplane. He was slapping his bare feet on the floor in time to the music. Tufts of black hair sprouted from the joints of his big toes. Kim had a sudden urge to walk over and stomp him with her boot heel. "Sam'll be back in a sec," Richard drawled, blowing smoke. "He's out getting falafel with Eli. Something the matter?"

"Yes, something's the matter." She laid it out for him as brutally as possible, relishing how it soured his high. She watched the bloodshot eyes dilate with horror. Bad trip. Hah. "So that little deal we talked about?" she wound up. "Eli's Uzis?" Richard was nodding like a surfer-dude bobblehead. "Well, it's going down tomorrow. And we need a brother to make the drop."

"A brother?"

"You know—black person—Negro—colored guy? One of those. Otherwise the Panthers won't play ball."

"Got it. Chocolate mule." Whereupon the door opened, and Eli and Sam walked in.

Kim looked from one to other, held up a hand, and darted into the bathroom. She rummaged for pills. Aspirin—Valium—anything to calm her down.

When she returned to the living room, the three guys were slumped side by side on the sofa. The three fucking stooges. At least Richard had killed the music and snuffed out the joint.

Sam stood but when he saw her expression sat down again. "Jesus, Kim. Richard told us about the—about what happened. Are you sure it was Lee in there? I mean—"

"What do you care?" she spat in his face. "You weren't part of it."

"I'm sorry, Kim. Sorry for you. This is—"

"Sorry!" She was screaming. "Sorry everything's fucked to shit? Sorry my people got blown up? You're *sorry*? *Sorry!* Why didn't you say something before, Sam? You knew what I was up to. It was no secret. But you did nothing. You said nothing. You never lifted a finger, never tried to stop me—not once. You made believe it wasn't real. Lee told me I had to get rid of you unless you joined up with us. No shit. But I was too nice to listen. Too stupid. Now Lee's gone and my entire fucking life is ruined—and *now* you care?"

"You're blaming *me*? I was supposed to—what?—talk you out of it?"

The little catch in his voice was gasoline. "ME ME ME. All

you ever think about. Pity me. Love me. Take care of me. Be my girlfriend. You're so full of shit, Sam. You just want to get into a good college so you can sell out and make a bundle of money. You won't sacrifice anything for anyone. Ever! Not one fucking thing." Richard and Eli slid off the couch and tried to slink into the bedroom, but she rounded on them. "Cowards! Motherfuckers! I can't believe I cooked for you two assholes." She stomped over to the plastic table and upended it. Dishes, roaches, weed bag, ashes, album covers, plastic forks, and beer bottles cascaded to the floor. "Clean it up, bitch!" she screamed. No one made a move. "Oh no, let the *girl* do it—that's what they're for." Richard kicked through the debris and Eli followed him into the bedroom. The door clicked shut. Now it was just Sam. He sat there paralyzed on the sofa, his eyes begging for mercy. But Kim was just getting started. She stood over him. Was he going to cry? Sweet innocent little Sammy Stein—the last romantic. Bullshit. As it turned out, Sam was everything she hated. He was a chauvinist pig, just like all the others. He wanted to bind and gag her. His little woman. He didn't care about her—he just wanted to brag to the boys. Look at my girlfriend. Isn't she cute? She fucks me then she brings me breakfast in bed. She thinks I'm a real man. One day she's gonna have my babies. Eyes blazing, they stared at each other. "I know you want to hit me. Isn't that how you boys fight it out?" She took a step closer. With the nail of her forefinger she scratched a white ragged path across his chin. "If you were worth anything, you'd let me have it." Sam put the tips of his fingers on her stomach and pushed her away—but she was back, swinging a slap against the side of his face. He made no move to defend himself. She hit him again. "*I hate you, Samuel Stein!* I never want to see you as long as I live!" She turned her back, stomped over to the bedroom door, and flung it open. Richard was on the bed with his arms crossed behind his head. Eli, curled up on the floor mattress, was reading a magazine. They stared up at her without moving, their eyes round. She could smell their sweat. "You think this is a game but it's not," she said, watching them shrink. Her voice rose, quavering, but she kept herself from shrieking. "This is war—them or us—there's no middle." She drilled her eyes into Richard's. "Don't forget tomorrow. Tell him." She shifted her gaze to Eli. Then she slammed the bedroom door behind her and was gone.

ELI WAS ALREADY SNORING, but Richard couldn't sleep. There was a light burning in the other room—the yellow strip glowed on the floor—so he slipped off the bed, stepped over Eli, opened the bedroom door, and shut it again behind him. Sam was huddled on his mattress in fetal position, arms clamped around his head, shoulders trembling.

"You still alive?" he asked softly. No answer. "What you need now," he went on, moving to the kitchen, "is a visit from our friend Jack."

"No," Sam mumbled into his arm. "No company." But Richard was already sitting beside him on the mattress with two jelly glasses half full of Jack Daniel's. He grabbed Sam's shoulder and shook it until he wriggled away and sat up. "Drink. Don't sip—just pound it back, man." Sam did as he was told, then he quivered all over as if he was going to sneeze—or puke. Richard was already pouring another shot. "Salud—down the hatch!"

"God, what is that stuff—turpentine?" Sam sputtered.

"Jack Daniel's, buddy—a friend indeed for a friend in need." They settled back side by side, letting the flames subside. Richard stretched and cracked his ankles. "So." He prodded Sam with a knee. "Wanna talk about it?"

Sam stared into his empty glass. "No." He sighed. Long pause. "I can't believe she blamed me."

"Forget it. That was crazy talk, man. She was out of her head—I mean, who wouldn't be, under the circumstances?" Sam shrugged. Another silence. Another sigh.

"She's right," Sam finally said almost inaudibly. "I'm never gonna amount to shit. I'm nothing—always have been—always will be."

"If *you're* nothing . . ."

"You don't *understand*, Richard. You've got all these cool friends. You know about music. Your father's famous. I mean, look at how you wowed Leon. You *stand* for something. You . . . Kim . . . even Eli. But I don't have a cause—I don't have a girlfriend—all I've got are my fucking report cards and SAT scores."

"I'm going to prove how wrong you are. Okay? Quick—answer without thinking—just say whatever pops into your head. What would you do if you got drafted?"

"Go to Canada."

"What would you lay down your life for—country, idea, movement?"

"Israel."

"Seriously? You'd throw Uncle Sam under the bus for a bunch of crazed Hebrews?"

"I dunno. It's what popped into my head. I mean, without a homeland, the Jews don't stand a chance. Look at history—the Holocaust—"

"Eli will die of joy. And, buddy, I gotta say, you're gonna look *so* sexy in your IDF uniform." Sam jabbed him with an elbow. "Hey, I made you smile. One for the team. What about a person? If you had to die for someone, who would it be? Don't think."

"Tutu."

Richard shook his head. "You'd choose the *maid* over your *mother*?"

"She saved my life once. When I was little. I totally owe her."

Richard shoved his face into Sam's. *"My baby!"* he wailed. Sam covered his face with his hands, but Richard kept talking. "Your brother Ron told me the whole story in like junior high. He was laughing his ass off. We both were."

"It's not funny. Tutu's the only one who's ever looked out for me. Still is." He turned away. "Okay, now your turn. What would you die for? Quick."

"Drugs," Richard shot back. "Oh wait, drugs and sex. No—drugs, sex, and rock 'n' roll."

"God, Richard, you're even shallower than I thought."

"You only go around once, man." Richard let his bare leg brush against Sam's—they were both in their underwear. "You might as well have a sweet ride. I'm going out high"—he stretched his arms over his head—"and mighty."

They lay on their backs and stared at the ceiling. Then Sam, without prodding, started up again. "What I said about Israel, you know, dying for a cause? Never gonna happen. That's not who I am. Not how my brain works. I don't know how to explain it—I'm not abstract. What matters to me is not ideology but people—*life*—the holiness of life. There's this line from a Wordsworth poem that I love: 'With an eye made quiet by the power of harmony, and the deep power of joy, we see into the life of things.' That's my—I don't know—mission. *To see into the life of things*. I feel like the only time I come close is when I'm out in nature. Does that make me evil? To love nature? To want to save the world from being paved and drilled into oblivion? The power of harmony:

that's *my* revolution. So yeah, I guess Kim nailed me. I do want a girlfriend. I wanna live someplace beautiful. I want kids—kids are cool! I want to travel. I want to meet amazing people and hear their stories and maybe write about them. I know it sounds lame—but I've got principles too. I hate the war in Vietnam as much as Kim does. I hate Nixon and the bombing. What cops are doing to black people in every city of this country is criminal—and yes, the Panthers are the only ones trying to stop it. I'm not saying we should turn our backs on all of that and hide out in the woods. We have to keep marching. Resisting. Organizing. Whatever. But blow shit up? Shoot cops? Decide who lives and who dies? That's just wrong. That's what *they* do. We're better than that."

Sam was gasping. His face was red and tears were leaking from the corners of his eyes. Richard lay beside him, listening to him breathe, watching his stomach rise and fall under the T-shirt. "You know." He rolled toward Sam. Heat was radiating from him. "You should write all that down."

"Yeah, right."

"No, seriously, man. It's important." Richard felt himself get hard. *Never try to fuck your buddy*, a little voice whispered in his head. But this was different. Sam was hurting. This would be *good* for him. "You know," he whispered into Sam's neck. "One day, when you're in your big house in the country—with the garden and the little woman and the kids jumping up and down on your lap"—he hooked Sam's T-shirt and drew it up—"you'll look back on this night—and you're gonna be grateful. . . ."

"You're creeping me out." Sam squirmed away. "It's not nice to make fun of someone when they're down. . . ."

"Oh, you want nice?" Richard skimmed his forefinger across Sam's undies and outlined the shape imprisoned inside. He felt Sam shudder. "I can be nice." He went very, very slowly. "So nice."

His fingertips plowed the runnel of muscle feathered with down. When he got to the bulge at the edge of the elastic, he went crazy. "Never forget this," he breathed. "Beautiful"—he wiggled the tip of a pinkie into Sam's spigot—"something beautiful we can do for each other"—circled the head with the pad of his thumb—"and no one ever has to know. . . . We're free, Sam—anything's allowed. . . . But"—rising, he rolled Sam over on his back and sat on him—"I gotta come first. . . . Otherwise . . ." (*Otherwise you're never going to let me near you again.*) "Please—trust me. . . ."

Sam tried to topple him.

Richard reached for the gap in his undies. "You know you want to see it."

"I already have," Sam managed to gasp. "Don't you remember?"

"Yeah, well, it's grown some since then." Richard wriggled free of his undies and there it was in all its glory. He pinned Sam's shoulders with his knees. Sam had that same dazed expression Richard remembered from when they were kids and he had lured little Sammy to his bedroom one sweaty summer afternoon and locked him in to play strip poker. By the time they were down to their tighty whities, Richard was hard as a rock. Sam bugged his eyes when Richard took it out and bounced it at him. "Go on—grab on—it's not going to bite," he taunted. But Sam—he couldn't have been more than ten—just gaped like an idiot. That dumb stricken look. Who knows what would have happened if the Rineses' damn maid hadn't started pounding on the door?

Richard moved it against Sam's lips. "Take it."

"No."

"You're killing me, man." He clamped a hand around Sam's jaw and started to twist his head side to side. Gently, slowly. "Let's finish what we started."

"No." Through clenched teeth.

Richard's blood was singing in his ears. "Yes." Anything to get inside. "You wanted it then—you want it now. Be a good boy, Sammy." He flattened his palm over Sam's face and pushed. He felt Sam's lips part and then the teeth sinking into the fleshy mound below his thumb. "You little . . ." Richard, recoiling, balled his hand into a fist—but before he slammed it into Sam's jaw, the kid was up and off the bed and barricaded in the bathroom. "Mother fucker," Richard heard him shouting over and over behind the locked door.

The pain drove Richard wilder. He brought himself off, moaning and writhing, all over Sam's mattress. He had it coming. Then he rolled over on his back, and in that spent instant everything clicked into place. *We need a brother to make the drop*. Richard suddenly knew who. Pure genius. *Never fails—I always get my best ideas with a cock in my fist.*

JESUS CHRIST!

Sam sat on the toilet lid with his face in his hands and those two words pounding over and over in his skull.

Jesus Christ!

Little cartoons bubbled up and spliced together behind his shut eyes. Richard's stiff cock waving under his nose. Fourteen-year-old Richard tracing a line with his finger between his little-boy nipples. Leon's voice in church vibrating inside his chest. Tutu crying her eyes out the day JFK was assassinated. Kim taking his dick in her hand and planting it between her legs. His mother flapping her hands between him and his furious father at the dinner table, trying to put out the fire burning between them.

Was he queer?

Jesus Christ!

He would have done it. He was hard the whole time. The first time he told Richard no he didn't mean it. It would have served Kim right. *Free love, you know? Don't be so fucking conventional.* She'd probably fucked Richard herself, for all he knew. Revenge sex. But then, right before he surrendered, something killed the current. He was ten years old again and locked in Richard's bedroom while the maid pounded on the door: "What you boys doing in there?" In a heartbeat he went from wanting Richard to wanting to kill him. The heat coming off his body was suffocating. The smell of his sweat made him sick. He gagged at the idea of that meat in his mouth. *Cocksucker.* Maybe he was just scared. He didn't care. He didn't think. He just had to get away.

Were there any bridges left to burn?

Sam raked his fingers through his hair, got up from the shitter, and met his face in the mirror. He stared at the bloodshot eyes, the red stubble dust on his chin, the blotchy freckles. He could practically hear Tutu's voice: "I *told* you to stay away from that boy."

Now what?

He could slink home with his tail between his legs, ask forgiveness, move back to his room, and finish the school year. He could track down Kim and beg her to take him with her down revolutionary road. He could sneak up on Richard while he slept and smother him with a pillow. He could jump out the window and be done with it all.

Kill yourself because your girlfriend slapped you and your roommate wanted a blow job? What a pussy.

When he figured the coast was clear, he crept out of the bathroom. He kicked the foul sheets off the mattress and collapsed. He had to make a plan. Tomorrow was Saturday. He'd call Leon first thing—tell him he was in trouble, needed a place to crash. But what about Tutu? She'd be back in Harlem that night. What if she threw him out—or told his parents? No way was he going back home. He'd have to blow town. He could hitchhike to Vermont—to the place where they skied. There had to be a commune somewhere around there—there were tons of communes in Vermont. He knew how to grow stuff! He'd be a natural on a commune. Sam shut his eyes and conjured up a big rambling white clapboard farmhouse, hippie girls with braids baking bread in the kitchen and little blond kids chasing each other around the porch. Morning glory vines twining up the columns. Apple trees blooming in the orchard. Plowed fields stretching out to hazy blue hills. *Welcome to Eden, Sam.* Yeah, except that up in Vermont it was still the dead of winter.

Sam found a pen and opened his notebook. GAME PLAN, he wrote at the top of a blank page. *Move out tomorrow—no matter what,* he scribbled. He left the tip of the pen on the page until the ink blotted. Nothing. He was alone. He'd failed at everything. The world hated him. Even his parents were happy he was gone. Tutu and Leon would tell him to pray—but he didn't believe in their God. He didn't believe in anything. Except pain. That was the one true thing. Sam dropped the notebook, went into the kitchen, yanked open a drawer, and pulled out a long skinny knife that had been sharpened to the vanishing point. He took it back to his bed, sat down, grabbed the worn bone handle in his right fist, and set the blade down on the string of vein that threaded his left wrist. He pressed until a tiny red bubble surfaced on the skin. *Deeper?*

He sat there, transfixed, until the bubble broke and pooled around the tip of the blade. Before he could decide what to do next, he heard the bedroom door open and Eli tiptoed out and into the bathroom. Sam dropped the knife, blotted his wrist on his bare thigh, turned off the lamp, and pulled a blanket over his head.

Chapter Twenty-One

Richard and Eli were still asleep when he left the apartment. He'd be back later for his stuff—right now he just needed out. He couldn't imagine what he'd say to Richard and he didn't care. *Let's finish what we started.* Well, it was finished now.

Sam crossed Tompkins Square Park and headed west on Tenth Street. It was one of those days when everyone on the street treated him like he was invisible. Pedestrians jostled him, trod on the backs of his sneakers, jabbed his ribs with their elbows. It was like he'd become a ghost, a disembodied spirit. Maybe he had. March was a week old, and though the cold was still fierce, the light was brighter, whiter, more penetrating. Rusted fire escapes zigzagged from the brick tenement façades like abstract art installations. Saturday—but people were already rushing up and down the avenues on their mysterious urgent business. Everybody but Sam. He was down to his last twenty with no idea where he was going to get more. *What the fuck*, as Richard would say.

He went in the first diner he came to, sat at the counter, and ordered up the three-grease special—eggs, bacon, and hash browns. It was too early to call Leon or anyone else. For company, he had *Crime and Punishment* and his notebook. He flipped open the novel, tried to pick it up where he'd left off, and quit after reading the same sentence five times. He cracked the notebook and, while shoveling in the grease with his left hand, started writing.

Everything happens for a reason—that's what my grandmother always said. God's plan, I guess. His will be done on earth as it is in heaven. So there has to be a reason for all the shit that's going down right now. The brownstone explosion. Kim's rage. Richard's—what should I call it—attempted rape? uncontrollable lust for my irresistible ass? Random events—or—or what? The hand of God? The end? The beginning?

Maybe this is what a revolution feels like. Attack and counterattack. Incidents and accidents. Fire and backfire. Fire—seriously? Is this the moment of truth when the Movement morphs into a real revolution—with guns and bombs and blood running in the street? Or are Kim and her cronies just fantasizing like a bunch of—well, like a bunch of students who don't know shit about shit and have no idea of how little they know?

Which is it?

There's no doubt that something's happening. Something that maybe has never happened before. It's in the air—in the water—in the clouds blowing off the dark fields of the republic—in the grit ground under our heels on every sidewalk. We're different—from them—from our parents, our teachers, even from the kids who don't have a clue and maybe never will. You can tell who's on which side just by the vibration. Our brains are wired differently. We hear the weeping guitar, they hear noise. We see beauty, they see money. We want peace, they want law and order. They tell us we are privileged, but we don't want our privilege. We want to be free. We are free. FEEL FREE—that should be our battle cry.

But is it really a battle or just a mood?

Sam put his pen down and looked around at the men hunched over the counter beside him. The guy to his left—fortyish, balding, paunchy—was reading the *Times*, and there it was, above the fold right smack on the front page: A grainy shot of a smoking crater on a downtown block under the headline: TOWN HOUSE RAZED BY BLAST AND FIRE. Jesus. Until now, Sam had half-believed Kim was making it up. When he tried to read over his shoulder, the guy glared nastily and twitched the paper away. *Excuse me, sir,* Sam wanted to say, *but do you think the time is right for violent revolution?* He buried his head back in the notebook and kept writing while the food congealed on his plate.

Everything's connected: the war in Vietnam, the systematic state-sanctioned slaughter of America's black men, corporate greed, imperialistic expansion. The media. The message. Everything's connected, but extreme polarization makes it impossible to tell truth from lies. Let's say Kim's got it right. Let's say there is a revolution—that Kim succeeds in uniting the Panthers and the Weatherman and together they bring down pig-state Amerikkka. Then what? Huey Newton becomes president? Abbie Hoffman secretary of state? Do they even have a plan beyond blowing everything up? Have they stopped to consider that a bunch of kids might not have the experience to run a country? Maybe they're all just crazy—delusional—spellbound by all the media attention—victims of their own fantastical groupthink? It's happened before—it could be happening now. The coming days will tell.

I know it sounds weird, but I think what's at the heart of this revolution is the same thing that tore the country apart in the Civil War: slavery. Only this time it's not just the enslavement of black by white. This is an uprising against every kind of slavery. The enslavement of poor by rich. The enslavement of the third world by the first. The enslavement of gay by straight. The enslavement of women by men. The enslavement of men by their own manly bullshit. The enslavement of everybody by money—or lack of money. Internal and external slavery. Mental and economic slavery. If we can end all of those slaveries, if each one of us can free ourselves, if we can love another, then and only then will we truly be free.

But it has to be universal. No one's free if anyone's enslaved.

I keep coming back to Tutu and Leon. Tutu was born with nothing and she'll die with nothing but she has a kind of power—the power of her voice. Leon is an invisible grocery store bagger, but his singing can break your heart and heal your soul. Why aren't they free? Like I told Richard last

> *night—it all comes down to the power of harmony. Not unison but harmony. Voices blending into something bigger, fuller, higher, more inspiring than any single voice could ever reach by itself. Every voice equal—not the same but equally valued. That's the real revolution. If Leon is as free on the street as he is in his church, if Tutu's as powerful in the dining room as she is in the kitchen, then we've won.*
>
> *We will win. We have to. The world is going to be ours. We will inherit, whether they like it or not. We have started this revolution—peaceful or violent remains to be seen—and the world to come will never be the same. We'll never be the same. We can't be stopped. We're everywhere. Without real leaders or a clear ideology, we have spontaneously risen up, taken power into our own hands, refashioned the world. In fifty years, when they look back, they might hail us or hate us. But one thing is certain: this era, this year, this season, this moment unfolding around us right now is the dividing line between before and after.*

Sam covered page after page, never lifting the pen. He let it gush from his fingertips. He forgot about Richard. He forgot about Vermont. He forgot to call Leon. *I don't have the answers*, he scrawled. *But at least I'm asking the questions. Taking it in and getting it down. This is what I live for.*

RICHARD PICKED UP ON THE first ring.

"Are you alone?" Kim didn't even bother with hello.

"Just me and Eli—Sam was gone before I got up. No idea where he is." *Crawling back to mommy if I had to guess.* His hand still hurt from the bite. What if Sam had given him rabies?

"All right. Good. It's going down this afternoon—four o'clock—north end of Central Park. They'll pay you three K—not a penny more. You ready?"

"You know it." *Jesus, could they even get the guns out of the warehouse by then?*

"What about the mule?"

"Leon'll be there."

"*Leon?*" Kim gasped. "*Sam's* Leon? Tutu's grandkid? *That* Leon?"

Richard felt the blood pounding in his ears, but he kept his voice steady. "He's perfect. Got a car—clean record—one hundred percent certified Negro."

There was a pause while she turned it over. "Cool," she finally exhaled. "Everybody comes out ahead. Okay. They'll be in a late-model black Olds. Right where Lenox enters the park."

"He'll be there." *What if he says no?* There was no Plan B.

"Okay."

"Sweetheart, you're going to be the queen of the underground."

"Don't fuck me over, Richard. Everything's riding on this." God, if Sam ever found out.

"Don't sweat it, Kim. Inconspicuous-looking car—Leon at the wheel—and *you know what* in the trunk. It's covered."

"It better be."

LEON WAS ABOUT TO TAKE a shower when the phone rang. "Leon, my man, Richard Rines here." *Who?* "You know—Sammy Stein's roommate?"

It took a moment to click. "The producer's son."

"Bingo. In fact, that's what I'm calling about. I've been thinking over what we talked about last night—you know, introducing you to my dad—maybe set up an audition?"

"No *way*." Leon beamed, dancing from foot to foot.

"*Totally* way. Your voice is amazing, man. But first" —static nipped at his ear— "I was wondering if you could do a little driving job for us."

"Us?"

"Dad, actually. There's this crate of LPs that never got delivered—Aretha's latest album—and you know how hot Aretha is right now. Well, all the regular company drivers are tied up this weekend, and when I told Dad about you . . . and how you have a car and everything . . ."

"My uncle's car."

"Right. But if you could borrow it—and get those records from the warehouse and bring them into town—Dad would like totally owe you."

"Owe *me*?" Leon tensed. That's not how it worked.

"With Dad, it's all about favors. He never forgets. This will be your foot in the door—the rest is up to you."

"Wow. You sure don't waste any time, Richard." But he was wondering: Why *me*?

"Like I say, those records are flying off the shelf—"

"So when do you need this job done?"

"Today? Like this afternoon?"

Leon thought it over. It sounded kinda fishy, but what did he have to lose? He had the day off from the supermarket and he still had the keys to his uncle's car. Granny would kill him if she ever found out, but she wasn't due home until that night. "Shouldn't be a problem," he finally said.

He could hear the hard swallow on the other end of the line. "Cool. Cool."

"So where exactly am I driving?"

"Teaneck, New Jersey. But don't worry, my cousin Eli will go with you—he works in the warehouse part-time. You just pick him up in front of the Orange Julius on the corner of Broadway and 181st Street—right by the entrance to the bridge. Say two o'clock? He'll make sure you find it."

"Sounds like a plan."

"And of course we'll pay you. I think Dad said three hundred bucks—once you make the drop."

"The drop?"

"You know"—more static—"deliver the records."

"Right. Wow. Thank you, Richard. Orange Julius. Broadway and 181st Street. Two o'clock this afternoon. I'll be there."

"Groovy, man. You're not gonna regret this."

Leon hung up the phone and clapped his palms together. First the Rabbi—then Irv Rines—and now the money for the demo. Everything was coming together. Leon stretched his neck as long as it would go, raised his eyes, and whispered to the ceiling: "Thank you, Lord, for answering my prayers."

KIM PUSHED DOWN THE CRADLE, let it up again, fed in another dime, and dialed Jesse's number. Jesse was in the Weather Bureau—central leadership—one of the higher-ups. They weren't supposed to communicate by phone—too risky—but Kim was desperate. She was on the verge of giving up when Jesse answered. "Heading out the door," he said. "We're meeting at Diomedes Diner on Fourteenth. Those who are left."

"Lee?" Kim breathed.

"Gone. Her and two others—everybody's freaked. You need to be there. War council."

The diner was ten blocks uptown so she started walking. *War council*—Jesus. Those guys were so full of themselves. Too bad they sucked at revolution. Until yesterday, Kim had thought Lee knew everything about everything—but it turns out she didn't know shit about making explosives. The bomb she gave Kim to plant in the downtown draft center had also misfired. It was set to go off at midnight when the Whitehall Street office building was dark and empty, but instead the fucking thing blew up in a cleaning lady's face at nine o'clock. Kim only found out about it because she'd gone down there after slamming out on Sam. She'd had a bad feeling after the town house blast, so she decided she better return to the scene of the crime. Though it wasn't a crime—it was a necessary act of revolutionary provocation. Or that's what it was supposed to be. It was nearly midnight by the time she got there but the street was pulsing with ambulances and police car lights. Kim lingered in the shadows outside the building for as long as she dared, eavesdropping on the cops and emergency crew. The bomb evidently blew when the cleaning lady jostled it. A piece of shrapnel lodged in her right eye and blinded her. Of course she had to be black and the mother of four children. Now her blood was on Kim's hands. Not to mention that she'd be in federal prison for the rest of her life if the pigs ever caught her. After that, she couldn't sleep—and anyway, where would she go? So she killed the night making the rounds of greasy spoons, fighting off horny assholes, trying not to think, not to blame herself, not to crack. When it got light enough to see, she found a pay phone and made the calls. First Jeff. Then Richard. Then Jesse, who told her about the war council—as if those turkeys knew anything about fighting a war.

Kim barely breathed as she darted through the East Village

streets, randomly changing direction, ducking in and out of shops and alleys. When she got near the diner, she melted into the shadow of a recessed doorway across the street so she could scope things out without being seen. You couldn't be too careful—especially now. Diomedes looked like every other shopfront on Fourteenth Street—foul, run-down, sleazy, and depressing. The last place the FBI would come looking for surviving Weathermen. No one entering or leaving; no cars idling nearby; no undercover agents (though how would she know?) in evidence. So she crossed the street and pushed her way inside. They were already there—six of them hunched around a booth, five guys and a pretty dark-haired girl Kim didn't recognize. She scooted her butt aside to make room for Kim. The men barely looked at her.

She'd missed the beginning, but it made no difference because no matter who was speaking, every other sentence was the same: "I still can't fucking believe it."

"Is there any question—any shred of possibility?"

"Zilch. You gotta face facts, man. It's over."

"I still can't fucking believe it."

"The first bloodshed—now it's real."

"We should have tried to stop it."

"This is war. You can't stop a war."

"You think the pigs could have blown the place up—like a preemptive strike?"

"No way. The bomb went off accidentally—there's no other explanation."

"You know, the last time I talked to Lee she wasn't a hundred percent."

"Meaning?"

"Meaning she was having second thoughts about the nails. About killing that many innocent—"

"*Nobody's* innocent. Not one fucking white person in this country is innocent."

"So what are you saying? She blew herself up to save *them*?"

"It's a theory."

"Well, as a theory it sucks."

"So what's the plan now?"

"I'll tell you this much—any one of you tries to bail, and you're done."

"What are you going to do—pop us with your BB gun?"

"Cool it, you two. Fighting's not going to bring them back."

"No, fighting is the *only* thing that will bring them back. Fighting the pigs."

"We gotta get out of here. All of us. Lie low for a couple of weeks. I know this place upstate. . . ."

"I have a friend in the Seattle cell. . . ."

"Berkeley is my choice. Anyone have a car?"

Kim felt a knee riding up between her legs. Jesus—these guys were apes.

"I've got some more bad news, as if we needed any," she broke in. All heads swiveled toward her. Kim took a deep breath and told them about the induction center misfire.

"That sucks."

"Everything sucks."

"At least the cleaning lady didn't die—one eye, right?"

"Means and ends—it's a trade-off."

"Yeah—but . . ." It was no use. No one was listening. To these guys, Kim was invisible—except when they were trying to fuck her.

They broke half an hour later. The plan was to blow town and hide out upstate for a while. They'd need two cars. No one even asked Kim if she was in. Just as well. Her deal with the Panthers was the game changer. These guys had no clue.

She and the other girl left together—Deedee was her name. A couple of years older than Kim by the looks of her, long shiny brown hair, high cheekbones, and slanting feline eyes, one green, one blue.

"How do you stand them?" Kim asked her as soon as they were out of earshot.

Deedee laughed. "I don't." She looked Kim up and down, reassessing. "Were you and Lee tight?"

"I guess." Kim paused. "I mean, I barely knew her—but she was everything. She was who I wanted to be."

"Yeah, same here." They fell into step on the sidewalk. "So are you going upstate to their hideout?"

Kim shook her head. "Got some business to attend to first—then—who knows?"

"Need a place to crash? Cause if you do, you're welcome to hang out at our collective. The Radical Sisterhood. Women's liberation, honey, that's the *real* revolution. We're never going to be free until we free ourselves of their chauvinist bullshit."

"Right on to that, sister."

"Why don't you come check it out? It's just around the corner." Deedee flashed her a lopsided grin. "You look like you could use some sleep."

Kim felt the knot between her eyes relax for the first time in two days. Sam. Richard. Eli. Jesse. If she never saw another man again as long as she lived, she would die in peace. *Women's liberation: count me in.*

Chapter Twenty-Two

Eli had been in New York six months now but he still didn't really know his way around. Tenth Street—Tenth Avenue—uptown—downtown: who could tell the difference? Everything was *up* in New York. Up, high, straight, crowded, and dirty. Wherever he went, it all looked the same. If he needed to get someplace, Eli just tagged after Richard. But not this time. "If we were seen together it would totally blow the deal," Richard told him. "Ever since I blabbed in Max's, those mafia goons have been tailing me all over town. But you're in the clear, man. You just need to connect with Leon and everything will be cool." Richard spread out a tattered subway map and showed him the route. He made him repeat the details so many times that finally Eli lost his patience. "Stop to worry," he shouted, "I was in the army."

"Yeah, smoking dope and stealing guns."

"No *stealing*—I was given."

"Whatever. Just remember: you can't trust anyone. Not even

Leon. As soon as those brothers hand him the cash, grab it and take off. Got it?"

"Got it."

"And don't forget, Leon thinks this is about *records*. You know—music, singing, rock 'n' roll, boogie-woogie? The less you say to him the better."

"My lips are smeared."

"Good—keep it that way." They clattered down the steps together. Eli reached for the knob of the battered front door, but Richard stopped him. "When we hit the street, don't turn around or wave or anything. Just keep moving, okay?"

"Okay."

"All right. See you back here at five o'clock. Six at the latest." Eli snapped off a mock salute. "And don't come back without the cash, cuz."

SAM HAD TO GO BACK there at some point to get his stuff, but he couldn't face it yet. The prospect of seeing Richard made his stomach turn. It was a nice day, sunny, not too cold, so after breakfast, he started walking, randomly following his feet. He got as far as the New York Coliseum at Columbus Circle. "New York Flower Show" proclaimed the big black letters on the marquee. "Spring Is Here!" When he was a kid, Sam used to go to the flower show every year with his father. Love of plants was one of the few things he and his dad shared: coaxing seedlings from the earth, watching the tomato vines climb the trellis, tugging (gently) at the ripe fruit—not to eat (Sam hated vegetables) but to admire and show off to his mother and Tutu. Growing stuff was Sam's baseball—something that came naturally, that he was good at and liked to do. Then Dirty Face started calling him a pansy and he quit. All that remained was the yearly trip to the flower show. And here he was again, like a homing pigeon. Sam stood on the sidewalk outside the Coliseum as people converged from every direction; without thinking, he let himself be swept into the flow. The lobby was warm, and the hyacinth smell he so loved as a child was still there, though with undertones of cigarette smoke and cheap perfume he hadn't noticed as a child. He was about to join the ticket line when he spotted the price list posted beside the windows: Admission: Adults $10, Children under 12 $5. So much for that. He beat his way back against the human current until he was free. Free to do what? Try Leon again? Head to Vermont? Take the train uptown and wait for Tutu outside her building? What did it matter? No one anywhere was thinking about him, waiting for him, wondering where he was. It was like he'd been erased. Edited out of existence. He stood on the sidewalk with his hands in his pockets and his chin on his chest while pedestrians rushed around and through him as if he were a ghost.

KIM WOKE TO THE SOUND of voices weaving around her head. Where was she? Whose clothes were these? She was about to panic—then the memory rose to the surface: she was in the loft/squat of the Radical Sisterhood women's collective. Deedee had brought her here after breakfast when she confessed she'd been up all night. Deedee insisted she use the shower, borrow an outfit, and catch some winks on the sofa. She must have fallen seriously asleep. What time was it? Kim lay there in a daze, staring at the flaking paint on the pressed tin ceiling and listening to the voices at the other end of the huge room. A kettle whistled and went silent. The kitchen?

"Wait—you *slept* with him?"

"Just once—though we weren't exactly sleeping."

"Did you suspect anything?"

"Nothing. I totally thought he was one of us—just another horny rad with a fro. Jew-fro."

"What? He's Jewish?"

"Jewish, Italian, black—Jeff is anything he wants to be."

Jeff? Fro? Kim sat up and shook the sleep out of her head.

"Who outed him?"

"It was just one of those things, you know. Brianna totally had the hots for him—I have to say he was a pretty good fuck—so when he kept blowing her off, she decided to, you know, stalk him. Find out what he was up to. You're not going to believe this, but she actually broke into his apartment."

"Seriously?"

"Seriously. I think she did some guerrilla training when she was in Havana. Anyway, she rifled through his stuff—and that's how she discovered that radical Jeff is an FBI pig."

"An informant?"

"More like a plant. Brianna found his college yearbook. Get this—Jeff went to Princeton. The FBI must have recruited him in college because he looks so—you know, radical scruffy. He passes for black on account of the fro, but Jeff's as black as my Great Aunt Fanny. Still, you gotta hand it to the dude—he infiltrated the Panthers, which is fuckin' hard to do."

At which point Kim was on her feet and bulleting back to the kitchen. "Excuse me for butting in"—she had her hands in the air like it was a stickup—"but are you two talking about Jeff the Red? Tall skinny guy with a red Afro out to here? Part black, part white, part whatever?"

"The very one. You know him too?"

"And you're saying he's an FBI plant? One of *them*—and he's infiltrated the Panthers?"

"That's the word on the street. Just came down the pipeline. You can't trust anyone these days, know what I mean?"

Kim's heart began to race. "What time is it?

"One thirty. Why? Someplace you need to be?"

"Oh god" was all she said. "Oh Jesus god. I'll be back—I can't explain now." She grabbed her bag off the couch and ran for the door.

CRAZY CITY, CRAZY COUNTRY, ELI muttered under his breath as he strode toward the subway. Six months was enough—more than enough. Once he had his share of the money, he'd be on the next plane back to Tel Aviv. He missed the sun. He missed the beach. He missed Hebrew. He missed the beautiful tan girls. He even missed his family. "New York is so exciting!" everyone said before he left. But he was finished with excitement. He was ready to go back. But first . . .

Step one: turn left, go five blocks, look for the Eighth Street station, get on the uptown train. He walked with his arms pinned to his sides so no one jostled him on the way—no mean feat on these mean streets. Were New Yorkers blind? Eli hated how they were always poking their shoulders and elbows into him—and then glaring like it was his fault. He had his pistol—a nice little Beretta Pico—zipped into the right pocket of his parka and he didn't want to risk having someone brush up against the spiny lump. "Hey, muthafucka, what you got in there—a gun?" Next thing he knew, there'd be a crowd pointing and shouting: "Look out—that guy's got a gun—somebody call the police." *Po-leese*. Crazy land!

But with thieves and murderers and junkies crawling all over the streets, you'd have to be a crazy *not* to carry a gun. What was the big deal? In Israel everyone had a gun and knew how to use it. After his two-year stint in the army, Eli was the best shot in his unit. "I can't believe that fuckup numero uno turned out to be our prize sniper," his major had marveled. Which explained why Richard tapped him to seal this little deal. That was bullshit about being tailed by the mafia. Richard wanted a marksman. Nobody had to know about the pistol unless he needed it. And tomorrow, before he went back to Israel, he'd give it to Kim if she wanted it.

Now there was a piece of work, Eli thought as he stepped on the train—*five stops, get off at Times Square, find the long dark tunnel, transfer to the A express.* Kim would be perfect in the Israeli army—if it wasn't for her politics. Small as she was, she knew how to look after herself and she could talk circles around any guy, especially Sam. Poor Sam. He had it coming. Eli had known schmucks like Sam in the army—first they were all tortured and writing poetry and shit but after a couple of months they ditched the notebooks and got real. That's what Sam needed to do. He should be in boot camp toughening up. Instead he had to go and fall for Little Miss Mao. *Revolution my ass.* Revolution was for people at the end of their rope—people who had nothing to lose. Like the pioneers who settled Palestine. Like the concentration camp survivors. The problem with these Americans was that they had too much—too much money, too much dope, too much sex, too much freedom. Kim was always going on about power to the people but didn't she realize that as soon as people had power, they made other people suffer? The more power, the more suffering. Sam claimed that the only power he believed in was the power of the pen—and look where that got him. A gun was quicker, louder, and easier to understand. No matter the language, with a gun everyone got the message.

At Times Square, Eli wasted fifteen minutes searching for the tunnel to the A line, and when the uptown train finally pulled up, it was so packed he had to elbow his way through the door. It was like a sauna in the car, but he was too pinned in to unzip. Inches before the Fifty-Ninth Street station, the train shuddered to a stop and all the lights went out. Five minutes of limbo, then without warning the lights and the heat came roaring back on, the train crept to the station platform, and when the doors opened, all the white people stampeded off. All except Eli. That was another crazy thing about America. Everybody talked about race all the time—but it was like they were talking about strangers. Blacks and whites never hung out. They didn't live in the same neighborhoods or eat at the same restaurants. They must be scared of each other. Eli saw the way Richard and Sam tensed up when a bunch of black guys passed them on the street. What was the big deal? In Israel, color made no difference—black, white, brown, blond, freckled, Afroed, ponytailed, side curled—everyone was Jewish. Or else they were Arab, in which case they were the enemy no matter what they looked like. At least there was no phony Black Power bullshit.

At 125th Street, three brown girls in miniskirts and scuffed knee-high boots got on and attached themselves to the chrome pole next to his. Eli couldn't tell if they were high school students or hookers. Maybe both? It was obvious from the way they flashed their eyes and snorted that they were talking about him. He could only make out a couple of words, but he liked the sound of their laughter. Especially the short one in the middle with the beads braided into her hair and the boobs jutting out on either side of her bag's shoulder strap. As the train hurtled forward, Eli caught and held her eye. With one arm crooked around the pole, he swiveled toward her. "Come here often?" He'd heard Richard use the line a dozen times in bars and it never failed—but these girls just laughed harder. "Yeah—can't get enough of this place," the one with the beaded hair said snidely. Eli racked his brain for what Richard would say next. *Well, I'm here all the time and I've never seen you before. What's a pretty girl like you doing in a dive like this?* That obviously wasn't going to work. So he just beamed out his widest grin, winked, and patted the top of his head. "Your hair—so cool," he said. She looked him up and down while her friends covered their mouths and shook. "What are you, Spanish? Puerto Rican?" "Israeli," he answered, trying to get her to look at him again. "Man, you are seriously lost." *"Denise!"* one of the friends hissed at her. "Well, he *is*," she hissed back. *Just keep her talking*, Eli thought. *Maybe you can get her number.* Two stops later, the friends sat down, but Denise didn't join them. She didn't respond much to his barrage of questions but she'd quit laughing at him. The other passengers weren't staring at them anymore. By a stroke of luck, Eli and the girls got out at the same stop. He checked his watch—he still had twenty minutes before he was supposed to meet Leon. The four of them walked to the turnstile together, Eli and Denise a few steps behind. He didn't get her number but he did make a date—or tried to. The only place he could think of was the Orange Julius where Leon was supposed to pick him up. "What if we meet at Orange Julius—just us—five o'clock—yes?" By then his pockets would be bulging with cash. "Then I take you someplace nice." He said her name—*Denise*, so pretty—and smiled.

"You Israel boys don't waste any time" was all she said. But at least it wasn't no.

Chapter Twenty-Three

It was early afternoon by the time Sam got back to the apartment. Panting from the climb, he threw open the door, but the place was empty. No trace of any of them except for the faint reek of Eli's aftershave. "Pack," he said out loud, but he didn't. He needed a plan and he didn't have one. It was windy out on the street. He couldn't just wander around with his backpack. And what if Kim came back to look for him? What if she wanted to make up—get back together? "Fat chance," he said. He polished off the last of the donuts and grabbed his backpack off the hook on the wall. If worse came to worst he could always go home. His mother would take him back in a heartbeat—and even his father had probably forgiven him by now. Forgiven him for what? Being honest?

But if he went home, what would happen to Tutu?

Sam slumped back on the sofa and let his hands dangle between his knees. Tutu cared about him. She believed in him. She had devoted almost twenty years of her life to raising him. And in all that time, she'd never let him down. Not once.

But what was he to Tutu? Honestly? A bed to make. A mouth to feed. A plate to wash. A job. Maybe that's why he was having so much trouble with that story about Leon: the truth was that he didn't want to write about Leon—he wanted to *be* Leon.

"Well, that ain't gonna happen, Sammy boy," he said out loud—and the response chimed in his head: *Quit talking to yourself, child. Folks gonna think you're crazy.*

Maybe he was. Maybe all writers were crazy. Maybe you *had* to be crazy to be a writer. Look at Dostoyevsky. Look at Baudelaire. Look at Poe and Melville and Emily Freaking Dickinson. Whack jobs every last one of them. Sam brushed the donut crumbs off his notebook, shut it, and surrendered to fantasy. Someday he was going to be as famous as all of those guys. Famous and rich. He'd buy his father's company, fire his father, and let the workers take over. He'd buy Tutu a marble headstone—no, a mausoleum. He'd dedicate a novel to Kim. "To K, the first." And she'd read it and show up at his door—his penthouse suite—in tears. *Oh, Sam, I was such a fool. . . .*

He was so submerged that he nearly fell off the couch when he heard a key rattling in the lock. Top lock, dead bolt, lower lock, creaking hinges—and there was Kim, wild-eyed and pale as a cloud. Where did that weird tie-dyed blouse come from? "Oh, Sam." It was like she'd mind-read his daydream—and the next moment she was in his arms, her face against his chest, her sparrow bones trembling in his grip. "Oh god, oh god" was all she said. Then she broke away and started talking fast. "Listen, Sam, listen." She stood before him but she wouldn't look at his face. "I've done something stupid—really, really stupid—and I need your help. I can't trust anyone else and I can't fix it myself."

"Anything," he breathed.

She started to pace. "Remember those Uzis that Eli's always bragging about?" She didn't wait for an answer. "Well, we made a deal to sell them to the Panthers."

"We?"

"Okay, I made the deal—this morning—on a pay phone on St. Mark's. Only I just found out that it's a trap. It's not the Panthers but the FBI."

"What? The FBI are buying Eli's guns?"

"Not buying—seizing. I was tricked. Royally fucking tricked. God, I'm such an idiot." Pacing with both hands balled in her hair. "It never occurred to me that Jeff could be an FBI plant. COINTELPRO, they call it. Counterintelligence something blah blah bullshit. Don't ask how I know—but I found out and now I'm screwed. Instead of actual Panthers buying those Uzis, it's gonna be FBI agents masquerading as Panthers. As soon as they hand over the guns, Eli and Leon will be arrested for trafficking in stolen weapons."

"Leon?" Sam caught her and spun her. "*Tutu's* Leon?" She nodded. "What the fuck does—what did you do—don't tell me—it must have been Richard. . . ." His brain was sparking faster than his mouth could spit out the words.

"Sam." She laid her hands on his shoulders. "I don't have time to explain. Yes, it was Richard's idea to rope in Leon—but that doesn't matter now. We've got to head them off."

"We?"

"Okay—you. The FBI is onto me, remember that agent you blabbed my name to at the rally? And now there's something worse. I can't tell you. The less you know the better. They're closing in. But *you're* clean, Sam. No record. No contacts. No trace. You could head up to the park. . . ."

"What park?"

"It's all going down in Central Park at four this afternoon. But if you got there first, if you intercepted Leon, if you warned them off—"

Then you'll love me forever and the world will live as one.

"I'm sorry about last night. I'm sorry about everything. I loved you, Sam—I really did. I still love you. You're beautiful. You're brilliant. You're going to be a great writer. But . . ." Their eyes met. "But you're totally clueless. Can't you see what's going on? Everything's on fire—the whole country—Jesus, the entire world! And you had no idea. You missed it. You want to be a writer but you completely missed the story. Wake up, Sam. You have to commit to something—something bigger than having a girlfriend. I've been trying to tell—"

But whatever she was going to say got swallowed by the knocking—pounding—on the apartment door. "Open up!" a voice boomed. "Law enforcement."

"Shit. Shit shit shit," Kim seethed. "Four o'clock. North end of Central Park where Lenox comes in. They'll be in a black Olds." She was moving toward the window.

"Wait!" Sam shouted. Kim opened the window. Sam started to tremble. "Kim—*please*," he was crying and begging. "Whatever you did, it's not worth . . ." but she was already out the window and onto the fire escape. Up, not down.

LEON GOT A BAD FEELING as soon as Eli sat down in the car. The guy had weird hair, his aftershave smelled like roach spray, and half of what he said was impossible to understand. "Turn zhere—change zeh lane!" Whoever taught him English had left out "please," "thank you," and "excuse me." But once they crossed the bridge into Jersey, Leon settled in at the wheel and let Eli talk. The guy obviously liked to run his mouth—even more than Sam—and he wouldn't shut up about some girl he just met on the subway.

"Brown like you, Leo."

"It's Leon."

"And so warm—"

"Hot, you mean?"

"Yes. A hot brown chicken."

"How come you're running after our folks? White girls aren't good enough for you?"

"Of course!" Eli roared. "White—black—pink—who cares the color?"

"Okay, okay, I get it. You like the ladies." Leon sized him up out of the corner of his eyes. Compared to Richard, Eli was a toad—but you never knew what girls saw.

"Eight—no, nine ladies since I come to New York. Not so bad, right?"

Leon nodded, eyes on the road.

"But no browns till Denise."

"The hot chick you met in the subway?"

"So hot." Eli laughed like a kid cracking up at his own joke. "But tell me, Leo"—downshifting to a confidential tone—"are they different, the brown girls? More—you know—sexier?"

The hell I know, Leon was thinking, but he bluffed. "You better believe it."

Another gust of laughter. "I do believe." Pause. "So tell. How many girls you have had?"

As in had sex with? "Well," Leon took a deep breath, stalling. "I don't want but one, but Shauna won't even look at me."

"Make her look!" Eli fired back—and he pushed his face so

close Leon thought he was going to kiss him. "Like that. So she can't look apart. Then smile with all the teeth—see? Then say her name with just the lips moving . . . *Shauna Shauna Shauna.*"

"Thank you, brother," Leon said when he finally stopped howling. "I'll try it next time I see her in church. *Shauna Shauna Shauna.*" He practically sang it. The front seat shook with their laughter. That must be his secret, Leon thought—he gets them laughing. But nine? That would be on his conscience all his life.

Leon exited the highway onto a glaring four-lane artery lined with strip malls and used car lots. A couple of miles down, Eli told him to turn right into a warehouse parking lot. "Uncle," he said, pointing to a short frowning man in a black overcoat waiting for them out front. Leon pulled up next to him, lowering the window so he could ask where the loading dock was, but the man brusquely motioned him out of the car. "You wait here," he barked as he slid behind the steering wheel. "Eli and I will load up the—"

"Records!" Eli yelled.

"The records—and then you take over again."

Leon paced the parking lot in the chill March sun for a good fifteen minutes before the Chevy reappeared from behind the warehouse. The car's trunk was two inches ajar and a tail of frayed rope dangled over the fender. "So much record we not close," Eli explained.

"Well, as long as nothing bounces out on the highway."

"You make sure that don't happen," the short man said, fixing Leon with a hooded stare. "Otherwise you get bubkes. Understand, junior?"

Leon knew not to ask what bubkes meant. With guys like that there was nothing to do but smile and go, "Yes, sir."

Neither of them said much on the ride back to the city. It was like bubkes man had killed the fun. No jokes, no more advice on getting with the ladies. Leon flipped on the radio and sang along quietly. It was funny about white folks—you go from buddy to lackey in the blink of an eye. At least no one had called him "boy."

Leon assumed they'd be dropping off at one of the big music stores around Times Square so he was surprised when Eli told him to take the bridge back. "You sure you don't want the tunnel?" he asked as they rolled toward the toll booths—but Eli just shook his head. Fifteen minutes later they were back in front of the Orange Julius. "Wait a minute here," Eli told him. Then he hopped out the passenger door and disappeared inside the restaurant. "No Denise" was all he said when he returned to the car.

"Are you crazy, man? You said you had a date for five o'clock and now it's"—Leon glanced at his watch—"three thirty. You really think she's gonna spend all day waiting on some strange white dude who hit on her in the subway?"

"Not strange," Eli said morosely.

"She'll be there at five, trust me." But Eli just grunted. "Meanwhile, we got a trunkful of records to deliver and you still haven't told me where."

"Drive," said Eli. "Lenox Avenue—down."

"Downtown on Lenox? Okay, whatever you say."

AFTER BLOWING FIFTEEN DOLLARS on a fancy haircut, Richard decided to pay a call on his pal Bill William, a conceptual artist who supported himself and his six children with a sideline in dope. Richard hadn't been to Bill's in a while because he owed him money (he owed everyone money) but in T minus two hours he'd be flush, and it wouldn't hurt to pre-order.

Bill's loft on Lower Broadway was the kind of place Richard wished he lived in—cast-iron columns, high ceiling, wide-plank wood floor big enough to play basketball, dusty shafts of light angling down through huge arched windows. God! The killer parties he could throw in a space like that. One day—maybe soon.

Bill looked none too pleased to find Richard grinning and bobbing at his door, but he brightened up when he heard the amount of coke involved. "You're shitting me, right?"

"Wrong."

"I won't ask where the money's coming from."

"Don't." Richard winked.

"Okay. But it's gonna take me a couple three days to lay my hands on that much product."

"Take all the time you need. I'm not going anywhere." Richard picked his way through the mattresses, clothes, books, and toys so he could examine the works in progress that Bill had hung on the loft's brick walls: huge blank canvases stenciled in primary colors with a single letter or word. A six-foot-high "GREEN" in saturated kelly acrylic. The letter "B" in glossy enamel stripes of black and yellow. "COOL" spray-painted in a prism of blues. Richard emitted the requisite burbles—"Whoa, awesome, yes, wow, that green totally pops, I'm loving these"—just enough to warm the cockles of Bill's drug-jaded heart. It worked. Bill extracted a tiny rock from a lacquer box on his drafting table and began chopping lines. "Just a taste, my man—this shit will be dumping down in drifts once you cop the cash."

Nose numb, eyes snapping, brain tingling, Richard clattered down the steps and joined the freak parade on Lower Broadway. "Seventy-Six Trombones" from *The Music Man* began to thump inside his head. Richard skipped to the beat. His head wouldn't quit swerving. Tendrils of air coiled around his neck and down his back. Wow. Everyone was so beautiful. That Puerto Rican girl with the velvet cleavage. That guy with the ponytail so red it was shooting sparks. And the boots—every foot bound in supple vintage leather—burgundy, ruby, maroon, ebony, banana, burnt sienna, apricot. What a stroke of luck that he had his camera in his backpack. Richard set the pack on his knee, gently lifted out the used Canonflex R2000 that was his prize possession, hung the strap around his neck, and started snapping. No one on the sidewalk gave him a second look. He checked his watch—such a perfect little machine, so shiny, so intricately coiled, so cool the way the black leather band perfectly matched the hairs on his wrist. Ten to three. He still had time to get to the park. He could be there for all of it. Wait! He *had* to be there. What was he thinking? Never forget the money. Like Daddy always said, it pays to be close when the bills change hands. No telling what that crazy Eli would do with $3K in his pocket. Trust no one—not even your cousin. Waste nothing, no matter how wasted you are. *Click, flash, click, flash.* Yes! He'd photograph the deal going down—and then sell the pictures to *Interview.* Film noir, film blanc, film ultra verité. Life morphing into art morphing into money. Rich *and* famous. Fucking genius.

Richard's sneakers barely grazed the sidewalk as he glided to the subway.

IT WAS AFTER THREE BY the time Sam got rid of the feds. He was sure they would bust him when Richard's hash pipe came tumbling out of a kitchen drawer, but they weren't interested in drugs. "Just tell us where your girlfriend is, and everything will be fine." That's what the big one kept repeating. And Sam kept saying, "I don't have a girlfriend. Do I look like I have a girlfriend?" The little one didn't talk. He just riffled through drawers, turned mattresses upside down, broke the backs of books, and shook out the pages. Sam's notebook got swept into his briefcase. Ditto with five canisters of film under Richard's bed. All they found of Kim's was a box of tampons under the sink and a pair of panties wadded up in a corner of the bathroom. "Yours, I suppose?" the big one sneered. "My sister's," Sam replied without thinking.

Without thinking was the only way he was going to get through this.

"We know Kim Goodman is your girlfriend," the little one yelped at him when he was done trashing the place. "And we know you stole one of our agent's notebooks. Your prison term's going to be a lot shorter if you cooperate. Starting with: where the hell is she?"

"My father's a lawyer." Lie #2. He was getting the hang of it. "Would you like to talk to him? And by the way, where's your search warrant?"

"Go fuck yourself, sonny," the big one said.

"Why don't you show me how it's done."

They were about to kick the shit out of him, but a glance passed between them. The big one stomped over to the window and threw it open. "Hey, maybe she's up on the roof."

Not anymore, she isn't.

"You'll be hearing from us," the little one said. "It's gonna take more than Daddy the lawyer to save your punk ass."

And they were gone. Sam pressed his ear to the door. At the top of the stairs, two flights up, there was a door—sometimes locked, sometimes not—to the roof. As soon as Sam heard it click, he grabbed his coat and headed out. Down.

. . .

TEN BLOCKS FROM THE PARK, Eli told Leon to pull over onto a side street and stop the car. "Here's what's gonna be," he said. It was getting cold—the car's heater was feeble—but Eli's face looked red and sweaty. "Maybe no need—maybe—but I bring just in case." He took the pistol out of his parka pocket and let Leon get a good look at it.

"What the hell you need a gun for a record delivery?" Now Leon was sweating too.

"Listen. Listen—I tell you—so we both come out safe and no bad shit."

Leon sat there shivering while Eli laid it out for him: When you get the money envelope, pass it over and let me count it. Then, and only then, hand over the goods. Make them lift out the crate—not you. Don't wait around. The second they get the records out of the trunk, take off. If there's any trouble, there's this—and Eli patted his parka pocket.

These white boys totally tricked me, Leon was thinking. *Richard, Eli—maybe Sam was in on it too. Irv Rines my ass. I'm nothing but the delivery boy on a drug deal.* If Leon could have ditched the car and walked away, he would have done it. But the foreign guy had a gun and he looked like he knew how to use it. And what would he tell his uncle?

"Now turn the block and go back on Lenox," Eli said. "Ten minutes to go."

RICHARD WISHED HE'D SKIPPED the haircut and saved his money for a cab. The uptown subway was crowded and slow and reeked of garlic breath. He kept worrying someone was going to pinch his camera out of his backpack. By the time they got to Ninety-Sixth Street, his high had unraveled. Everyone was looking at him like he was some kind of freak. A rich lost honky with an expensive haircut. He thought about bailing and taking the train back downtown—but he was broke and a big thick pile of cash was waiting for him just a few blocks away. Besides, it was such a cool idea. If the truth ever came out, no one would believe it. Leonard Bernstein's radical chic money bouncing from the Black Panthers to the back pocket of Richard Rines's blue jeans and from there up the noses of the Max's crowd. It was like one of those Rube Goldberg machines. And anyway, Richard was planning on holding back a few hundred—for a rainy day.

SAM GOT OUT of the subway at Lexington and 110th Street and ran up the stairs. Shadows were lengthening. When he hit Central Park, he could just glimpse the silver skin of water shining between the trees. He never knew there was a lake up here. A rim of dirty ice near the shore. Bare branches shivering above. The city seemed to be holding its breath. Sam sprinted the long block between Fifth and Lenox. A couple of mothers strolling babies turned and muttered. A kid stuck out his leg to trip him, but Sam steered around. There was a car pulled over just inside the park—exactly where Kim said it would be. One black car. Not Leon's. Which meant he wasn't too late. Right?

ELI SHUT HIS EYES and pretended he was back on the West Bank. He'd done operations like this lots of times in the army. The trick was to get in and out fast before anyone knew what was happening—because once you had a bunch of bystanders milling around, things went south fast. Women and children caught in the crossfire. Human shields seized by the bad guys. Media appearing out of nowhere with cameras rolling. That's when your major handed you your ass on a platter. Not this time. No majors. No Palestinians. But still, a wad of cash and a couple of crazy black revolutionaries on the other end of it. Luckily, Uncle had thought to pry one of the Uzis out of the crate, pop in an ammo clip, and stash the machine gun under a towel on the backseat. Just in case. By the time the Panthers realized they were short one gun, he and Leon would be home free.

When Eli spotted the car inside the park a block away, he slipped the black-and-white checked keffiyeh scarf out of his left parka pocket and tied it around his head. Richard's idea. The Panthers would be spooked by a white guy, but with the Palestinian scarf on, he'd look like an Arab terrorist. If things got hairy, he'd shout at them in Hebrew—they'd never know it wasn't Arabic. Then he'd say, "Brothers!" and raise a clenched fist and everyone would be cool.

Leon's hands were shaking so violently he could barely hold the steering wheel. "Not worry," Eli whispered to calm him down. "Almost there."

THERE WAS A CLUMP of trees—thin naked hardwoods—beside the park drive and Richard ambled casually into their striped shadows. Kneeling, he took up position with the camera. The black car parked ten yards away was pointing north—uptown. Richard held the camera up to his face and squinted through the viewfinder. Two guys—both wearing ski masks. Weird. The

Panthers didn't wear masks—or did they? Black berets, leather jackets, ammo belts—but masks? He focused and clicked off a few shots, then lowered the camera. Sure enough, there was Leon's Chevy cruising very slowly across the intersection and easing to a stop across the road from the Panther vehicle. He watched through the viewfinder as Leon rolled down the window and leaned his head out. Richard saw his lips move but he was too far away to make out the words. *Click. Click, click, click, click, click.*

SAM BROKE INTO A FAST walk when he saw Leon's Chevy pull to a stop across from the black car. Kim had told him to abort the deal—but how? Race out screaming and waving his arms? Bad idea. The FBI goons would just open fire. What about this: make like a crazy person—the city was full of them, all ages and colors. Howl, froth at the mouth, dance around in circles, tap on the window of the FBI car, shout out something about Jesus, turn fast to give Leon the high sign, keep on babbling until they split.

Sam pulled his shirttails out of his pants, unzipped his jacket, ruffled his hair, crossed his eyes, and staggered toward the cars, dragging one foot behind him. Crazy as a fucking bedbug.

"WE GOT THE RECORDS in the trunk," Leon shouted to the driver of the black car, jerking his head back and to the side. "Let me see the money."

A man in a ski mask got out of the passenger side of the car and walked toward him. The driver stayed put.

"Tell him, 'Hands to sides,'" Eli muttered through the scarf.

"Hands to the sides," Leon called.

The man dropped his hands and kept moving. "Show us the guns, motherfucker," he barked. If he thought he sounded black, he was a fool.

"Guns? What you talking about guns for?"

"Shut up and get out the car," Eli spat. "Go to trunk, untie rope, but don't open till they give the money. Remember: money first. Do it."

Leon got out and went around to the rear of the car. While he fiddled with the knot on the rope, the masked man reached into his pocket and pulled out a fat white envelope. "Want this?" Leon nodded. The knot came loose, and the hood of the trunk glided up. "Let's trade."

Leon had his hand out for the envelope when out of nowhere some raggedy guy with his coat pulled over his head spun in front of him. "Jesus saves," he shouted, turning circles with one foot dragging behind, "but only the righteous!" The voice was muffled by the coat. He swerved at the masked man. "Arms for the poor! Arms for the poor!" he yelled, dancing from one foot to the other. Then quick as a knife he pivoted to Leon and screamed full in his face: *"Tutu loves you—now get the hell out of here!"*

"Sam?"

At that moment, the air exploded in deafening cracks. It was Eli, bearing down on them with a small machine gun cradled under his right arm. He fired off two more rounds high in the air and then, freeing his left hand, he lunged for the envelope, tearing it out of the masked man's hand. "Back in car," he screamed at Leon. He lowered the weapon inch by inch until it was aimed at the heart of the masked man. "Uzis yours," he said. "Take and go. No bullshit."

"Hands up! FBI," the man shouted, reaching into his pocket.

But Eli didn't wait around to see for what. He got off a round at the man's feet—

"It's a trap," Sam was shouting. "They're—"

Leon was already behind the wheel. Eli dove in beside him. The car lurched forward, and the crate tumbled out of the trunk onto the asphalt. *"Leeee-onnnn,"* Sam's voice screamed over the engine roar.

SAM WAS RUNNING but he veered off the road and into the bushes when he heard more gunfire. He doubled over on the ground, his side burning. Through the film that hazed his eyes he could see the flashes of fire blazing from the passenger window of the blue Chevy. He turned around. The masked man had dropped to his knee and was returning fire. He motioned behind him with one hand and the black car took off, giving chase. The Chevy disappeared into the shadows and the gunshots ceased. The black car sped by. Like a zombie, Sam staggered after them deeper into the park. He heard footsteps slapping the pavement behind him and there was Richard at his side. *Where did he come from*? They fell in together for a moment, too winded to speak, then Richard sprinted on ahead, his camera swinging from side to side.

They made it. They made it. Those goons will never catch them now.

Sam kept walking. He rounded the bend and there was the water he'd glimpsed from outside the park. Harlem Meer. The sun was behind the trees now and the surface of the lake looked like lead, not silver. He pitched forward. People were jogging beside him now, streaming across the grass toward the lake, and Sam got swept along. As he approached the mud- and ice-crusted shore, he saw Richard's back, bisected by the camera strap. Richard's arms were raised as if he was snapping pictures, but when Sam got close he could see that both palms were clapped to his forehead. He kept going. There was the black car, idling next to the lake, a plume of exhaust spewing from the tailpipe. A crowd was massing on the shore—a small crowd but getting bigger by the second. Sam joined them. His gaze inched from the mud to the ice to the rippling open water until it snagged on the shelf of blue. It could have been a raft. It could have been the bottom of an overturned dinghy. It could have been a submerged barrel. But it was the roof of Leon's car, sinking agonizingly beneath the surface.

The water, the water. Dead in the water.

He could already hear the wail of sirens.

Chapter Twenty-Four

Tutu was in the kitchen when Sam's parents brought him home on Monday afternoon, but she wouldn't talk to him or look at him.

"Any news?" she asked his father, but his father just shook his head.

Sam went back to his room and shut the door. Less than two months had passed since he'd last set foot in this room but it felt like a lifetime. He lay on the bed where he and Kim had had sex that day she came to dinner. He laced his fingers together behind his head and stared at the ceiling. Breathing, staring.

Eli died clutching an envelope stuffed with Monopoly money. He went into shock from the bullet wound to his shoulder and drowned before they could tow the car out of the water.

Kim was gone. Underground, whatever that meant.

Richard had a lawyer—or rather Richard's father did. Sam had a lawyer too.

Leon was in critical at a maximum-security hospital. The FBI agent had shot him through the neck, possibly grazing the larynx. The doctors induced a coma so they could get a ventilator down his throat. If he recovered, he might never speak—or sing—again. If he recovered, he would spend God knows how many years in prison: trafficking in stolen weapons, conspiracy, assault.

Sam looped it all through his mind again and again. The faces of his friends—former friends—popped out at him one after another like cartoon mice from a hole in the wall. He tried to grab them but they wriggled through his fingers and disappeared. "Get Together" by the Youngbloods tracked through his mind on infinite repeat. *Come on. Come on. Love, love, love. Right now, right now, right now.* Was he going crazy? He shut his eyes, stuffed a pillow over his head. But he couldn't stop the music or erase the faces.

SAM STAYED ON HIS BED until he heard his parents close the door to their bedroom. Then he counted to ten, got up, padded down the hall, and stood at the bottom of the stairs. He mustered the nerve to climb.

He knocked. Three times Tutu told him to go away—but then his hand opened the door, his feet shuffled across her bedroom carpet, his knees crumpled until he was kneeling in front of her chair. His head sank toward her lap but he snapped it back before it touched her.

"I told you, go away. You deaf?" Sam put his face in his hands and shook his head. "You think crying's gonna help?"

Sam let his hands fall. "I can explain."

"No you can't. You've done enough already. You took my baby—"

"He's not dead," Sam pleaded. "The doctors said—"

"I don't care what the doctors said. You took his life. You and Richard and that girl of yours." She kept her voice down but the words burned him. "What have we ever done to you—except serve you? Now they've got my baby chained to his bed—chained . . ." Her voice broke.

"No. No. No."

"Don't you tell me no. They're gonna lock that boy away for the rest of his life. *If* he lives."

"No."

"Watch."

"It was all a mistake. . . ."

"Get out. I curse you, Sam Stein. You hear me? I curse the day you were born. I curse raising you up. I curse myself for bringing you to my home. I curse your friends. I curse your family. I curse the ground you walk on. May you live to eat ashes and grovel in the dirt. Now get out of my room and close the door."

He obeyed. What choice did he have?

Trembling, he trudged back down the stairs. He saw his hand reach for the doorknob. He heard his bare feet shuffle on the carpet. He was simultaneously himself and outside himself, as if he had fissured into two beings. Or rather two strangers: one inhabiting, one watching. A crazy aunt once told him that she woke up one night and saw God on the ceiling of her apartment. Now he knew what she meant. Only it wasn't God looking down at him. It was his other self—the hollow eyes of his own internal Dr. T. J. Eckleburg. Watching him. While he watched him watch.

ON APRIL 17, THE COLLEGE admissions letters arrived in the mail. Sam got into four of the five colleges he applied to—Harvard, Columbia, Princeton, University of Michigan—and was wait-listed at Swarthmore. In the days that followed, letters trickled in from all of them withdrawing their acceptance pending the outcome of the trial.

None of it touched Sam. He went to school and sat silently through his classes. He ignored the whispers that eddied around him. He did his homework. He took tests. Mr. Coffin fired him as editor of the student newspaper—"It's for the best, Sam"—and appointed Dirty Face in his place. Dirty Face tried to make it up to him, but Sam brushed him off. He brushed everyone off.

A letter came from Kim—he recognized the handwriting on the envelope but he didn't open it. He pinched the envelope between thumb and forefinger and shook. A single sheet whispered inside. He pictured her propped on a mattress in the back room of some row house in Chicago—or Oakland—or god knows where. Queen of the Underground. She probably had a boyfriend—or three. He tried to remember the smell of her perfume—lily of the valley. He didn't have a single thing that belonged to her. Not even a photo. She was alive—somewhere; he was dead—everywhere. The letter sat on his desk until other papers covered it. Eli's parents wrote him as well, but he didn't open that letter either. There was one thing he had to attend to: getting his driver's license. His mother took him for the road test one afternoon and he passed. The license arrived in the mail a week later.

His parents told him they loved him—something they had never said before, not once in his life—but he didn't respond. "We know you're not to blame, Sam," his mother said gently one evening at dinner, but Sam left the table, shut himself in his bedroom, and stayed there until everyone went to sleep. If he wasn't to blame, who was? He ransacked the past for the fatal juncture. If he hadn't said anything about Leon to Richard. If he hadn't invited Leon to Richard's apartment. If he hadn't gotten together with Kim. If he'd stayed home with Tutu on New Year's Eve instead of going to that party. If he'd kept his big mouth shut for once in his life. He wanted to slam his head against the wall, repeatedly, until he knocked himself out. But they'd come running at the first crack of bone on plaster. *What are you doing, Sam?* They'd lock him in a padded cell. Would that be worse?

He rarely washed. His face and back erupted in red clusters that burst and sweated pus. He heard Tutu tell his parents: "I'm not feeding that child till he bathes."

Sam ran the tub full of water, stripped down and submerged himself. He stayed in until the water chilled. When his teeth began to chatter, he got out, wrapped a towel around himself, and, without looking in the mirror, slunk out of the bathroom.

You're beautiful. You're brilliant. You're going to be a great writer.

But.

But.

BUT.

He ceased dreaming. He had no fantasies. No erections. No appetite. At dinner, he pushed around the food on his plate until they let him leave.

He slept rarely and never deeply. When he shut his eyes, he saw Leon's car listing to one side as water sluiced over the hood. It was like an electric shock every time. He sat bolt upright, his heart racing, sweat streaming down his arms. He kicked the sheet off, got out of bed, stood in the center of his room. All around him, the house ticked and sighed. Nothing had changed but everything was different. *Panic,* his brain winked at him. *Attack. Panic. Attack. Panic. Attack.* It took an hour to stop his heart from galloping—but afterward it was worse. Back in bed, cradled by his pillow, his brain careened down one blind alley after another. There must be some fix, a hidden escape hatch, a button he could press, a pill he could swallow.

No.

Nothing.

Ever.

I curse you, Sam Stein.

He quit going to school—what was the point? He saw no one, did nothing, asked for nothing.

As the body dwindled away, his hearing became more acute. Without opening his door he could eavesdrop on every room in the house. Tutu, wailing, told someone on the other end of the line that Leon was still chained to the hospital bed even though he was in a coma. There was a guard posted outside the door night and day.

Hearing her cry made him cry. *Have a good cry—it will help*. It didn't.

His father barked into the phone, "We'll get to the bottom of this. We'll get those kids off, don't you worry." He must be talking to Richard's father. *Those kids*, as if he and Richard had pulled some prank. Whoopee cushion on the teacher's chair. Hiding the key to the cafeteria.

"He won't tell us anything, but we're not giving up. It's a stage—he'll snap out of it—and when he does . . ." His mother talking to Kim's mother.

They unscrewed the lock from his door so he couldn't barricade himself in. They stared at him every night at dinner until he gulped down a couple of swallows of the disgusting egg-and-milk shakes Tutu made him. "Let him starve for all I care," he heard her muttering in the kitchen—they all heard it but they said nothing. *They're scared of me*, he was thinking. *Otherwise they'd can her.*

He knew his silence was driving them wild and he relished it. The only pleasure he took anymore was seeing their eyes beg him to stop. Never. It was like the repeating telephone dream where the person on the other end of the line refuses to speak: you know he hasn't hung up, you can hear him breathing, but no matter what you say or how you implore, he won't respond. *I beg you*. Silence: the power of madness.

One Friday morning toward the end of April, his father opened the door to his bedroom and ordered him to get out of bed. "You've been holed up like this for weeks. It's time to put it behind us, son." He waited for Sam to say something. "Okay." He exhaled wearily. "We're going to see the lawyer. I took the day off from work, so the least you could do is cooperate."

Sam squeezed his eyes shut and the sinking blue hood shimmered before him. He and Richard were standing side by side in silence when they dragged Leon's car out of the water. By then, the lakeshore was packed solid with cars, police, jabbering onlookers, all the faces stained red by the strobing lights. Sam caught a glimpse of Eli's bloody parka as they laid his body on a stretcher. Richard's fingers twitched at his camera.

Sam opened his eyes to his father's creased face staring down at him. "Half an hour." He felt like puking but there was nothing in his gut. He was so thin his jeans sagged around his hips. "Get washed. Shave. Eat something, for god's sake."

The lawyer, Arnie Berg—a wiry bantam in a three-piece charcoal suit, with black sideburns flaring over raw razored cheeks—smiled at him like he was an invalid. "The pretrial hearing is scheduled for next Wednesday. We know you're innocent, Sam."

Oh yeah?

"You got in over your head. Way over. And I'm going to get you out."

He heard his father clear his throat. He placed a hand on Sam's forearm. *Restraint.*

"You don't have to say anything if you don't want to. In fact, better if you don't. Take the Fifth, that's all you have to do—I'll take care of the rest." Sam just stared at the dark stubble on the lawyer's cheeks. "Doesn't matter. Eli's dead and there's no way to connect those guns to you. . . ." Sam flinched. "Or Richard. You didn't know anything about it. You were roommates but he kept you in the dark. It was all Eli and Leon."

"No, no, no." Sam pounded the lawyer's desk with his fist. "Leon had nothing to do with it."

"Easy, Sam, easy. Doesn't matter. Leon's in a coma anyway. You don't have to say anything. Just play dumb. You didn't know. You're just an innocent kid—an honors student."

Sam started to cry, silently, only the tears.

"Think about it, Sam. It's you or him. You and Richard. Maybe you made a mistake. . . ."

"Go to hell," Sam spat through his tears. Why wouldn't they just leave him alone?

"I'm not blaming you. We were all young once. These are crazy times. You got your whole life ahead of you. Don't throw it away for some—"

"I'm not listening to this bullshit."

"Yes, you are," his father said. "And watch your mouth. You're going to do everything Mr. Berg tells you to do. You don't have to lie."

"If it's not the truth, it's a lie. It can't be both."

"You don't have to say anything, got it?" Berg's sweetsie tone was gone. "Just let us do our job. You'll thank us in the end. Believe me."

. . .

AFTER EVERYONE HAD GONE to bed, Sam crept out of his bedroom and up the half-flight of stairs to the den. The rear wall of the room was lined with shelves where his mother carefully arranged the books that no one read. An entire shelf was devoted to the stout red-and-gold-spined volumes of *The World Book Encyclopedia*. Sam tipped out the second of the two S volumes (SO–SZ), carried it back to his bedroom, and shut the unlockable door. He read the suicide entry twice, then he went back for the R volume. *Roman empire, suicide in*. "In ancient Rome, suicide was considered an honorable way for political prisoners and enemies of the state to end their lives. The stoic philosopher Seneca, after being implicated in a plot against the Emperor Nero, reputedly opened his veins with a dagger and bled to death in warm bathwater."

Sam rummaged in his desk until he found his Swiss army knife—old, gummed shut, rusty, but still serviceable. He pried open the large blade, watched it glint in the light of his desk lamp, then jabbed it repeatedly into his arm until a bubble of blood rose to the surface. The first stroke was the hardest. After that it didn't hurt a bit.

He rinsed the tiny wound in the bathroom sink, scrubbed all the knife blades clean, and went to bed. That was the first good sleep he'd had since Eli died.

HE WOKE THE NEXT MORNING to the sound of Tutu shouting and wailing into the phone. "Oh, thank you, Lord Jesus. Glory. I knew the good Lord wouldn't take my boy."

Sam sat up in bed and cocked an ear. Leon had come out of his coma. He still couldn't say anything, but his eyes were open. He was able to turn his head from side to side. When they spoke to him, he blinked and sound came out of his mouth. Not words—but something.

Sam's mother gave Tutu the rest of the day off and drove her to the station so she could get to the hospital before visiting hours were over.

For some reason the news made Sam desolate. If he could see Leon again, talk to him, explain, beg forgiveness. But he knew it was impossible. There was no way out. He felt the rage rise up his throat and gag him. When he was little, Tom and Ron used to gang up to torture him. Tom would twist his left arm behind his back; Ron would grab his right arm and force him to sock himself in the jaw. Over and over again. *Why are you hitting yourself, Sammy? Why are you hitting yourself?* The more he thrashed, the harder they made him punch. They harder he punched, the more insane he became. *Why are you hitting yourself?*

"Going to the library," he shouted to his parents when he left the house an hour later. He could have driven now that he had his license but he knew they didn't trust him with the car. It was a two-mile walk. He was light-headed by the time he got there. He had to lean against a wall and shut his eyes. Silver stars revolved on the backs of his eyelids. Better than a sinking car roof. In two and a half hours he absorbed everything the town library had about suicide. Famous suicides in history: Mark Antony, Ernest Hemingway, Adolf Hitler, Marilyn Monroe. Most common ways to do it: Jumping, drowning, gunshot, intentional electrocution, poison, self-immolation, starvation, self-strangulation, carbon monoxide, cutting. Trends. Demographics. Warning signs.

Cutting worked better if you kept the wound submerged so the blood would not coagulate. Consuming alcohol before and during also hastened the process—something to do with arterial constriction.

That night, after he left the dinner table, Sam sneaked into his parents' bedroom and got the key to the liquor cabinet out of his father's top bureau drawer—just where his brothers had told him it would be. After they closed their door for the night, Sam went down to the basement with a flashlight. He studied the labels. There must have been forty different bottles. He knew that proof corresponded with potency, so he finally chose the bottle with the highest. Smirnoff Vodka, 80 proof. Back in his bedroom, door shut, he took a swig. It twisted his throat and burned his windpipe. Two more swigs. Then he went to work with the knife, whittling away on his forearm. This time he pressed deep enough to make the blood trickle down his arm in a little red delta. He could go deeper.

TWO NIGHTS LATER, after Tutu went upstairs, his parents sat Sam down in the living room for a talk. They spoke in hushed, murmuring voices, barely more than a whisper. The hearing was being delayed a week in the hopes that Leon would recover sufficiently to be able to testify—or at least nod or shake his head in response to questions. So it was going to be his word against Leon's—his and Richard's. Berg was working with Richard's lawyer. They had it all mapped out. Berg had assured them that Sam and Leon would not be in the hearing room at the same time. They were trying to talk Tutu out of going—too hard on her heart. Leon had a lawyer too—state appointed. Of course they felt sorry for him—everyone did. They were going to do everything in their power to see that he got the lightest sentence possible. They wouldn't forget. Later, when he got out, they would do something for him. Money. A job. A place to live. They owed Tutu that much. *Just remember, whatever they say, whatever they ask, your answer is: "I don't know. I wasn't there. No one told me anything." Your record is clean. You're an honors student. Innocent.*

"When it's over, you can think about reapplying to your colleges," his mother said.

Sam loved the "your," as if Harvard was in his back pocket. Like a comb.

AFTERWARD, SAM SLUNK BACK to his bed and curled up in the fetal position. He was trembling so violently that he bit his tongue. He grabbed the pillow and wrapped it over his head. Why couldn't he just die?

THE NIGHT BEFORE THE HEARING, a Tuesday, his parents left the house at 7:00 p.m. for a dinner party. He and Tutu were home alone.

"Don't bother cooking," he told her. "I'm not hungry."

"You're not the one giving the orders around here," she told him, the longest sentence she had spoken to him since she cursed him to his face.

Sam sat staring into his plate until she finally gave up and took it away. "You're gonna die if you don't eat," she said. "You look like a skeleton as it is."

"So?" was all he answered.

He could tell she had more to say but she pressed her lips together and glared.

He had until midnight, eleven at the earliest. Tutu would go to bed by eight. That gave him three hours.

"I'm going to take a bath," he mumbled before leaving the kitchen. "To save time tomorrow morning." Their eyes met but she still didn't speak.

Okay, that's it, then.

He ran the bath at nine o'clock. So hot it scalded his fingers. As if that mattered. The Smirnoff bottle was half full and he chugged down as much as he could stand and set the bottle down on the rim of the tub. Then he locked the bathroom door, stripped naked, and eased himself in. Like boiling vodka, he thought. His body looked like a white worm suspended in the water. He hated every square inch of himself.

Open the veins. *Now more than ever* . . . His right hand trembled as the fingers closed around the knife. He'd been practicing. He knew how to do this. He had it down. His head was spinning. His vision was cloudy. He took another swig. Press. No, stab. That was the only way it would work. He sank the blade into the vein on his left wrist and pushed and the blood ribboned out. Was it enough? The water turned red. The tide of blood rose up over his chin, his mouth, his eyes. He could feel his heart beating in his wrist, pulsing blood into the water. Wave after wave. The red rose up and stained the whites of his eyes. There was nothing left. Nothing left to love. Or hate.

He went under.

TUTU WAS DRIFTING OFF when a shiver jolted her awake. Someone walking over her grave. An angel—or devil more likely. She opened her eyes and listened. That child said he was taking a bath. She'd heard the water running—what, half an hour ago? But she hadn't heard it drain. She looked at the clock by the side of the bed. Nine forty. Even Sam couldn't stay in the tub that long. Skinny as he was, he'd freeze as soon as the warmth went out.

Let him freeze.

Then she heard a clink and a muffled crash like shattering glass.

Heart aflutter, she heaved herself out of bed and down the stairs.

Chapter Twenty-Five

She scrubbed away all the blood. She swept up the shards of the Smirnoff bottle. She washed the towels and rags that she had twisted around his forearm to stop the bleeding. She fixed him coffee so he wouldn't nod off and pass out in his sleep. But there was nothing she could do about the splintered trim of the bathroom door that she had pried open with a crowbar.

When Mr. and Mrs. Stein came home just before midnight, she told them everything.

SAM HEARD THE THREE OF them murmuring around the kitchen table until deep into the night. Tutu's alto, his mother's soprano, his father's baritone. The only words he could make out were "poor Sam."

Poor pathetic Sam. Couldn't even pull off his freaking suicide.

He was drifting off when Tutu came into the room. He heard

her breathing and then he felt her cool, dry palm on his forehead. "Oh, Sammy. If you'd've gone and died . . ."

HIS MOTHER WAS THE FIRST one in his room the next morning. "You don't have to do this, Sam. Your father has been on the phone with the lawyer. They make exceptions for . . ."

Medical emergencies. Failed suicides. Miserable losers rescued by their maid.

"Yes, I do" was all he said.

His mother helped him button the cuffs of his sleeves. Only half an inch of bandage stuck out past the left cuff. If you didn't look, you wouldn't even notice it.

HE FELT LIKE THEY WERE driving him to an execution. As the suburbs coagulated into row houses that metastasized into skyscrapers, Sam's gut went cold. It was his first time back in the City since what his parents referred to as "the accident." They spent an hour getting to Lower Manhattan and another half hour parking the car. Outside the federal courthouse, Sam craned his neck back until he could see the tongue of blue caught between the fangs of the office towers. His last glimpse of sky.

The hearing room was hot, crowded, and overlit. The back rows were filled to overflowing with men in cheap suits with plastic-sheathed badges dangling from their necks—the gentlemen of the press. The judge looked like a rabbi, stern but kindly. Richard sat up front on the left with his lawyer and his parents. Sam scanned the room: no sign of Leon. Tutu hadn't come either—his parents convinced her it was better not to. Sam slumped down between them; his mother put her arm around his shoulders; the lawyer opened his briefcase with a resounding snap of the latches. Sam stared at his ragged fingernails and tried not to bite them. The wound on his wrist tingled. The judge's voice droned on, the reporters scratched at their steno pads, the stenographer clicked into her machine. Sam tuned all of it out. His heart was stone. His brain was mud. None of it reached him. The sooner it was over the better.

He began to tremble uncontrollably when Richard took the stand. His wrist throbbed. He couldn't tune out the scratchy seducing voice. "I met Leon Carter on a Friday afternoon—I think it was the sixth of March. Sam was writing something about him for the school newspaper and he thought it would be cool if we all met him. All meaning me, Kim, and Eli, my cousin from Israel. Leon seemed like a good guy. I liked him right away. We talked about music. Sam tried to get him to open up about his childhood and stuff like that. I don't remember much about what Kim said. Anyway, we shot the breeze for a while and then Leon hit the road. Before he left, he gave us each his business card. I thought it was kind of funny that he even had a business card—but I noticed that Kim grabbed hers and shoved it into her pocket. Yeah, I knew Kim was into radical politics—Black Panthers, SDS, all that stuff—but Leon didn't seem like the type. He talked about church, singing—he seemed so genuine. Totally weird that it was all a front. Anyway, Leon left and I thought that was the end of it—but Kim called him later that night. I was in the bedroom, but I could still hear her side of the conversation. She told him she had a contact who could get the Panthers some guns—Uzis—I distinctly heard that word. I had no clue the contact was Eli—none, zero, zilch. Eli never said word one—I found out about it all later.

After." Richard's cleft chin began to tremble; he paused to collect himself. "I loved Eli, I really did. He was nuts, but . . ." A deep sigh. "Anyway, Kim and Leon worked it all out over the phone. I think it was Leon who came up with the plan. He knew the Panthers would never trust a white guy to run them guns—but if it came through him it would be cool. Yeah, the guns were Eli's—but he totally got caught in Leon's scheme. Eli couldn't have cared less about the Panthers and all that revolution crap. I still can't believe he's dead. . . ." A sob racked his shoulders. He hung his head and the black hair spilled down over his face. He was done.

Then it was Sam's turn. His heart was pounding so hard he thought the wound would reopen. The blood roared in his ears as the clerk swore him in. His voice was barely audible; the judge had to ask him twice to repeat "I do." The lawyer gave him a hard stare and began: "Was Leon Carter a friend of yours?"

Sam hesitated. "No."

"What did you know about Leon Carter's involvement with the Black Panthers and other radical groups?"

"Nothing."

"Did you have any idea that Eli Nagel and Leon Carter were trafficking in stolen weapons?"

"Eli," Sam began. His lips were trembling. "Leon . . ." He started to choke up.

"Take your time, Sam."

Sam felt an iron fist tighten around his heart. He was on the verge of passing out. But he fought it down. "Eli Nagel," he began again, croaking out the words, "is dead because the FBI set a trap." Adrenaline shot through his veins. His mind cleared. "Leon Carter is an innocent victim." He heard his parents groan and a gust of voices whip through the room. "Totally. One hundred percent. Innocent. The only thing Leon did wrong was to get involved with me and through me with Richard Rines." He didn't look at Richard but he could feel the fury beaming his way. "Leon wasn't a radical. He wasn't a gunrunner. He wasn't a trafficker in stolen weapons. Leon Carter was and is a poor young man who fell into a trap—a trap masterminded by Richard Rines and sprung by the FBI." The gust amplified to a roar. The judge banged his gavel. "Go on, Sam." Sam sat up straight. He cast his eyes to the back of the room, where the reporters were bent over their pads writing for all they were worth. "The FBI infiltration of radical organizations is an established fact. Weathermen, Panthers, Women's Strike for Peace, Revolutionary Youth Movement—there are agents masquerading as revolutionaries in every radical group in the country. They don't just spy—they instigate and foment. The FBI is to blame for the death of Eli Nagel and the shooting of Leon Carter." The roars broke into shouts. "Leon was duped. He thought he was transporting *records*, not weapons. Ask those phony Panthers who fired the shots—they know the truth. Leon is a clean, sober, churchgoing young man whose life has been ruined because of me. No, I didn't know anything about the Uzi scheme—but if it hadn't been for me, Leon would never have met Richard, and if he had never met Richard, he'd be bagging groceries and driving a cab and singing his soul out in church every Sunday instead of being chained to a hospital bed."

"Are you saying," the judge interrupted, "that your friend and roommate Richard Rines is lying under oath?"

"Yes." And now he turned and looked full on into Richard's glittering eyes. For a second, Sam's breath caught in his throat. Richard had been his friend. How was this different from snitching? "That's exactly what I'm saying. *Let the black guy take the fall.* That's what this is about. That's what it's always been about. I can go to college. Richard can get a fancy job in the record business. Who gives a rip if Leon spends the rest of his life in prison?" Richard had his face in his hands. "Who's gonna know? Who's gonna care? Well, I know and I care and every one of you should care too. You can go ahead and lock me up—but please, please, don't punish Leon Carter any more than he's been punished. Leon's innocent." Sam raised his head so his voice would project to the back rows. "Can you hear me back there? Leon Carter is innocent and deserves to be free." The room erupted but Sam's voice could be heard soaring over it all. *"Free Leon Carter."* The judge furiously pounded his gavel. *"Free Leon Carter. FREE LEON CARTER."*

Chapter Twenty-Six

Later, after he'd gone back home and knelt before Tutu and gotten her forgiveness (on the promise that he'd never try to hurt himself again), after the dinner that his mother cooked ("If ever Tutu deserved a night off"), after his parents told him for the twentieth time how proud they were of him for telling the truth, after he and his father washed the dishes and talked about the start of baseball season ("No way in hell the Mets are gonna pull it off two years in a row"), after his parents went to bed and the house fell silent and all its secrets and lies and aching disappointments settled like dust, Sam shut himself in his room and opened a fresh notebook.

Kim was right—I totally missed the story—or part of it. I missed the story of how friends can trick and hurt and even kill one another—not out of meanness, or not only out of meanness, but out of blind passion and invincible selfishness. Yes, I'm to blame, at least in part. I should have seen it coming. I could have stopped it. But Kim was also wrong. I didn't miss it—not all of it—I lived it—I was there. You don't have to blow things up to make history. You don't have to shout from center stage. When the audience leaves the theater, they become the actors: people trade roles all the time. History is as much the record as the deed. Without witnesses, without someone to see and write what they see, it might as well never have happened. I am the witness. My power is the power of the voice, the vision, the memory. It might take fifty years, but before I die I'm going to figure out how to tell this story. My story.

First step: go see Leon.

THE NEXT MORNING, his mother shook him awake. She'd spoken to the doc treating Leon: the bullet had penetrated the trachea but missed the larynx by a couple of centimeters—meaning there was a chance he might one day sing again. *Might*, she repeated—but Sam was levitating. He borrowed the car and drove Tutu to the hospital. "Last time they were only letting family in," she said as he backed out of the driveway.

Sam turned to look at her—she was sitting in the passenger seat beside him dressed in her church clothes—and shook his head. "I'll wait" was all he said.

Acknowledgments

I could not have written this novel without the love and support of my family. Our daughters, Emily, Sarah, and Alice, have aided me in innumerable ways—perhaps most of all just by being such delightful, tolerant, and accomplished young women. My wife, Kate O'Neill, has been with me and beside me every step of the way. I'm grateful to Kate every day for her love and for keeping me sane, honest, grounded, and perpetually on my toes. Thank you for living this book—and so many others—with me. And extra thanks, Sarah, for navigating the labyrinth of permissions requests on my behalf.

Many individuals generously helped me trace the history and genealogy of the actual woman on whom the character Tutu is based. I'd like to single out Karen Sutton for answering countless emails, for sharing her deep knowledge of African American family history, for guiding me through old Baltimore neighborhoods, for aiding me with contacts in the Northern Neck of

Virginia, and for reviewing a draft of the book. I'd also like to thank Brenda Campbell, Bessida Cauthorne White, the late Catherine Scott, Helen Wynn, Virginia Thomas, Julie Cardozo Haynie, Edward Haynie, Stanford Crockett, Carolyn Jett, Hilary Derby, Catherine Bennett, Ruth Ball, and the Reverend Kelvin P. Evans and his congregation at the Mount Vernon Baptist Church in White Stone, Virginia. The staff of the Mary Ball Washington Museum and Library provided valuable assistance with the history of the Northern Neck, both during and after slavery. Thanks also to Nisi Shawl for putting me in touch with Aaliyah Hudson, who read this book in manuscript and made many valuable suggestions and corrections.

For help with understanding the zeitgeist of the 1960s and the mindset of young revolutionaries, I'd like to thank Alan Senauke and Kit Bakke. Thank you, Deb Caletti, for astute professional advice at a crucial moment.

My friends David Williams and Lyanda Lynn Haupt are enduring sources of writerly camaraderie and support through dark times (bright times, too). I'm grateful to Seattle7 Writers for connecting me with a wide circle of gifted and inspiring professional writers. In ways I can't really disclose but always rely on, I'm grateful to the mystic company of the Unspeakables. My friend Karen Pennar read a draft of the book and caught an embarrassing number of errors and oversights—thanks for saving me from my own carelessness. Jack Levison and Tony Robinson, dear friends both, helped me penetrate passages in the Bible. Carol Doig has intrepidly picked up where Ivan left off as my mentor, adviser, and friend: her continuing comradeship is a treasure. Thanks also to my old friend Jim Moran, who has listened patiently, commented wisely, and supported staunchly.

I've been blessed with a terrific team at Penguin. Many thanks to Kathryn Court for her passionate support of this novel—and for handing it over so gracefully to Patrick Nolan and Victoria Savanh. Kathryn, Patrick, and Victoria bring a light touch and an elegant manner to the business of editing and publishing—ideal traits for this writer. Trent Duffy did a superb copy edit—what luck to have an exact contemporary drill down into the myriad period details. Clarence Haynes reviewed the manuscript and provided many incisive suggestions for revising and re-imagining key scenes and characters.

I must single out my agent, the divine Jill Kneerim. Over the years, Jill has become not only my fiercest partisan and best reader but also a beloved friend. And huge thanks to Lucy Cleland at Kneerim and Williams, who co-agented the book with Jill. Lucy is a brilliant fiction editor with an intuitive feel for the psyches of people on the page. I gratefully adopted every single suggestion she made—all of which improved the book immeasurably.

Thanks to Mary Whisner at the University of Washington School of Law for helping me untangle a thorny legal thicket. And thanks to Drs. Janis Mercker, Peter Esselman, and Joost Knops for help with medical questions.

I'd like to thank Pam Royes for inspiring me to write this novel in the first place. Because of Pam, I've become involved in a wonderful literary organization called Fishtrap in Wallowa County, Oregon. I'd like to thank Nina McConigley and my fellow participants in her wonderful fiction workshop during 2018 Summer Fishtrap. Thanks also to Shannon McNerney, Fishtrap's executive director, for her continuing leadership and support.

Barnett Kaplan assisted me in crucial ways from start to finish—many thanks.

My brothers, Bob, Dan, and Jon, and my sister-in-law, Susan Senauke Laskin, lived alongside me through this period of time—fifty years ago, incredibly enough—and they refreshed my memory on many forgotten details. Thanks, Sue, for your unfailingly loyal support of my books. Thanks, Dan, for your writerly advice and example.

And finally, I'd like to thank my parents, Dr. Leona Laskin and the late Meyer Laskin. Mom and Dad always told us boys that we could do anything we truly wanted to do—words to live by, as it turns out.